BEHIND THAT MASK

BEHIND THAT MASK

HARRY STEPHEN KEELER

WILDSIDE PRESS

To
Bob Gontier,
a real 100-percent square-shooter.

CHAPTER I

The Artist

Yin Yi, expert wax worker, gazed reflectively over the waxen head he had just completed for Captain Barraby's Dime Museum and Chamber of Horrors, of Davenport, Iowa. So that he might get the tout ensemble, as it were, of the whole thing, exactly as it would be gotten by those thrill-seekers who ultimately would be visiting that time-honored institution of morbidezza located some two hundred miles west of Yin's Chicago studio, he held against the forward-sloping side of the base on which the waxen head was reared the small black placard which Captain Barraby had forwarded him by mail. A simple oblong of heavy 8-ply bristol board, the placard was some 3 inches deep by 5 inches or so long, thickly inked over its smooth surface with fuliginous ivory-black, with edges neatly beveled by a safety razor and neatly gilded as well, and lettered in gold letters by some commercial artist in Captain Barraby's home town. Its brief tale ran:

ELISHA BUSHMAN
World-Famous Murderer!
Executed 1894

This kindly-looking gentleman of the mauve decade fell in love with a burlesque queen, and in order to flee America with her, strangled his wife, poisoned his mother-in-law, and cut the throats of his two daughters, later shooting to death 3 policemen who were sent to capture him. He was hanged in Eastern Penitentiary, in the heart of the City of Philadelphia, April 4, 1894.

"Ts, ts, ts!" Yin Yi clicked critically; and his next words to himself, spoken in Chinese, to be sure, proved that he was criticising neither his handiwork nor the position of the black card, but the sad and gory tale thereon. "How unnecessary that this estimable gentleman should have wound up on the gallows. For was it not Chu Fu, the old Wise One, who once did say 'The Careless Thief, in Stealing a Bell, Forgets to Hold the Tongue of the Bell'? Now, of a truth, this estimable Caucasian gentleman assuredly must have known considerably in advance that he would have to dispatch those who were encumbering his life, were he to realize his amatory ambitions.

Why then, why indeed, did he need to end up with his neck enshrouded in a hempen noose, that must have scratched fearfully the tender skin of that region?" He reflected a moment deeply, and morosely. And then nodded sagely: "**Ai**, that was it! He just forgot to hold the tongue of the bell!"

Now he stood alongside the waxen head a large photograph, somewhat faded, it is true, with the years, and obviously taken from some ancient album. It was held upright in a simple unfinished photo-easel, made of pine sticks. And standing off a few feet, in his wax spattered blue smock, he squinted his eyes as does the true artist the world over, in contemplating his handiwork, then while referring to a typewritten notation, bearing the ornate heading of Captain Barraby's institution, which read:

> Make exackly photagraphic, Yin, except put a slight stare into the bloater's eyes, like what you did on that other murderer. I find it makes the land-lubbers what comes to my museum shiver a bit, like they was standin' naked in a noreaster. Also cast him in nearly colorless wax, Yin, sos he's pale as a goast, but take your bresh and hand him a good bright consumptive tetch on his cheekbones.

Outside, perhaps, of the good Captain's requirements as to the eyes, the head was a most perfect replica of the large photograph; indeed, it could hardly have been more perfect. Both the 2-dimensional photo and the 3-dimensional waxen reproduction thereof showed a gentleman of about 42—the dangerous age, to be sure, for all such!—with his chestnut brown hair parted in the middle, as was the custom in that mauve decade. Nor was the hair on the waxen bust something that had been recreated merely in wax, nor was it a thatch of vegetable fibres, but real hair, fine silky human hair, and Yin had had to buy it, at so much per ounce, downtown, inserting it generously over the waxen scalp with the noisy chattering automatic electric hair-implanter, and, around the actual hair line, painstakingly hair by hair, with the hand needle—a mere needle with the top third of its eye broken off, and sunken halfway in the head of an inverted wooden clothespin. Indeed, were it not for that crude and improvised tool, the shorter, stiffer bits of lighter-hued hair comprising the effigy's eyebrows and eyelashes would never have sprung forth so bewilderingly lifelike as they did, and as they invariably do in waxen busts, the world over. The sitter—who, however, had not in this case actually sat!—wore a flowing voluminous brown mustache of the type known as the "walrus" which Yin, being only after all a waxworker, had selected complete, after much thought, from the huge collection of available beards and mustaches in the huge stock of Monsieur Peloux, the same Monroe Street toupee artist from whom he always bought his human hair. The coat, or at least the brief upper fraction thereof, which enshrouded the waxen head, was a vivid check, with the absurdly short but wide lapels of the '90's, hemming in not a modern tie but a huge flaring purple cravat, as well as a very high stiff collar. The fractional segment of coat Yin had had specially made for him by Chee Lee, the old deaf tailor around the corner, and the antediluvian collar and tie he had obtained at Schmidt's, the North Clark Street theatrical costumer. The defunct Mr. Elisha Bushman's dainty shell-like ears were seemingly too small for his otherwise normal cerebral dimensions, but the photograph showed that Nature had endowed him with just that precise abnormality; and his kindly blue eyes—Yin always got his eyes at Nicol and Frimpton's, the Van Buran Street glass-eye wholesalers—popped most beautifully from his head, thanks to the precise way in which Yin had set them in the inch-thick wax shell which recreated Mr. Bushman for modern inspection. The various semi-globular pots of wax, held rigidly each in its surrounding water jacket, and each with its fixed thermometer rising from the wax compartment of the double-container, and all hanging just now on the rack across the room, showed from where the exact stearin must have come which gave Mr. Bushman his extreme paleness of complexion; and the several cans of tints which stood on Yin's workbench, just under his small skylight, showed exactly whence had come the hectic flush that artfully adorned Mr. Bushman's cheekbones, and which had been first applied and then neatly worked into the very wax itself. Mr. Bushman was, in short, his own photograph come to life—staring affrighted at the 3 officers who had come to get him—a blush at his own criminal misdeeds just rising to his face.

"Well," quoth Yin, lapsing into the current English of the year for a change, "that's done, I guess. One hundred bucks, minus $3.65 for hair, $2.25 for the mustache, $3 for the coat lapels, $1 each for the cravat and collar, $6 for the glass eyes, and $2.50 for expressage to Davenport. A profit of $80.60 for two full days' work. Not so bad. Not so bad. Hotsy-totsy, in fact—if I have the phrase correct!"

He gazed about him now, speculatively, at the much-confused interior of the unique studio on the fringe of Chicago's Chinatown. The speculation always arose at this juncture of a job, being nothing more than a fleeting intention to straighten things up and set things aright. But, being a true artist, such righting of things never took place—and the big whitewashed room always continued to exist in exactly the condition it was now in. Wax-spattered benches lay here and there, and over to one side sat the large modeling and casting table, with its plaster-of-Paris encrusted troughs, and the battery of electric lights just above it, focussing downward, when necessary, on the truncated wooden cone on which Yin always made his preliminary model in quick-hardening fine clay. Two large iron kettles of as yet untinted wax stood on ringstands in huge water pans, each on a one-hole gas plate connected by rubber tubing to the wall. A pine board lay across two small saw horses, over its surface a weird assortment of peculiar smoothing and shaping tools laid out, tools by which a waxen cast was evened out to life-like reality. Barrels stood here and there, of fluffy shredded paper-maché, for filling hollow casts where it was so desired; and various kegs of cement and triply-ground French plaster-of-Paris stood more or less underfoot about the floor. The low north-exposed skylight, angled stiffly upward, its frosted panes facing the rear alley, cast a chromatically perfect daylight into the small niche where Yin did the most meticulous part of his wax-smoothing and his wax-tinting. A rickety flight of uncarpeted steps, with an equally rickety wooden balustrade, ran up the side of the high room, ending in a narrow door which marked Yin's ascetically simple bedroom and living room that comprised just his narrow iron cot, his cooking cupboard—and his old boxwood upright piano! Two broad show windows gazed out on the narrowest street of Chicago's Chinatown, but permitted none to gaze within, since, were one outside on the sidewalk, one found both windows painted downward half their heights with opaque red paint to which was added, on the left one, in green letters, the English words "Yin Yi, Wax Worker," and on the right the three Chinese characters equivalent therefor; and, a few feet back of each plate glass window a dusty brown velveteen drape rose upward to where it hung by a brass-ringed curtain pole stretched clear across. In the left expanse of window—in front of the brown drape, of course—was a dusty waxen head of a Chinese girl, with black bangs and melting appealing black eyes; in the right, a document of some sort looking something like a diploma, with a gold seal and several ostentatious signatures, framed in black wood and resting against an invisible upended brick, its glass surface flyspecked as well as dust enshrouded.

Stepping now to the tin washbowl which reposed on a low partially knobless washstand near the west wall of his studio, Yin Yi surveyed himself, for a change, in the large mirror with unpainted wooden frame which hung above the washbowl, the while he stripped off his blue smock, and washed and scraped his long lean yellow fingers. His study of himself revealed no more, no less, than it always did reveal, but which never at any time lost its compelling interest for him: a neatly built young mongolian of not more than 29 years of age; impeccably dressed in dark blue serge of excellent material and good cut; with squat flat nose and enormously high cheek-bones set in a flat ochre-tinted face, jet eyes fearfully oblique, hair a glistening black, and rendered even blacker yet by the two unsmiling rows of even white teeth with their one strikingly visible all-gold incisor in the upper front, its dull, satin-finish surface gleaming in all lights with a sort of mocking radiance. Behind him, on the opposite wall, a wooden pendulum clock ticking away showed the time to be 3:30 in the afternoon; and were one but able to interpret the Chinese daily leaf calendar alongside it, with its peculiar representations of a crescent moon, a dragon beneath the moon, and a fish above, one would have seen that the top leaf was proclaiming the date to be October 29th.

His satisfied survey of himself completed, even as his ablutions came to an end, Yin dried himself on a towel, the while gazing cautiously about the room as though to make sure that none of those slant-orbed urchins who played at times out on the sidewalk were lurking, curious-eyed, under his casting table or behind a paper-maché barrel. Then, apparently convinced that he was quite alone, he stepped to a battered old-time wall phone protruding from the wall not far from the washbasin, and raised the receiver to his saffron ear.

"Please to give me Webster 6900," he directed in a low voice.

He waited, his Chinese stolidity marred only by a slight impatient tap-tap-tap from the toe of one well-shod foot.

But as he waited, a shadow darkened the door of the shop. And a loud bell tinkled as the door opened, tripping some lever near the top. **"Kai dai!"** muttered Yin—which was a good round Chinese oath. He dropped the receiver back upon the hook instanter, cutting off his connection short at whatever point it had then advanced to. An old Chinaman, clad in the typical black rubber-like blouse, with pajama-like fasteners, stood inside the door, hands encased within his sleeves.

"Greetings, Yin Yi," he said imperturbably in Chinese.

"Greetings, Ancient," returned Yin Yi, also speaking in Chinese. And proceeded thereafter to use that tongue—but in the **tsou** or formal form, which a younger Chinese, no matter how disparaging or supercilious his words may be to an elder, instinctively uses for the form of his address, and which the older one, strangely, uses to the younger—to keep the latter in his place! "But who mayest thou be?" added Yin Yi. "Methinks I have seen thee shuffling around these sidewalks somewhere."

"'Tis true," conceded the ancient, but with manifest asperity in his tones. "Like yourself, I was once young, and leaped and sprung like a doe who had drunken rice wine. Today I hobble along, as you too, someday, will drag thy weary way."

"Thou art not a bringer of particularly roseate pictures," commented Yin Yi, with a grunt of irritation. "And so who, again, art thou? And what is thy errand with me?"

"Sing Ling is my name," said the old Chinaman. "And I am errand boy for Kai Gee Lai, the milliner of Chinatown."

"Ah yes—Kai Gee Lai. I pass his shop always when I go to the Noon Fang restaurant, where I dine when too tired to cook. What dost wish?"

"Honorable Kai desireth me to ask what will be the cost to him of 6 heads made, upon which he may rest hats, instead of, as heretofore, resting the hats upon sticks?"

"Just pretty-girl heads—not reproductions of any particular picture nor person?" asked Yin, businesslike.

"Ai."

"The six, in such event, would cost him no more than $100," said Yin. "For I happen to possess a goodly number of old plaster casts, made from both comely Chinese girls and equally comely white girls. Which fortunate possession, on my part, renders unnecessary a large part of the labor otherwise required in such artistry as mine. I have also bought, of late, at tremendous discount, a large supply of wax that makes it possible for me to quote a pri—"

"Kai Lai does not wish wax heads," pronounced the ancient.

"Does not wish wa—why?" inquired Yin.

"If thou walked, young one, as do I, on the grass-slippers of our ancestors, instead of upon the delicately shapen white man's leathern shoes which grace thy extremities, thou wouldst know the reason why, the moment thy feet trod Chinatown's sidewalks! Even today, though it be the third turn of the 40 and 1st moon in the 7th cycle of Kwong-Sui—you, I presume, call it October!—the sidewalks are hot and their heat penetrates to the very withered soles of my feet. And if thou wert, likewise, observant when thou rushedth to the Noon Fang restaurant, thou wouldst note that Kai Gee Lai's show window faces the west—and that the hot sun beateth its way daily therein—even as it doth at this moment. In short, I have wasted 9 and 90 words of discourse, to say that waxen faces, placed in Kai Lai's shop window, will melt." Sing Ling paused a moment, as though to allow his words to osmose into his hearer. Then he went on "Honorable Kai, however, while in New Orleans recently, did see in a Negro millinery store, like placed to the Southern sun as is his to the Northern, heads which were of hard rubber, though touched upon the cheeks with a dab of red to give the suggestion of reality. He did inquire of the proprietor, who assured him that such last forever, and can be ever changed with a little brushwork; and that the New Orleans sun cannot melt such. Kai Lai wishes me to inquire whether thou possess the craft to make heads of rubber?"

"Ha!" snorted Yin Yi, his artistic soul affronted. "Canst not read a line of English, ancient one?"

"Nay. An unmelodious tongue, that in its intonations riseth and falleth perpetually like—like the roller-coaster in Riverview Park; that scurrieth, in its cadence, madly hither and thither like a he-dog frantically seeking a mate whom he hath scented somewhere in the vicinity. An outlandish tongue, at best, and one not at all necessary in Chinatown."

"A very necessary tongue," corrected Yin Yi, with some asperity of his own, "do you have intercourse, social or business, with whites." He shrugged his shoulders at the hopelessness of making old China see life through younger Chinese eyes. "Well, ancient, couldst thou read that tongue, thou wouldst see that that paper in yon north window is a certificate showing my graduation from the Rubber Technological Institute of Indianapolis, Indiana, where I was born and where I spent my earlier years. For thy benighted benefit, it means that in addition to the trade which I learned by being apprenticed for 7 long years to Song Chew, the great Indianapolis wax-modeler, now alas dead, I also possess the additional craft to do anything in rubber that man can do. I can, if necessary, make thee a big rubber stamp that would carry all the characters found in the old men's Prayer of Chongwi, presented exactly as painted on rice-paper by thy very own brush, so that thou couldst, on each fete day, stamp thy prayer on innumerable squares of the gold and silver prayer paper—the **gum gnun yee chee**, as you term them—and burn a hundred times more of them than thy ancient rheumatic wrist can create with brush and ink pot; also could I, were I of a mind to demonstrate my additional craft, cunningly coat thy shoes—didst thou deign ever to wear such!—with infinitely thin rubber from tips to soles, so that thou wouldst ever be carrying an invisible pair of overshoes, and making thee able to walk dry-footed in rain or sleet. And I can, likewise, at no more than $7 a head, cast thee—or anyone else—a fair semblance of a standard Chinese girl in hard rubber, or soft rubber, of any hue. But that, ancient one, is not art."

"Nay, but it is practicality," pronounced Sing Ling sagely. He paused. "However, Honorable Kai does not wish a fair semblance of a beautiful Chinese girl. Or any other kind of girl. He wishes a mere rough and unobtrusive headlike form, that will hold properly a hat, but that at no moment will detract the attention from his creation which sits atop it. Or canst thou not perceive the reasoning underlying his desires?"

"My reasoning faculties are so extremely developed," remarked Yin calmly, "that even when it goes counter to my business advantage, I am constrained to admit the existence of wisdom wherever wisdom truly exists. Kai is, of course, right: the white milliner utilizes such beautiful heads, such as I can, of course, create, that people do not look at the hats! Well, I can give Kai what he wishes; but, I again emphatically say, it is not art."

Sing Ling gazed innocently at the other. "From thy frequent emphasis on art, I presume thou classifieth thyself thus among workers? Thou art, in short, an artist?"

"Would I receive commissions from all over the United States, were I not?" inquired Yin, derisively.

"Why then art not rich?" pursued Sing naively—but relentlessly.

"Because though my art is a rare one, and its workers are few, it supplies the needs of a field that is greatly limited. And so I must needs pluck my living on the few jobs that arise here and there, now and again, and are delegated to me from far as well as near, because of my far-flung fame."

"Then thou art famous too?" badgered the old man cunningly.

"I am indeed fam—say—dost thou grow sarcastic with me?" inquired Yin suspiciously, his face darkening. "If thou dost," he added meaningly, "change thy tone, if not thy words. For thy enlightenment—and the whole rest of Chicago's Chinatown from Archer Avenue to 25th Street, and from Wentworth Avenue here to the railroad embankment, dost thou wish to carry the information forth—I am not only an artist, but am that rare thing, an artist with a daring and strictly individual point of view in all things he does, as to what constitutes true and real human beauty, be it masculine, or be it feminine. Moreover, I am a poet, capable of blending the words in either of two quite unlike languages into magic phrases that charm the hearer, white or yellow. I am also a musician of no mean sort, as thou might guess, couldst thou see my piano upstairs in my simple living room, with also my mandolins—or **yeong kum**—lying atop it. Only a month ago, in the earlier moon of 7th Kwong-Sui, did a bird, trilling vaingloriously and pompously upon my sill upstairs cease his song in deference to myself, the greater master, who ran but idly over the keys. And wait—open not thy withered lips to bandy further words with me. I am also a scholar of no mean attainments, for I am able to reconcile the curious old theory of Mencius that time is substance, with certain modern theories by one Ein-stein, that time is non-existent and is in reality space. And being a scholar, I am, consequently, a philosopher, a philosopher of the deepest and most profound type, so much so that nothing painful that will ever in the future befall me will so much as make me even shrug my shoulders, because I know it to be written for me even now on the book of Destiny. I am also—don't go ancient—an actor a consummate actor, able to render the so-called Ham-let of one Shakespeare, more perfectly even than recently it was rendered on the talking screen at the Golden Dragon Cinema at State and 22nd Streets. No less a man than Sir Alfred Leets, greatest Shakespearean tragedian in the world, upon whom I called recently at the Stevens Hotel to modestly demonstrate my talents, did say that were it not for my Chinese blood I would have undoubtedly made my mark as a thespian upon the American stage. Moreover—pause a moment longer, ancient, and obtain some more information for that rabble out there in Chicago's Chinatown!—my histrionic ability is basically natural, and dependeth not on melodramatic lines written by white playwrights, since I can do the chamber act from that great play of the Yuan period known as **The Auspicious Hour and the Beating of Hang-Niang** better even than Mei Lan-Fang, the great Chinese actor, who rendered it here in Chinatown's own theatre but 6 months ago. I am again, in addition to all things I have enumerated, a logician of high acuity, able to perceive the flaw in any train of reasoning, as well as the most subtle error in any presumed sequence of cause and effect. And lastly, I am—but not of my own doing, to be sure!—a handsome and practically perfect example of my racial type. By which— and all my other talents—I wield a magnetic power by which I can charm the heart of yellow maid or white maid, at my will."

"I am pleased," said Sing Ling plaintively, "that it was granted me by Fate that before shuffling off of this old earth, I could meet and converse with a man who possessed all of those attainments." He blinked gravely once or twice as he spoke, but his wrinkled face remained a triumph of impassivity. "To have met such a man as you, Yin Yi," he added solemnly, "is to have fittingly climaxed a long and eventful life." He withdrew one long-nailed hand from one capacious black sleeve. And put its skinny fingers on the knob of the door. "I will convey to Kai Gee Lai thy quotations, as well as the fact that thou art trained in the working of other pliabilities than wax, particularly in that single one which we did mutually discuss. And he will no doubt call thee for a conference, if thou wilt deign to honor his shop with thy presence." And turning, the old man exited painfully, the bell above the door tinkling reverberatingly as he went out.

Yin Yi took no further chances, this time, of interruptions, and consequent eavesdroppers. He proceeded over to the shop door, and locked it tight by means of the long-shafted key protruding inward from its keyhole. And, key safely in pocket, he returned once more to the battered wall phone.

"Webster 6900," he asked again, in a low voice.

CHAPTER II

Plans—for Two!

Within a reasonable fraction of a minute, the answer to Yin Yi's call came. "Hotel State," a businesslike man's voice replied.

"Allow me, if you please," said Yin Yi, silkily, "to converse with Room 414."

There was a clicking on some small hotel switchboard, probably adjoining a day clerk's counter, and then, after a brief pause, a further receiver was lifted, and there came on the wire a woman's voice—a somewhat small, thin, but high-pitched treble voice, quite pleasingly sweet and girlish, however—although so childish in some of its intonations that one could hardly help but realize that the words spoken by it emanated from a tiny, perhaps even slightly petulant, Cupid's-bow mouth.

"Yes?" it inquired, friendlily.

At which Yin Yi did a very peculiar thing, the reason therefore being known best to him. He asked quite deliberately, and clearly: "Am I in connection—with room 514?"

This peculiar question, considering that he had specifically asked for room 414, plus the unmistakable tones of his own very distinctive voice, obviously conveyed to his fair hearer some sort of code message, for she replied at once:

"It's—it's all right, Yin. Nobody here but me."

"Good. Then I will await your call on the other phone." And Yin hung up promptly on his own instrument.

He waited where he was, however, tapping that well-shod right foot with the pointed toe. The call that would come back to him within the fraction of a minute would, he knew, emanate from a phone which had been installed at one time in a certain room 414 of a cheap South State Street hotel patronized chiefly by theatrical people of the lower class, by a small-time race-horse bookmaker who had permanently occupied that room over many months. And had in due course left it. And the telephone company, following its usual custom, had not yet removed the instrument, but had merely cut off its incoming service, being careful however to leave its nickel-hungry maw open for all further nickels that future guests of that room might care to insert in it in the meanwhile. And what was most important, however, was that the wires from that instrument did not go through the hotel switchboard, but went straight to the downtown automatic exchange which was now handling calls for pretty nearly all of Chicago except Chinatown and the two Black Belts. The expected call from that other phone, so desirably private as it now would be, came in a half-minute, jangling from the bell-box near Yin's elbow. He raised the receiver again. The same childish feminine voice was on the wire.

"It's me again, Yin. Dolly." The voice literally glowed with pleasure.

"And how is my sweet, wondrous flower today?"

"Aw Yin! What—what sweet things you kin say. It does beat ever'thing. No white man's got that there kinda language what you got."

"Think you so, my sweet? My fairest of buds? You compliment me far more than I deserve, I greatly fear. After all, I speak only that which rests upon my mind. And nothing else." Yin Yi paused a bare second. "I dreamed of you last night, angel, and so vivid was my dream, that all the day long, while I finished that recent job I told you I expected to get—yes, from Davenport—I found myself wondering when, oh when, were you and I going to see each other once more?"

"Gee, Yin, and for 'zackly that there reason I sure am glad you called. In fact, big honey-boy, I was a-goin' to call you pretty soon if I didn't hear from you. 'Cause somep'n unexpected's come up in my affairs. Yin, Herman called up from Milwaukee just a while ago. He don't never as a rule call in the afternoon, as you know, so I knowed when I heard his voice that somep'n had come up. Well, it had, Yin. He—he got that darned New York engagement. An'—an' it's for 3 long months, Yin. Startin', too, th' evenin' o' November 2. After that, a month on th' Southern circuit, down 'round Alabama. Then, thank God, Yin, he an' me comes back to Chicago so's he can work his act on the sideshow platform at th' Indust'ial Exhibits Fair here. Th' World's Fair is jes' far enough gone now, he says, that th' Indust'ial Exhibits Fair oughta pull—an' give the platform show a break for real coin. But anyway, Yin, this is gonna mean we ain't gonna have no chance to see each other for 120 long days."

"That is, indeed, an unhappy piece of tidings," pronounced Yin gravely, though philosophically. "That would leave you then, to be in Chicago, but tomorrow and the day after, if I underst—"

"Not tomorrow, Yin. I guess you done forgot me tellin' you I had a sister in Chicago. Well, not 'zackly Chicago—but Gary, Injiana. An' that tomorrow's her birthday. And that she's givin' a big dinner for all her kids—an' me, what's their aunt—with all sortsa doin's. Gee, Yin, on'y time durin' th' last 5 years that I 'uz within five hunderd miles o' her when 'twas her birthday. And I—"

"Quite, Dolly. I understand. I have, in fact, a deeply understanding mind on all such matters. She would never forgive you if you omitted honoring her birthday." He paused.

"But let's see," he calculated. "We have not only day after tomorrow, as I see it, but even part of today yet. We—"

"Not today," almost groaned the fair one on the other end of the wire. "Fate's just a-campin' on my trail, big honey boy. Herman's friend what played in th' same outfit with him at Omaha—that there darned hypnotist I told you about—is goin' through Chicago today, an' is to stop by the hotel here, anywhere's between now an' midnight tonight. Herman thinks the sun jes' sets an' rises with that there homely lookin' man, with his long hair, an' his waxed mustaches, an'—an' them gleamin' black eyes what'll nearly drive you critzy when they look into yours. An' he writ me as how I'm to greet the snaky-lookin' gazaboe without fail. So here I gotta set th' next 10 hours or so, and wait till he comes by and dishes me all the dirt—for Herman, o' course!—what's busted in the profesh around Omaha, and blows on his way to Buffalo where he's got a bookin'."

"Well, Beautiful, you are indeed, then, riveted for today where you now are. When, then, will you be coming home tomorrow, Dolly—from this town of Gary?"

"'Bout midnight, Yin; not before. Susie—yeah, th' big sister—wants me to meet her worser half, what works that crazy shift in the steelmills. And I'll be gettin' home with maybe no more'n a hour to spare, to catch Herman's call from Milwaukee, 'bout 2 in the mornin'."

Yin surveyed the transmitter calculatingly.

"Exactly when do you leave for New York, Dolly sweet?"

"At 11 o'clock at night, sharp, day after tomorrow, Yin. That bein' October 31st. What we white people, Yin, call Hallowe'en. It—but do you know what Hallowe'en is, Yin!"

"Oh, of a surety, sweet. That is the evening when people of your race go masked about the streets, ofttimes in strange costumes as well as masks. The one evening, outside of New Year's eve, when the law, it seems, permits them to go freely thus about. Of a surety I know your Hallowe'en. There will be clowning and merrymaking about the city, even in the very downtown district itself. I have, in fact, participated in the merry rites of Hallowe'en myself, though only back when I was a few years younger than I now am, and found life to be less grave and serious than I find it to be today. And— but you will be leaving Chicago, beautiful, at 11 o'clock that evening?"

"Yes, Yin. Herman says as how he wants to leave on that Broadway Express what goes out at that hour. In fack, he 'spects me to be all packed, such as what we have, which ain't much, you know; for I can pack it all in less'n twenty minutes' time. They're gonna let him cut that there last show there in Milwaukee—jest for that one last night—an' stick on a Hindu glass-en'-tack eater what's been a-tryin' for weeks to get hisself a tryout. They're lettin' Herman cut that last show, ya see, so's he can get away early. 'Bout 8:45, in fac'. Then all he'll gotta do is get his money. An' put together his swords an' knives an' fire apparanguses, an' hop that fas' train on th' Milwaukee an' St. Paul. The one what'll bring him in here at 10:30. He'll go by th' hotel here in a taxicab, pick me up—and we'll head for the 12th Street depot here with plenty 'nough time to unload our stuff in the stateroom on that 11 o'clock train. We'll be naturally havin' a stateroom, o' course."

"Yes, of course," granted Yin. He scratched his chin a bit. "Then, then," he said, a little disconcertedly for a true philosopher, "it would mean that if we are to see each other again—to dwell in each other's love, for the last time in 120 long days, it will have to be—"

"It would gotta be day after tomorrow, Yin—but c'n be any time or all the time, so far's that goes, from early mornin' clear up to an' includin' most any part o' th' evenin'. Up till—say 10 o'clock, that is. How—how—are **you** fixed, honey-boy?" There was a worried tone in the treble voice.

"Hm? Now during the later evening of that day, my sweet, which you call Hallowe'en, or October 31st, it would not be possible for me to be with you, or, rather, you with me, because of the fact that I have a vital appointment which means the payment to me of a very large sum of money—money which rightfully belongs to me and was wrongfully taken from me. That is, my sweet fairy, if it were merely a matter of giving up the money to see you, I would give it up—of course; but since you are free all of the day—and I have this appointment only during that evening—then we have indeed a whole delightful day for our tryst, and, alas, our last and only day for such a long, long while."

"Tryst? What does that there word mean, Yinnie-honey-wunnie?"

"A tryst," explained Yin patiently, "is a place and a time where two who are intensely fond of each other may be—er—secretly together for a number of fleeting, precious hours."

"Gee—tryst!—that's a nice word. I'm allus gonna remember that word. You an' me has sure had a lot of trysts, ain't we?" She giggled a bit.

"Sshh, sweet! 'Tis best not to speak damaging words out loud."

"Gosh no—not—not if Herman ever heard 'em," She snickered again.

"Exactly. For a sword swallower and professional fire-eater always has plenty of extra swords lying around. And probably a few pots of fire as well!"

"I'll say! You betcha life on that, Yin. Herman Gottlieb wouldn't never stand for no—" She broke off embarrassedly.

"No cursed mongol playing with his wife," laughed Yin. "No, Dolly, pride of race is ofttimes more sensitive than pride of mere marital possession."

"What—what does all that mean, Yin?"

"I will explain when next we are together." Yin Yi paused. "Well, the Fates conspire definitely to fix our tryst for day after tomorrow. Which, at that, will give me all of tomorrow to clean up a lot of loose ends which confront me on various delicate matters. For if you are to be far from me, I may go far, far too—during those 4 desolate months. To China, in fact, where my ancestors were born. I have long been intending to make such journey, and now may be the logical time to take it. I shall, of course, not remain there, for America is my natural home." He paused. "Well—all is settled then?"

"Yes, I guess it is. Except Yin—well—where we gonna meet—and where we—well, you know—gonna be—together?"

"Where," asked Yin Yi hopelessly and expressively, "could two such as you and I ever be together—for any protracted length of time? I a Mongolian and you—well—with a quite possessive husband! No, my little petal of a new blown rose, it must be the same place as always before."

"Gee—the cute little nest, Yin. I was hopin' you'd say as what we'd go there. Gee, but I sure love that place. It's so different like as what we white people ever do. So—so orimental—ain't that the word?"

"Perhaps, Beautiful, you mean ornamental—or perhaps—Oriental?" inquired Yin puzzledly.

"I guess I mean Oriental, Yin. 'Count o' them heavy draperies, an'—an' the big curtained bed, an' th' hangin' lamps, an' th' way the windows is all cut off from ever'thing. Gee, jes' like, when you're in it, that you've done stepped entirely outa the world, it's so away from ever'thing and ever'body."

"Yes, it is all of that, is it not? And I try to keep it just that way. Very occasionally, it is true, I bring people there who wish for some reason to be modeled—but who dislike coming into Chinatown. I can at least complete their sitting there—that is, effect the preliminary clay head—and achieve the more soilsome work here in the Chinatown shop later."

"Say, Yin, why for did you really fix up that there place? Was it really so's you c'd take care o' people what didn't like to go into Chinatown, or—now don't get mad, Yin!—was it—was it maybe so's you could have other wimmen? Ya see—I'm a little jealous!"

Yin laughed. "My best answer, Beautiful, is to repeat to you merely a saying once uttered by Chu Fu, one of our ancient wise men. Chu Fu said: 'If your skin is thin, never approach too close to a bramble bush'." He paused a moment. "But I **can** say, Beautiful, that never since I met **you** has any woman been in that place."

"O.K., Yin! Ain't nobody c'd ask nothin' more. But just you be sure you go to China while I'm gone! I don't want you 'round this city while I'm far,

far away."

"Quite so, my china doll. I am sure I shall leave for China in a few days or a week."

"Well, Yin, seein's it's the same old nest—that jes' suits me. 'Cause it's bootiful—and cause it's—it's safe. And now, Yin—will **you** bring supplies—or should I? We gotta eat, honey-bunnie-Yin, as well as—love."

"Of a surety. Except that we shall not just eat—we shall dine! The emotions are, after all, but a functioning of nerve cells, which in turn are but a product of metabolism. And metabolism depends upon nutriment. In short, emotions spring from nutriment! But worry not **your** mind with details of pabulum. For I shall bring with me the finest of Chinese food, which you like so well. Gamgots, I shall have, stuffed with minced pineapple. The rarest and most fragrant Fansang tea, which I import myself. Noodles that have been browned not in an ordinary oven, but in an oven hung with pendent strings of almonds, for it is not generally scientifically known that a Chinese noodle absorbs 3/16ths of its own weight in aroma. I may bring two boned hares, can I obtain them, but I shall assuredly have two stuffed cooked ducks—one a great duck and one smaller duck—but each jammed with parched walnuts. And—but I will not tantalize you by telling you all we shall set forth on our table. And I shall of course fetch two bottles of rare wine, the brown **how-sai** and the red **ching-we**, both of which have served your delectation before. Also, I think I shall bring, this time, a small bottle of the rare **muikwailo** cordial, although I fear you will like it not, since it is distilled from bamboo and only we Chinese, as a rule, like the taste of it."

"Aw, I'll like it, Yin. Never yet saw anything you liked what I didn't like, didja? Say—but this is gonna be swell. It's nice to eat—I allus did think that!—but it's nicer still when at the same time you're with somebody what loves you and says the sweetest things that ever a girl has hearn in her ears. And so, Yin, you'll be waitin', maybe, in the alley, like before so—"

"No, Dolly. I propose a slightly different procedure this time. But first, how early can you come?"

"As early as you want, Yin. 'Course you know I gotta be here—" Her voice took on a scared aspect. "—for that two o'clock ev'ry mornin' call Herman sends me from Milwaukee. Gee—it'd go bad with me if I wasn't on hand for that!"

"Of course. Of a naturalness. Well, I suggest you receive your spouse's call at 2 a.m. that morning. Then go back to bed, as you always do, and finish out your sleep. Arise early, however, and come to our place of rendezvous in that early, early morning before the alley and the courtway gets full of trucks and wagons. Instead, though, of going in to that cobbled courtway from the Clinton Street side, where we have entered before, go in by way of the alley on Harrison Street—where we went out last. Do you remember, sweet?"

"Oh sure, Yin. I know all that terr'tory. I been in Chicago lotsa times."

"Well then, dismount from the cab which you will board a half block away from the hotel, at the northwest corner of Clinton and Harrison Streets. Walk west on Harrison Street a half block to the alley. Turn down the alley. Two hundred feet or so, as you know. Then turn in again, into the inner cobble-stoned court. Go straight to the red painted door set in the brick wall. You have your key safe?"

"Gosh yes, Yin. I love that little Yale key. 'Cause you give it to me.

"Thank you my dear. It is I who am honored." Yin paused. "Well, just open the red door and enter, and close it. It will lock by itself. You will find yourself quite alone, of course. But the usual warehouse light, which burns night and day, will be burning as always, so that the many showcases piled about, as well as the cashier's desks and light fixtures and extra phone booths will not obstruct nor impede your progress."

"Oh, that junk won't bother me none, Yin. Anyway, you've cleared a good aisle to where your green door is." She paused. "And so, then, you'll be—"

"I will be in the—er—nest, as you term it. Thread your way around to the door of it—and tap on that door—say—5 times. I have an engagement tomorrow evening with a Chinese friend—a scholar—on the far north side; this engagement will undoubtedly keep me up quite late, and so instead of going clear back to Chinatown to complete my own slumbers, I shall in all probability just go back to the—er—snuggery, and complete my sleep there. I shall have everything straightened out, however, and in readiness for my queen before she arrives. Now, Dolly, is everything clear?"

"Gosh, yes, Yin! Sure it is. Ever'thing's clear as day to me."

"In which event, if you have no objection, I would like to offer a suggestion. Concerning this disciple of Mesmer who is to visit you today—yes, by that I mean the—er—hypnotist. I suggest, my precious, that you be exceeding guarded while in his presence. He could, you know, be a spy or emissary of your husband. And while the scientific laws of hypnosis are said to be indubitably such that you could never be forced to reveal information detrimental to your own interests, he could nevertheless project upon you, unknown to you, a psychic state in which you might possibly betray the fact that you were concealing guilty knowledge of some sort."

"I didn't get all that, Yin. Will you say it shorter?"

"Assuredly. Just this: Guard yourself—while around this hypnotist. Your husband may have sent him there to obtain an inkling of what lies back of your charming, mystic, inscrutable blue eyes—eyes which I am convinced contain the long lost Chinese blue found today only in the pottery of the Ming era."

"Yin, you slay me! You do, honest to God. Are my eyes really like that? Are they—but ne' mind. About this guy—he can't hypnotize me, Yin. He's more or less of a fake, anyway—he allus hires some of th' bedouins in whatever push he's with—them's th' hangers-on, Yin, with every pit or platform show—to shill for him. That means to play-off hypnotized, see?"

"Be not too certain of the paucity of his powers. The Chinese magicians of old combined the worst chicanery with true magic and true occultism. Confucius—yes, that other old Wise Man to whom I so frequently refer—did say: 'Only the foolish cock-pheasant goes to slumber when the sun is eclipsed.'"

"Don't worry, Yin. He's a fake, I tell you." Her voice dropped confidentially. "An' anyway, Herman wouldn't send him around to snoop. Herman'd come rarin' here hisself like a wind outa th' North, if he was on the war-path, an' prob'ly blowin' fire outa his nostrils like he does in part of his act!" She giggled openly in spite of herself. But subsided quickly. "But I won't let Gimlet-Eyes get my eyes—if that'll make you feel more comfortable."

"It was not my own comfort, sweet—but yours, which I held in mind," declared Yin. "However, my words of advice were merely an admonition, at best. You cannot be hypnotized—if you are on your guard, and **will** not to be. Always remember that! Well, all, I believe, is clear now."

"All's clear," she repeated. "Clear as day. My heart's all a-pumpin' a-ready thinking about bein' with you again. Gee, but I **sure** do love you, Yin. I—" She stopped "Expec' my 5 taps on the inside door—not the red door, o' course—at about 6 in the mornin', Yin. Which'll give us—"

"One full and entire day together," said Yin, "the while the late fall sun rises—flows across the sky outside of our arbor, seeing us not, nor seen by us—and sinks into Chicago's smoke again. Rare viands to eat. Wine to speed the blood through our veins. Love, to make the heart beat faster. And then—long desolation—for four interminable months."

"Ain't it awful? It drives me nerts to think of it. Seems—seems like a lifetime."

"But time," declared Yin scholastically, "is in reality a quite non-existent entity. And the future already exists in space-time, except that our consciousness has not yet traveled to the point where it lies. And the proof of my observation rests in the fact that the future invariably becomes, somehow, the present. Very well, fair Nordic, with hair of corntassel hue, matched only by skin of the softness of a baby's, I will await five taps the morning after tomorrow."

"Bye, Yinnie-bunny!" And a faint pecking noise like a kiss came over the wire, followed by the clicking of a severed connection. At which Yin Yi deposited his own receiver back on the hook.

He stood by the phone ruminating.

"Somewhat of a complication, to be sure, that our tryst must be October 31st, of all days! Since I must send her home by not later than 8 in the evening. At least if I am to see a man at 8:30 whom, if he does not concede my just demand, I must kill. And, killing, must do it in such a manner that those wax-workers who in future years make models of famous murderers may never receive the deplorable order to create one of 'Yin Yi, Famous Murderer!' **Hai-law!** How, therefore, to make quite certain of that? How indeed? Since I must not be as the lazy, who use a long thread, nor the stupid, who use a crooked needle. How, then, to avoid both? I must—" He turned toward his waxen specimen of handiwork, gazing popeyed at him from across the room. "But, if I mistake not, I already have framed the exact answer to such a problem. The clever thief holds the tongue of the bell he steals. How simple!"

CHAPTER III

The Great Idea!

Doctor Hippolytus Zing, Numerologist—Doctor, **not** through any medical degree, but by virtue of a Ph. D. degree, Poggtown College, Iowa, 1908!—leaned back in his rickety swivel chair and regarded his brother Sebastien sadly. He sensed, did Hippolytus Zing, Ph.D., that the other's roving gaze about the big office, looking out as it did on the lugubriously dark interior court, its floor carpeted with thin worn and here and there threadbare carpet, its several propped up bookcases with here and there a glass pane missing, and the big terrestial globe in one corner now unreadable through much thumbing, was highly critical. Hippolytus Zing was glad, in fact, that Sebastien, well dressed, clean shaven and all—4 years Hippolytus' junior, but looking in actuality, only 40 instead of 46!—was not riveting his eyes upon him, Hippolytus. For he realized that his own shiny black clothes were baggy, his black Windsor tie frayed, his shirt dirty, and that his 50 years of age had given his face jowls and bags. He knew, in short, that he was unsuccessful—even though one of those bookcases held two books by him on Numerology, and even though his tiny pamphlet, the **Numerological Gazette**—issued **if** and when he could get it out—held the latest findings in Numerology.

But now, alas, Sebastien was gazing directly at him.

"Hippolytus," the latter said, "don't you think you made a great mistake in taking up Numerology as a life work?"

"No more so," said Hippolytus haughtily, "than did you—in becoming private secretary to a Steel Company president."

"Yes—but look what I've gotten out of it, Hippolytus. I've been prosperous—well taken care of during the years—had voyages to many places and all. And now that President Elliott Muncibar is going to the Himalayas—**I** go with him."

"I suppose," muttered Hippolytus, "that he'll be wanting to dictate letters concerning steel operations—up in Tibet?"

"Well, not exactly, Hippolytus—no. But he wants to do a book called

'40 Years in the Steel Business'."

"Or," put in Hippolytus caustically, "'How I Stole a Million'!"

"Oh come now, Hippolytus. That's no way to talk. Muncibar made his fortune honestly, and, as his secretary, I've fared well. It's only **you**, Hippolytus, who are at fault. Here you are—50 years of age—a really great numerologist, as such things go I fancy—who has studied every aspect of the fool subj—that is, the subject—but here you are, putting out your poor little magazine when you can, your two books selling to a few bugs—"

"Not bugs, if you don't mind," ordered Hippolytus.

"All right. But here you are. With nothing. Nothing but a cottage on Buckingham Place in which you live, so heavily mortgaged that I've just had to—"

"Don't rub it in," begged Hippolytus, "because you just loaned me $200 cash to get an extension on my mortgage—from the nigger plutocrat who holds it. You'll—you'll get a second mortgage for the money."

"Oh hell, Hippolytus, I don't want any second mortgage. I wouldn't even have your cottage—as a gift. It's just that I'm worried about **you**. Here you've virtually wasted your life—it's all over, Hippolytus—and by God, Hipp, you'll—well unless, Hipp, you catch hold of the tail of Success somehow during the next ten years—you'll have to fall back on the Old Age Pension."

"Well, that wouldn't be so bad," pronounced Hippolytus Zing glumly. "It'd be better than trying to scrape together the rent for this piece of area here in the Interstate Life Building!"

"Exactly," said Sebastien. "All you take in from clients—and subscriptions—and book sales—has to go out to pay for this very area—only in order to take in more!"

"Well—what do you want me to do?" Hippolytus asked. "What **can** I do? To make more subscriptions? And sell more books? And get more consulting clients? What the goddamned hell **can** I do?"

Sebastian was reactively silent.

"Well, I suppose you've got to advertise."

"Advertise? For God's sake, Sebastien, there's scores of numerologists doing that. And most of them—all providing competition to me—not even knowing the science."

"Yes," admitted Sebastien Zing, "I suppose that's the trouble. The competition. Yes." He was silent. "Well, I guess you've got, Hippolytus, to publicize yourself in some way so that your name will go all over the country—so that everybody will rush out and order your magazine from his newsdealer—and your books from his bookseller—so that, in short, people will fall over each other calling for appointments."

"Oh—yeah? Well how in hell, Sebastien, can I do **that**?"

Sebastian was silent.

"Darned if I know. Confess to a murder—I guess!"

"Confess to a mur—what do you mean, Sebastien?"

"Well, I was only joking—at first. Then, a second later—after I enunci-ated the idea—I grew a bit serious."

"Well, what do you mean—confess to a murder? What kind of a mur-der?"

"Oh—some unsolved murder, of course. No murder, Hippolytus, where the police have their eyes on the actual murderer—much less have him ac-tually in custody—for in such a case they'd kick your threadbare behind galley-west out of the police station if you even so much as tried to claim the authorship of the murder. No, Hippolytus, some murder that has failed utterly and completely of solution. Don't you know of any?"

"No, I don't. In fact there are none, at present in Chicago, of that cat-egory. However—one may occur. At any time. And it—but listen here, Se-bastien, you must be crazy. If I confessed to a murder, I'd get hung."

"Oh you poor ass, Hippolytus. I don't mean to hawgtie yourself that way. No, I mean some murder which—listen, you have certain classes in Numerology, don't you?"

"Yes. Two—during two afternoons a week in Handel Hall. I get $3 for conducting each. Then, again, I have private classes three nights a week—in a private home—on the West Side. I get 10 cents from each person attend-ing—and average $2 for each class."

"All right! That takes care of the hanging! Confess only to such a murder as has been done—or will be done!—during one of your classes. In short, Hippolytus, have a half dozen alibi witnesses. But long before they read the news of your confession, and come forward, you'll be in print on the streets all over the world—'Famous Numerologist Confesses Murder'—and you'll be made. You can later just say the police forced your confession."

Hippolytus gave vent to a derisive laugh.

"Your ideas, Sebastien, are so damned foolish they are—they should be called 'scrooey.' Yes. If I were even involved by the police to the extent that I had to confess murder, I'd—I'd be professionally ruined. I'd—" He took out a dappled fountain pen, with a gold band, and started to write a check. "Here's a check, Sebastien, post-dated 6 months—for that $200."

"Your checkbook is dirty," commented the latter quite freely. "And also your cuffs. So where, oh where, is the ancient tin fountain pen you used to use? Surely you aren't starting, Hippolytus, to buy $15 pens?"

"No—Christ no! This one was loaned to me by Jack Kenwood, the rack-eteer who issues the **Ultrapolitan Magazine** across the hall. Not a regular magazine, you understand—but one that's sold to cockroach tradesmen, as a local advertising medium, by virtue of a lot of spurious 'big names' in it. It—but about the pen. Mine went on the Fritz while I was witnessing some paper of his as a notary—and he magnanimously—the stinkingly lucky pup!—told me to keep this of his till mine started flowing again! It's even got his name etched on the gold band here. He—lucky devil! He makes plenty, all right, on his **Ultrapolitan**."

"Well," said Sebastien, "it's sort of too bad, don't you know, that **he** can't get murdered! Then **you**—with a quite innocent means of having his pen—could get yourself picked up somehow—and confess you killed him. And no opprobrium attached to you at all—thereby."

"Quite true. Only Kenwood isn't murdered—and won't be—and I've got to return his pen eventually. So—what?"

"So—what?" echoed Sebastien Zing. And rose. "Well, I've had my say. Which was all in the manner of rough suggestion anyway. I've tried to emphasize, Hippolytus, that you've got to do **something** desperate. To advertise yourself. You've only 10 years of active life left. 10 years in which to make money. And to make a competence for your old age. You've the goods—but not the market. In short, the clients. And I only suggested confessing to a murder in sheer desperation myself. That was all."

And Sebastien Zing took up his bag.

"When do you leave for the Himalayas?" asked Hippolytus, changing the subject.

"In two hours! In view of the fact that this is 2 p.m.—October 30th. I'll be aboard the Aquitonic this time tomorrow."

"I see. Well, I'll return this money in due course. And I'll—listen, Sebastien—about this nut idea of yours—how in hell, Sebastien, could my confession to a murder—even if I could clear myself and charge police coercion—**help** me in my profession?"

Sebastien Zing scratched his chin.

"We-ell—to be sure—I hadn't thought of that. But, starting out as I now am, for the far spaces of the earth, I'd only say, Hippolytus, that you'd absolutely have to make it a numerological murder—i.e., you'd have to give a motive, based on numerology, why you murdered the victim!"

Hippolytus Zing gave a disgusted gesture with his two hands. And arose himself.

"It's time for you to go, Brother-o'-Mine," he said. "Your brains are commencing to get addled."

And the other, shaking hands, swung his bag to his free hand, and was conducted to the door by Hippolytus Zing.

"Good Luck," said the latter, grumpily. "Write me—from some Buddist monastery."

And Hippolytus Zing closed the door upon his radical brother.

And, inside its threshold, stood thinking. And the more he thought, the more—

"His idea—his idea," he said, scratching his own chin, "isn't nearly as crazy—as it sounded at first. By God—it isn't! A numerological murder! Committed—the gods willing —during the hour of one of my classes. It—it would go around the world, in a single night. 20,000,000 people would read it. My books would be mentioned. My theories would be published. My magazine would be advertised. People interested in Numerology would be curious, afterward, to see me. People—by the Gods—Sebastien **did** have the answer. A numerological murder! Hippolytus—if you play your cards— you're made."

And he sat down at his ancient desk and commenced writing with the beautiful dappled gold-banded fountain pen of Jack Kenwood, the prosperous racketeer across the hall!

CHAPTER IV

"Invest Such Murder with a Chinese 'Angle'!"

Mr. Nisaku Sato—alias "Eichii Tokanami,"—head of the Chicago branch of the Japanese Secret Service, gazed down on the greenish, ever-mysterious Chicago River from his window high up in the Merchandise Mart, Chicago, and re-read, again—for the third time—the communication he had just received from his chief, Chosoburo Kusumoto, head of the entire System, in New York, and which he had painstakingly—oh, ever so painstakingly—decoded.

It read—when decoded into Japanese: [1]

> Arrange to have followed passenger with short grey beard, stockily built, age about 50, arriving Chicago today October 31 on Chicago Flyer known as train No. 6 New York Central Railroad. He will be riding in coach Number 5, Lower Berth Seat No. 4. Assign to this exceedingly grave matter your full complement of 5 Japanese agents and not less than 4 of the 6 non-Japanese in Chicago who are accepting each a monthly stipend from Nippon, but excluding white C-8 and Persian C-12 the two such being excluded because of their unwillingness to commit homicide for Nippon. It will be perfectly correct to entrust white C-11, who I have down on my record here as being formerly NY-15-xx, white C-3 and white C-13 with the full details of the matter, but give separate and garbled instructions to the Negro C-27 omitting specific details as to this matter having a bearing definitely injurious to China insofar as he evinced slight pro-Chinese leanings on the Edgewater Beach Hotel affair. The passenger hereintofore described in this wire has upon his person, and may by the time he arrives Chicago have in a bag he carries, the 13th Coin of Confucius. But because of visual difficulties and absence of required lenticular appurtenances we are certain that he does not know up to the time of his disembarkation from the train the identity of the coin or its probable value. It is but a question of time after he detrains however that he will contact someone who will apprise him of what he has, or will obtain same from him, either by open purchase or assignment as a numismatic specimen, or by purchase for the weight of gold in it. The first thing you are to do therefore is to have this

---

1   Author's Note: This communication was also presented in an earlier novel, "Finger Finger."

man followed without fail to his lodgings wherever they are. The minute he departs therefrom have them combed and searched thoroughly. In the meantime dog him at every step and record every person he succeeds in contacting, particularly as to whether they possess numismatic knowledge or not, or connections in that field. Strike quick and at once, to the ultimate extent, if any indications arise that he has actually passed the coin; or, if in doubt, search the quarters or place of business of such suspected recipients the moment he or she leaves such quarters or place of business, and do exactly likewise with respect to any such place as such may repair to. No one knows that the 13th Coin has been stolen in New York, and it may continue to be unrecognized as such in Chicago. In following up such individuals as this bearded man may contact, and taking certain measures with them that the situation dictates, be apprised please of the following exception which you are to note carefully: To-wit: a young man, aged about 27, with blue eyes, residing on Oak Street in the first block west of Dearborn. Due to my agent NY-31's manipulations of raincoats aboard this train this young man now has the bearded man's raincoat and the other has his, which contained an elaborate graphical sales chart of some sort. This young man was in frequent conversation at times aboard the train with your quarry and may have obtained the latter's name or address or possible eventual hotel, or the latter in turn may have obtained a clue to the young man's identity. If this prove to be so, the latter may, on discovering he has lost this chart, succeed somehow in getting into telephonic touch with the bearded man and either go to his quarters or have the older man come to his on Oak Street in order to re-exchange the apparently transposed raincoats. Be cautious, and so instruct all agents, that this young man is not to be regarded as a suspicious contact inasmuch as he has a quite logical and innocent reason for contacting our man. If our man makes any alarming move any time, subsequent to his obtaining lodgings in Chicago or leaving them, that in any way threatens our re-obtaining the coin, have the agents then trailing him induct him into their car if they have such available, either by a trick, or by force if the whereabouts permit, or at the points of concealed guns, and rush him to hideout Number 3. There, if coin is not on his person, force its location from him, as well as a brief signed confession that he stole it from the Cyrus Weatherford Museum, New York City, at 3:45 October 30th, using the guard's keys. This will clear a certain guard in the museum whom we are trying to protect, at least for the immediate present, if not for all time to come. Once you obtain the coin from your bearded prisoner, or its location, and have the confession, I suggest he be permanently put out of the way so that he cannot later repudiate his confession. If you have difficulty in using the Japanese agents during the full daylight from 3 o'clock to 6 o'clock, I suggest that you confine yourself to the whites only for the direct work during those hours, but take full advantage subsequent thereto of the fact that it will then be Hallowe'en and that the city will be more or less in masquerade costume. Once evening comes, your work may be tremendously facilitated and the agents' powers greatly enhanced by their opportunity to go freely about masqued and costumed and to rapidly shift their positions with respect to themselves and their various objectives. See therefore that each has available to him a cheap costume and cheap mask which may be donned and later discarded when necessary. The agent or agents are to kill instantly and swiftly if confident at any time that the coin has changed hands to a recipient who will prove to be a custodian dangerous to Japan's interests, and providing opportunity to thus strike is then present; but agree, between all of you in conclave, that such killing must if possible be invested with a subtly Chinese angle inasmuch as the ensuing police investigation may result in the fact coming out that the victim had contacted the Confucian coin owner or actually had the Confucian coin, and that would result in a roundup of all Japanese in Chicago, as well as all whites known to have Japanese affiliations, with probable third degree tactics unpleasant and dangerous for all, insofar as the white agents do not possess the resistive stamina our Nipponese have. The object of the Chinese angle to any killing is because the Chinese, down to the last man of the entire Chinese race, are the obvious aspirants for possession of this coin, and the investiture of such killing with a concrete Chinese flavor will point the finger of suspicion to the few representatives of the Chinese government in Chicago—or to some Chinese who may have had business, social or other contact with the victim. Except I must caution you to be most subtle in what traces you leave: the Chinese murderer never leaves clues, and betrays himself at best only in the method of his killing, or in the more psychological aspects of what he does. And the Chicago police, particularly those who have had Chinatown experience, are by no means fools if too mephitic a herring is drawn across the trail. So subtle, subtle, subtle there, my good friend Nisaku—in whatever you do; and impress that fact on each and every agent, yellow or white. Keep me apprised in the meanwhile, via any safe outside phone connection, of all developments, including any obscurity you may happen to find in this wire. Also kindly acknowledge same the moment you receive it. Receive and check the complete story of my agent NY-31 who has been trailing this bearded man, and write me a full account of it as received by you. I believe him to be absolutely reliable and trustworthy, but it will do no harm to see whether his story remains unchanged at your end with respect to its version as rendered to me. I shall remain constantly here during the whole afternoon and all of tonight, if necessary, to receive your reports, and will not depart until I learn that the Confucian Coin is in the hands of Nippon. Banzai, to his Imperial Highness, the Son of Heaven!

Kichirobei Yamaguuchi, Importer.

Coming to the end of his reading of the decoded communication, Mr. Tokanami—that is, Mr. Sato alias Tokanami!—stroked the end of his smooth chin.

"Murder itself," he remarked to himself, "will, of course, be quite nothing, to regain this coin—and help thwart China's recovery of herself. But

Chinese murder—now what, precisely, would exactly typify Chinese murder? Hm! Murder —via hatchet, of course. And why not? Of course! My killer man, in this case, shall be provided with a hatchet. Yes—so it shall be."

And Sato pressed a button on the side of his desk.

CHAPTER V

In which Justice Is Arranged for a Humble Chinaman Named Yin Yi

David Rand, just back from his business trip to New York for his employer, Jack Kenwood, publisher of that very odd magazine The **Ultropolitan** (if "magazine" it could rightfully be called!) gazed hungrily about the walls of the big square 1-room office, trying to realize that he had really been away from Chicago for 5 long days. The light from the tall windows gazing far out over the western city, from their positions of vantage in the 11th story level of the Interstate Life Building, seemed to proclaim everything to be apparently quite unchanged. It seemed, indeed, to David Rand, that it was but yesterday that he had sat here in this same capacious "visitor's chair," in this very room with its cement floor and its bright Persian rug, its gleaming mahogany desks and filing cases, his back to that solid oaken entrance door whose panel bore Kenwood's name and his business, talking to Kenwood himself sitting behind his beautiful hand-carved desk standing here in the northwest corner and facing diagonally the entire office and the entrance door. Even Aline, working away at her desk, was dressed exactly as she had been when David Rand saw her last. Everything was unchanged. Unaltered. Except that, of course, Kenwood, with his black hair glistening, as it always did, like a seal's coat, was dressed today in a skilfully tailored dark grey oxford suit, instead of the blue serge he had last worn; and grey madras tailored-shirt cuffs peeped from his coat sleeves instead of the white ones that had last peeped forth. Only Kenwood's changed suit—and the changed leaf of the calendar on the wall, reading October 31—revealed the passage of those 5 days.

"And what, David," Kenwood was asking, now that the full details of that business trip had been detailed to him, "is the talk on Broadway about the Republicans fixing upon Senator Capman to lick the Democrats two years hence?"

"From all I heard here and there in the hotel lobbies," David Rand replied, "they're all betting that the Democrats will ride back in in 1940."

"Yeah? So do fleas ride into a cozy kennel on a fat dog's warm back!

I'm telling you that every man in America who votes the Democratic ticket in even the coming local elections should be taken out by his local sheriff and given twenty-five lashes on his bare back with a rubber cat-o-nine-tails till it draws blood!"

Rand started to expostulate, but Kenwood went on self-assertively:

"And every woman that votes it should be ducked six times in Lake Michigan in the middle of January in a ducking stool."

Now David Rand's choler started to rise—he felt the millimetres of his bloodpressure going up—because he happened to believe in the principles of Democracy himself, and moreover knew that Winsome One herself was going to cast her first ballot in that direction. Then he grinned. For he was used to Jack Kenwood and the latter's dogmatic utterances as to what was right and what was wrong, what should be done in the world, and what shouldn't be done, who should do it and who shouldn't.

"How do you make that out, Jack?" he queried placatingly. "I'm voting the Democratic ticket myself. Next week—and two years from now."

"Then you're a bigger fool than I thought you were," Kenwood bit out testily. "Here I put you down as having about 48 ounces of real brains, and it turns out you've got a hatful of dried peas rattling in your skullpan. You'll discover that—" He scratched his head sheepishly. And half grinned himself. "What the—am I shooting my mouth again? Good thing you two here know me. And I hope Winsome One over there isn't a Democrat. Of course," Kenwood added, and he was his more charming apologetic self now, "I think the Democrats are a bunch of upstart fakers who are pretending they cured the panic of 1929 to 1933, when it was already automatically mending itself. That they—well—never mind. November, 1940, will tell the tale."

Whereupon Rand told the other about the apparent puzzlement, there in the East, as to Capman's acceptance of the principle of currency inflation.

And heard Kenwood's theories to the effect that all currency invariably automatically inflated anyway!

But now Kenwood himself changed the subject.

"Well," he said, "any questions about the business—General Manager?"

To David Rand that sounded not so bad! And he asked one.

"How'd you come out at Topeka, Kansas?"

"Not quite so good as I expected—but not so bad either," Kenwood said. "They preferred to try 25,000 copies at the larger rate—rather than sign on the dotted line for the 100,000 at the cut rate." And he added, a bit ruefully: "I did think I could knock the deal across for one hundred thou, considering the downright ease with which young Veldon talked 'em half the distance into considering 10 thou at top rates. Maybe I'm losing my magic touch, David."

"Not you, Jack," Rand said, shaking his head. "Young Veldon was losing 'em altogether, if you ask me. That's the way I sized it up when I left here. You're just 25,000 copies to the good, that's all. And a plump order too, when you consider it alongside some of those 100-copy orders that Lyendrerth always sent in from that territory." I paused. "Anything else happened while I was gone?"

Kenwood laughed grimly. "Yeah, something. Something that's going to cost me five hundred berries. And I'm paying it out of my own sweet, kind heart—with no grousing and no grumbling. In other words: Invited guests kindly omit sackcloth—and ashes!"

"$500!" Rand echoed. "Who the deuce are you paying five hundred dollars to?"

"To a Mr. Yin Yi, Esquire."

"Yin—Yi?" Rand repeated slowly. "That sounds like a Swede—or a Chinaman."

"It is a Chinaman," Kenwood replied. And added, taking a malicious dig at him: "But Chinaman though he be—he has brains enough in his yellow skull to be a good Republican."

"That's good," Rand retorted. And paused helplessly. "What—what's it all about?"

"The damned gravestone marble ad, David," Kenwood said, frowning. "You know I was afraid of it when I took it. It looked to me then like that outfit was operating on a shoestring. But they talked pretty fast and loud and big—and their goods seemed to be the real McCoy. So I let 'em have that 2nd cover." He paused. "Well, it seems that during the couple of months they've been operating, the United States Bureau of Standards has been testing their product as to water solubility—and air resistance—and all that sort of thing—using acids on it, and solutions, and drying breezes, and what not, and found that an obelisk hewed from the stuff would rot entirely away in 5 years, and a headpiece in 1 year 3 months. Neither can the stuff stand freezing to 20 below—there it cracks. Nor can it stand focussed arc lights corresponding to the temperature of a mid-July afternoon, for over 2 hours without turning a nice brown, at which point it looks—so the Government says—like marble cake instead of marble!"

"Hm," David Rand commented. "I thought they had a really good thing. Everybody knows what a fearful cost there is to having a gravestone—or a monument—made for some departed one—at least out of the genuine marble."

"That's what made me leary of it," Kenwood said, "right off the bat. One can't afford, in this life, to fool with dead people's rights. No—sir! For the living relatives don't take kindly to being gypped. If they walk through a graveyard and see a beautiful stone that they've put up all cracked and browned and rotting to pieces—there's trouble in the air for somebody. I felt in the first place there was a jonah attached to that ad. And I see now that if their stuff really had been the McCoy, they wouldn't have been coming around here for our space."

"Well," Rand put in puzzledly, "if they only operated a couple of months, nobody saw his mother-in-law's headstone falling to pieces. So what happened? And where does the chap Yin Yi come in?"

"Well, the Government clapped a fraud order against 'em, that's all, before they even had a chance to properly shake their wings out. A postoffice inspector blew in here last Monday morning—you were **en route** towards New York then, you know—to let us know we needn't expect any further remittances from 'em, and lo—I knew the chap, personally. Walter Hardeen, his name was. I'd been drunk with him one night, anyway. Well, I was able to get far more of a lowdown on the affair, because of knowing him. See? It seems the District Attorney had found a couple of old **nolle-prossed** swindle cases against two of the three partners—and had put the screws to 'em: in short, give 'em the chance to quit business right where they were—then and there—and call it a day. Or go into Federal court. They elected to close up shop. There wasn't much to close up, Walter Hardeen told me, for they'd sold only about two 1-ton pieces of the stuff and one 500-pound piece—and caught but 3 stock-holders, one for $10 worth of stock, one for $20, and one for—ouch!—five hundred bucks."

"Five hundred? You don't mean the Chi—"

"Yeah," he nodded. "This Chink wax-modeler in Chinatown here. It seems he got hold of one of the copies in that 100-copy order that Charley Longabaugh sold to the Noon Fang Restaurant dawn in Chinatown. Remember the 100-copy order that cost us all our profit, because the Chinese message we had to have specially engraved to go on its cover? Well, the Noon Fang Restaurant mailed this Yin Yi one of the copies, because he's a star customer of theirs—eats there, or something—and he saw the ad right off the bat, and mailed in the coupon. He was interested primarily, it seems, in doping out the costs of a monument above his mother's grave, somewhere down in Indiana. They—and I mean of course the American Synthetic Grave-Stone Marble Company—had a salesman out to see him inside of 12 hours. And who in the devil do you think they had on their selling force—that went out to see this Chinese feller?"

"I give up. Who?"

"Golden-Tongued Kelly."

"Golden-Tongued Kell—good night!" Rand said. "And he was selling gravestone marble!"

"Gravestone marble **stock**," Kenwood corrected him. "For they were primarily out to unload their stock—not their marble."

"Well," Rand admitted grudgingly, "Golden-Tongue was the best salesman we ever had on our force here. That fellow could sell an electric ice-box at the North Pole."

Kenwood nodded. "I know it. Well, he took the poor Chinaman for his wad. Or part of his wad, anyway. I guess a Chink never lets all his eggs slide into any one basket. But he took him, for what he did, lock stock and barrel. On the stock end, too, instead of the marble end—can you beat it? And he took him purely on the basis of the logical features inherent in American S. G. S. Marble, too! He spread out in front of the fellow all the statistics and data about the gross business of marble in the U.S.A.—and the unfilled area in all the cemeteries—the number of people yet to die—the amount of life insurance now in force, and the proportion of life insurance known to be put into headstones and monuments—etc., and etc. Produced little cubes of real marble, and cubes of this phony; let him bust some of each with hammers, and crushed some himself with recording dynamometer pinchers. Showed him their patent papers on the stuff—the huge inevitable expansion of the synthetic marble industry—showed him how much Ford, Kelvinator, and Majestic radio stock sold for in its infancy—and how much it was worth today—and landed him purely on the logic of the thing. And logic, unfortunately, seems to be this Chink's weak point—or strong point. However you look at it. And the logic of that synthetic marble was unbeatable!"

"Yes," Rand granted, "except that acids and focussed arc-lights were stronger than logic! But go ahead. How did you get involved?"

"Well, Golden-Tongue walked in home with the Chink's check, and they cashed it, and paid G. T. his commission. A hundred bucks, too, their books showed, that Golden-Tongue got for his 3$1/2$ hours of statistical oratory. They didn't stop there, however, but went right on paying out. They paid—do you remember that $42 check we got about ten days ago—as against the first 2100 copies of our last printing mailed out—the last 2100 copies, that is, on our last American Audit Bureau statement?"

David Rand nodded. "Yes. I remember thinking they must be getting results, they were so prompt."

"They **were** getting results," said Kenwood moodily. "That $42 came out of the Chink's five hundred! In fact, they didn't stop with paying off Golden-Tongue and us, here. They paid some bits due their other salesmen, declared a partial liquidation on their own organization salaries, bought a little postage, and cleared their office rent to date. When they were closed up later, David, they had exactly $4.91 in their till. Well, the inspectors naturally notified the Chink to come in and see them. He did, of course—that was the same morning that Walter Hardeen came in to see me. They told him the doleful news. Notified him officially that the company was out of business, and had no assets whatsoever. That he had a dubious claim, at best, against the directors, two of whom were ex-crooks, and none of whom had a nickel."

"And so—he came in to see you?"

"Yeah. He came in the afternoon of the day that Walter Hardeen delivered me my end of the bad news. You were probably stepping out of the Grand Central Station at New York into 42nd Street, on or about that time. Well, he—and I mean the Chink—introduced himself, drew up a chair, and—"

"What kind of a looking old fellow is he?" Rand interrupted curiously.

"Old? Oh, he's not old. He's only about 30, as near as one can judge those things. Most Mongolian looking Chink I ever saw in my life. Flat in features. Face as impassive as a mask. Well, as I say, he drew up a chair, and stated his entire case just like a European lawyer summing up all the reasons why Uncle Sam should cancel the entire foreign debt. He at no time waxed angry, nor even emotional. He was icily calm, cool. The theme of his masterly discourse, David, was that I owed him the sum of $500, and that he would expect repayal of the entire sum to him. I asked him how he made that out. He said I owned the magazine which ran the fraudulent ad—and that therefore I should make good on all losses sustained by persons from it. That was a new one on me, I'll tell the blooming world! But there was a peculiar menace in this fellow's attitude. He was so damned quiet. He didn't frown, but he didn't smile, either. There was about his whole attitude the implied threat that I would best consider fixing this thing up. I can't say whether he silently conveyed the idea that he would shoot me—or that he would sic his tong on me—if he's got one—or that he would just throw one fine batch of publicity on the affair and us—take it to the papers, in other words. He's too perfect an actor and psychologist, you see, to let me know what the menace was; he knew I'd be more upset if the thing was unnamable. But, strangely, I didn't get sore because of the implied threat in his bearing. For his confounded logic overcame any feeling I might have that way; clearest brain I've ever encountered. I'd say—"

"He told you he was a Republican?" Rand asked quizzically.

"Yes."

"Well, that accounts for his clear brain," he badgered. "But go ahead."

"Yes, by gosh—it does account partly for it at that! Well, as I was saying, it was his confounded logic that struck me. When he got done with his arguments, David, I was quite sold myself—not only that I owed him $500—but that I owed him 6 percent interest on the sum for 29 days, and 7 percent accrued interest on the two added together—for 24 hours!"

"Why didn't you hire him to be one of our salesmen?" Rand asked facetiously.

"I would have," Kenwood returned unsmilingly "only, for one thing, he's got a well-paying trade—wax modeler: and secondly, because the asinine public that we sell to has a well-defined prejudice against Chinese. You know, David, believe it or not, the Chinese are, in general, a dam' fine race. I've always gotten along fine with 'em—in fact, I like Chinks; they're such philosophical, patient devils, they intrigue me—they appeal to me in some peculiar way. And as a rule they like me, too. But on with the story. This chap Yin Yi convinced me I owed him his five hundred bucks."

"And did you tell him you'd give it back to him?"

"Gosh no—not at that first visit! It was too much for me to digest. Five hundred bucks is a lot of money, you know. I made another appointment where we could talk later and at longer length—for I had to hop for Topeka—and I said we'd thresh the matter out further then, and to a final conclusion to save his time and my time. I had in mind at first maybe refunding to him the entire $42 we ourselves got from the synthetic gravestone marble people for those first mailing charges; even perhaps giving him a $100 bill to salve his feelings. For you see, David, he's in a position to do us a devil of a lot of harm. But he doesn't exactly know that, of course, because he doesn't have any inkling about the real low-down on all those cover names. See? But we couldn't stand any publicity centering about some poor Chink suing us for a lot of money, and resulting probably in our getting all written up, even though we're not legally liable for a cent. And on the other hand, I had to keep the grim fact in mind that here we'd gone and run off 100,000 of those covers—and now 80,000 of 'em would be unproductive so far as income from the 2nd cover went. That meant a staggering loss to us, either way it went. Nearly a thousand dollars if we scrapped the remaining ones, and re-ran the run with a new 2nd cover ad; or $1600 loss if we mailed the rest out at 6 cents apiece, and took in but 4 cents from the other two covers from the other two advertisers thereon.

"So I wasn't any warm, I'm telling you, about kicking in with any consolation monies to anybody—in the face of that loss. I sat there all of twenty minutes by myself, stewing and worrying about it—the huge printing loss, mind you, not the Chink. I was all alone then; Winsome had gone out on an errand long before even Yin Yi had left; and the Chink had long since bowed himself out as well. And about the time I began to think I'd better bestir myself about getting on to Topeka, who should call up but Sol Rosenberg. He said he was having trouble in getting a new supply of unstitched covers from Svensenjorg. So I called Svensenjorg up and started to raise Billy Hell. And whaddayou think, David?"

"What?"

"They—Svensenjorg's pressmen—had come a cropper on that last run.

They'd smashed the synthetic-marble copy electro at about the 20,000th imprint, and had taken the job off press for the time being till they could get a new electro straight from the marble company itself. They were leary, you see, of making another electro from the duplicate electro that they were using for the alternate imprints on that 'two-on' run, for fear it would give a foggy production. They'd written the marble company several times, but the outfit hadn't answered, nor had Svensenjorg pressed on with the matter, for his color presses were then busy with another big job. And so, David, we'd lost nothing! Not a blooming cent, practically. Old Lady Luck had been camping right on my tail. So I followed the old dame up. I called up Hinderfak, of the old brokerage company ad that we had up until this last run. They were glad as anything to come back on for that 80,000 fractional run that was open. And if you ask me, David, they haven't been able to get the space they need in some of those other mediums they had in mind when they got snooty. They'll be back for good, mark my words."

Kenwood paused.

"And so," he finished, "instead of having one big loss—I had no loss at all, to speak of!"

Rand started to ask a question, but Kenwood waved him imperiously into silence, as was the Kenwoodian custom oftentimes.

"And so I did some hard thinking," Kenwood went on. "Here, says I, we've run along beautifully all these months, never hitting a single snag or catching a dose of publicity of any sort, harmful or otherwise. And here one poor devil of a Chink gets accidentally into our smooth-running machinery and hurts himself—and thus us. And so I said to myself, says I: having saved a neat chunk of money thanks to that electro going bad—and being just about to expand in N. Y. as well—I says, says I, if David brings home the bacon, I'm going to pay the Chink off—his whole $500 loss—and consider it cheap."

He looked inquiringly at Rand, almost defiantly, as though he were ready to unleash all his verbal guns if the other dared to take issue with him.

But Rand fooled him, he guessed. "It really is cheap," he told Kenwood. "The Chinaman's story is just the thing for the sob-writers. And what you have to pay him back isn't but a fraction of what you make personally in one month. Be glad that there wasn't more of that stock sold, to widows and orphans and what not. Which makes me wonder if we hadn't better watch our step now on that tire-swelling mixture ad?"

"That's safe—because it does what they claim it'll do. This marble didn't. There was the rub!" Kenwood paused. "Furthermore, the old copybooks were right. Virtue is always rewarded! Didn't I at least make that 25,000 sale in Topeka—and cinch again not less than double what I intended to give this Chink? Something tells me, David, that he's the hunchback's hump for J. Kenwood, Esquire; that I'm going to have good luck for the rest of my days, now, just for settling with him. You know—oh, I say, Winsome, speaking of money—where's that $1500 in mixed hundreds and five hundreds you got for me at the bank today?"

Rand watched Winsome from the side of his chair where he was now seated, as she reached into her desk and brought the thin sheaf of money over. Lucky Kenwood—with his little **Ultrapolitan** gold mine! But now he, Rand, was going to get some of the larger crumbs, for a change. Kenwood took the sheaf carelessly from her, as though it were so much hay—shuffled the crisp bills about a bit, glanced at their denominations, and brought from his inside vest pocket another sheaf of bills, equally crisp, and about the same thickness.

"Gosh, Jack," Rand commented, "you've got enough there to pay off a dozen Chinamen!"

"God forbid," Kenwood said cheerfully. "The one doesn't worry me—he's my lucky talisman now—but a dozen would. Sixteen hundred—seventeen hundred—oh, I'll count this later." He tucked the resultant sheaf of currency back into his inner vest pocket and buttoned it up tightly.

"Aren't you afraid to carry all that money around on your person?" Rand asked him, curiously.

"No. Why should I be?"

"Well, you know—" But David Rand shrugged the rest of his words away. For he saw that dogmatically assertive glint rising in Kenwood's eye which portended an utterance to the effect that everybody in the world who was afraid of hold-up men should be compelled daily to drink a quart bottle of castor-oil—or some such affirmation. Instead, he glanced around at Winsome One.

"I suppose Yin Yi made love to you? Chinamen always do, to blondes."

"No," she said puzzledly. "Mr. Kenwood stepped out of the room once while he was here, but he only scowled at me when I tried to be pleasant and nice to him."

"Perhaps it was brunettes he liked. Or red heads."

Kenwood frowned a bit. Rand could discern, somehow, that it was purely unconscious on the other's part, and that it was at the fact that he, Rand, was bandying jests with Winsome One rather than the subject matter of their words. But Kenwood's face grew amiable at once.

And so David Rand delivered his bombshell.

"Jack," he asked, "how would you like to have, in place of that nondescript editorial—rather, Editor's Talk!—in the magazine, a talk by Gilbert Melbourne?"

"Hah!" Kenwood said melodramatically. "Are you trying to kid me, David? With Gilbert tied exclusively to Hearst—for $100,000 a year? Go home! Genial as I am this afternoon, my mind isn't capable of aerial acrobatics."

"No," Rand said, "I mean it. How would you like to have an Editorial Talk by Gilbert Melbourne? Which you could feature on the cover, by just an additional line of b.f. type?"

"How," asked Kenwood dryly, "would a blind beggar like to have his sight? How would a 101-percent superstitious guy like to get one of these 'Destiny Weight Tickets' out of a Malmgren drugstore weighing machine reading **'You'll Inherit a Million Dollars Tomorrow'**? How would a chorus girl like to catch the lead in her musical comedy? How—well, with the names we've already got on the mag, David, a final line—for future orders—saying 'An Exclusive Editorial Talk by Gilbert Melbourne' would just about lend the ultra-final touch. However, Gilbert hasn't gone insane yet, so he won't break his contract with William Randolph!"

"No," Rand said slowly, "Gilbert **has** gone insane—and has recovered."

"Lis-s-sten, David," Kenwood put in. "Is this what a trip to New York does to you? If so, I'll never send you there again. Gilbert Melbourne, I just read, got a salary raise of $25,000 a year, and a further long-term contract, and he—"

"All right, Jack," Rand said. "I won't devil you any longer. Be apprised, therefore, that I met Gilbert Melbourne across a table in the diner at lunch today. He had a bit of a wild look in his eyes—but was otherwise quite sane. Until, that is, he got onto the subject of Chinamen. And boy, oh boy, but he's 'off' there. Anyway, when we exchanged names, I naturally asked him how the devil—"

"—he had the name of Gilbert Melbourne of the Hearst Syndicate?" Kenwood commented, his face growing grave, for it was evident right away he saw the thing that Rand had stumbled upon. "And how was it? Just had it, eh?"

"No," Rand said. "His grandfather was an English convict named Jack Smith who was sent to Australia years ago—sure, the blighter I met was quite frank about his family history—and who settled in Melbourne, this convict, yes. And subsequently took the name Melbourne—Jack Melbourne, see?—just as Jack London is said to have taken the name 'London.' And so this Gilbert Melbourne's father was legally Gyles Melbourne—and hence he, Gilbert, became Gilbert Melbourne—"

"Listen," put in Kenwood tensely. "Has he got any certificate as to that legal name change?"

"Has he?" Rand ejaculated. "I'll say! He showed it to me. All stamped up with old Australian seals. He has his father's birth certificate—and his own—to boot."

"Zowie!" commented Kenwood. "Well—did you approach him—on a

deal for his name?"

"I did. Though I felt I was approaching a crazy man. And even found I was. He's absolutely nuts, Jack, against Chinks. For it seems some Chink accidentally killed his mother in Frisco, in a tong war. He—but when the waiter on the diner asked him, Jack, what he'd have to eat—and he told the waiter to bring anything that was good—and the waiter brought him chop-suey—I thought the guy would go bats. He wanted to pry up the heavy diner window and scatter the food out of the window. The waiter had to calm him down. And I also. Then he told me his story—over bacon and eggs. He said he would gladly kill a man if only he could send a Chink—**just one Chink!**—to the noose for the murder."

"Nice customer, this Gilbert. What about his alleged recovery—from his alleged insanity?"

"He showed me that. A certificate from the Iowa State Insane Asylum. Showing full recovery. Angrily he told me—we were all alone in the diner then—how he'd been sent there because he had advocated bringing capital charges against **all** Chinks, electrocuting them first, and then trying them afterwards! But the doctors had to let him out. His ideas were, they had to admit, not a delusion—only a 'paranoiacally tinged advocacy.'"

"I say he was nuts," pronounced Kenwood.

"I think so," agreed David Rand. "Anyway, he's coming in to see you— God knows when—he's going to phone you first, so expect a message any time of the day or night—this fellow doesn't apparently keep regular hours at all—doesn't believe in them—and he wants to come in, show all his papers and get the hundred."

"The hundred? What hundred?"

"I agreed, Jack," Rand now said, "to give him a hundred bucks for the use of his name on an editorial talk in our magazine. **The Ultrapolitan**. And I told him frankly just what it was—a purely local advertising selling device—and that we used our 'apparently' big names just as bait. Did I do wrong—or right?"

"Good God, David, you did the exact thing I would have wanted you to do. Only—why didn't you fetch him right along with you?"

"Oh, because he got off fifty miles out of Chicago—to see some distant cousin or something. If you ask me, he'll probably be catching the chilly shoulder pronto—and dive in on the next train. Which would be an hour after. Maybe not. Anyway, look for him any time between now—and a year from now."

"I will. And gladly. For with that certificate of his grandfather's name change—and his various birth certificates —and his legal discharge from that nut house—all of which I'll get photostatic copies of—we'll have all the big names in the country. David, I ought to raise your pay still again for that. But—but listen—who'll write the editorial spiel? That pale wandering one we've got won't do for a Melbourne."

"Of course not," said Rand quietly. "I'll write it. Have written it."

"You?"

"Sure. Did you think I could be connected with a mag—and not get the writing bug? I've written a sort of long Melbournish 'truish' 'talk' that for a long time I've wanted to get you to stick in instead of that thing we've got. But didn't have the nerve. Now that this fellow will sell his name—you've got to use it."

"Got to? How much?"

"Nothing. Does a new general manager charge fees?"

"We-ell, I suppose not. Where is it?"

"In my hip pocket—folded four ways! I intended to revue it still further—on the train. But never even pulled it out. Now I **will** put the finishing touches on it. Tonight."

"Okay! Bring it in—revised as you see fit—tomorrow I may change a few words in it myself. And this fellow?—You don't know when he'll be phoning me?—but you gave him the number?—Which number? This—or my apartment?"

"This one, of course."

"Okay! Well, I'll be ready for him—when he comes."

"'Okay' also say I," pronounced David Rand, relieved. "But please, Jack, please don't—"

"Yeah? Please don't—what?"

"Don't let out a damned word about your going to pay—or having paid—a Chink $500. He's nuts on the subject of Chinks. I hope he doesn't, by any fool mischance, come here **if** and **when** your Chink does. For he—but that wouldn't be likely to happen. No. Why, Jack, he'd gladly kill anybody who was even decent to a Chink—and kill himself, if needs be, just to send a Chink to the noose."

"The damn fool!" said Kenwood, without regards, this time, for Aline Creston's ears. "Well, I'll watch my words, don't fear."

And then abruptly terminated the interview.

"Well," were his words, "you'd better beat it, Traveller. Go on home and wash up and rest. Travelling's tiresome work. We've lasted the bigger part of a week now without you, and can go another day." He rose from his desk. "Expect you down tomorrow, as usual, David. To sort over various stray ends of the business before I go East early next week. But if you're tired, sleep late. No more time clock for you! You're virtually general manager around here now, you know."

With which, and a critical look at some inkspots on his well manicured hands, he gave David Rand a curt nod, and rounding the right side of his obliquely placed desk, left the room, and the sound of his footsteps going up the hall outside were audible.

Rand rose from the visitor's chair, took up his pig-skin bag, but strolled over to Aline Creston's desk. She looked up curiously at him, and smiled. He asked but one question.

"How about taking a walk tonight, Winsome—around 8 or 8:30? Or have you a Hallowe'en party on—somewhere?"

"No, I've no party on," she said. "And I'd like to take a walk. I do want to hear all about New York. And about Mr. Kenwood's curious cousin. He's told me about him."

"Drinkwater's a good scout," Rand told her. "But he doesn't make the error of thinking that I'm the mainspring here! He's coming in—but solely on the basis that Jack Kenwood remains in—and with us!" With which he turned away, but paused long enough to add: "All right then, Winsome. I'll be at your place at 8 sharp."

And, downstairs, David Rand hailed a cab, and ordered it to take him to 72 West Oak Street. That—Mrs. Sprudelganger's dilapidated and down-at-heel roominghouse—being the place he called "home!"

CHAPTER VI

The Case of One, Barton

A man who is Down—and likewise Out—never really comes back, say the Sociologists. For the thing in him which can make it possible for him to climb, is destroyed by the very fact of his "Downness"—and his "Outness."

But that—to one who might be familiar with the case of Barton—should make one smile.

For Barton was more than down. He was down—the "down" put in italics. And Barton was out. The "out" being spelled in capital letters. And yet Barton—

But here is the story of Barton.

Barton was apparently just an ordinary fellow, moderately ambitious, moderately energetic, and with a faint suggestion of possibilities. He spent freely from what little he earned, and saved little. During those days before he met The Girl, if you had asked him what success constituted, he would have said: "Success to me is partly money, but just as much so the happy faculty of being able to deal with big men on their own basis; to act with that poise and ease that money and success brings. To have a standing, a reputation. To have one's opinion asked and valued."

And these things Barton woefully lacked, for he was just an ordinary young man. In the presence of men only slightly above him in the corporation for which he worked, he was pronouncedly ill at ease, conscious of his own inferiority. He was the worm.

It was then that he met The Girl. According to all the standard laws on the subject, Barton should have been projected automatically upon the road to success, for The Girl was his mental, physical and personality ideal, such as he had entertained since his schoolboy days, but had never dreamed he would meet. It was, indeed, one of those rare coincidences, for Barton had written out on paper the delineation of the girl he wanted—and to cap the climax he had found the original of his own specifications.

"Man realizes his Dream Lady." Here is the motive for an electrifying ascension into the heights of success. Let us see how it worked.

The first thing Barton naturally began to think about was the subject of

Marriage. Marriage required money, and it meant children. And that meant more money. Now, more than ever, must he hold tight to that tiny bit of prestige which three years of fairly faithful toil for a big organization had produced. To lose that intangible thing was to weaken his financial grasp on the dread future.

Of course it was the old story—that the married man is more afraid of the whims and caprices of fortune than the bachelor. And Barton had already in imagination taken upon his feet the shoes of a benedict, in his super-cautious preparations against possible financial loss.

He became more humble and wormlike than ever. In his tiny depart-ment, the nature of which allowed considerable latitude in the way of or-ganizing developments and working out creative ideas, he lost his nerve completely—what nerve he had ever had. He didn't lose it consciously, of course, but he became in fact, nevertheless, spineless. Innovation meant to him possible demoralization of his little department, the calling of himself upon the carpet, the loss of his job and the precious three-year record of faithful service which he treasured as a miser hoards gold.

Thus it was that his department stagnated. And then it was that the spineless man, who could define success but who could never realize it on account of the damming back in a good brain of ideas which should have teemed for expression and translation into money for the firm, received the shock of shocks.

A succession of alarming symptoms which compelled him to consult several doctors caused him finally to wind up in the shop of a great specialist in medical diagnosis. The great man, after thumping him, testing him and making a genuinely thorough study over several days of the onslaught and nature of the symptoms, pronounced for him the name of a disease. Barton, with a catch of the breath, knew that a terrible pronunciatum had been made in his life, and with this slight information tremulously made special queries as to what the chances of cure or retardation were. The specialist, not know-ing how much Barton knew, told him that the condition could not be cured, nor could it be attacked in any way known to medicine or surgery. Nothing could be done!

It was then that Barton, with set white face, went to the nearest medical library—something, perhaps, that he should not have done—and thoroughly investigated this diagnosis. It was confirmed in the medical books. His sick-ness **did** mean death!

He went from the library and out upon the street. It was a sunny day. He leaned against a lamppost. He was very weak. He did not smoke a cigarette calmly as did the doomed characters in various lurid magazine stories he had read in his life. And a strange thought came to him: Why was he not act-ing as they? He felt very tired, soul sick, and so, so weak. He knew suddenly what it meant to be a trapped rat, and he suddenly seemed to glimpse faintly the answer to an old unanswerable question: What will happen when an irresistible force strikes an immovable body? People, in gay colors, passed him laughing in either direction, like great holiday streamers flowing into each other. A girl with a red coat passed by, and Barton half reached out his hand to touch it. Life had suddenly ceased to be life and had become a moving picture, a flow of unrealities on the screens of his dazed eyes, and while he knew he was only dreaming a dream he knew at the same time that the dream was never to be terminated by the sunlight of morning realness.

Of course it was no longer possible for him to hold his position. He never even went back. He had a few hundred dollars. He spent several weeks sitting on a bench in the park. She—The Girl—was out of the city. He must talk it over with her. He had withheld from her the terrible news.

Then it was that to him, idealist as he was, an equally terrible blow fell. He had written her only that a great tragedy had come into his life—that he was facing his black hour. He did not tell her what, reserving that for a face-to-face talk. Her answer came. It was brief. She had decided not to marry. His talk of his "black hour" had fallen into fertile ground. For he had reaped Desertion. And Barton's life, doomed to terminate in the most horrible of deaths, was crowned with the fact that he was brutally left alone in the shadows—for the reason that The Girl was a "Sunny day girl"—not a "Rainy day girl." Marriage might have been impossible, but at least ideals and constancy might have been saved.

He felt more tired and weary than ever now. He spent most of his time realizing that the three sisters, Clotho, Lechesis and Atropos, the mythical trio who spin the threads of human destiny, had knotted his thread and clipped it off close to the loom. He made no attempts to see The Girl. He was enough of an idealist to know that desertion in the black hour was the blackest of crimes, and he was now too bitter to attempt to gain the acme of pusillanimity—a meeting with her.

And so his money, badly depleted by his doctors' visits and fruitless wild treatments prior to his seeing the great specialist, melted away as mist under the summer sun. And so it was that he became reduced finally to one suit of clothes, the cuffs of which were ragged, and one flannel shirt. No longer could he even afford carfare. He lived as a rat lives, devoid of hope, bitter, tired of a solar system so unstable that the Great Love—its Pole Star—must waver.

And then, driven to the wall, without further hope of either life or love, he began to have faint glimpses of what he could have done with his old position, had he then known what he now knew: that inside of a year the Grim Reaper would have reaped his harvest; that Barton would be where the disastrous results of all the innovations in the world could not ruin him.

He ran into his old employer accidentally. "I've had much trouble," he said simply. The other stared at him. A new Barton seemed to be evolving: one in whose eyes stood lights and shadows which no man could fathom. His employer mentioned that Barton's successor was not doing well with his position. He suggested, as one suggests to a servant or a beggar, half chidingly, half pityfully, that the spineless man come back and fill out his old position.

Barton laughed. The laugh was without mirth. "I'll come," he said. For he knew now that work would serve to banish from his mind the horror of what was to come.

He groomed himself as best he could, and appeared the next Monday at his desk. He gazed at his work as a man views the pseudo-serious happenings in a drama. These details—such as filled and made other men's lives— these were the playthings with which he was to amuse himself until such time as the jailer unlocked the door for the execution. And he fell to play.

But now the old play was too dull. He played with ideas. They helped him to forget. He played as a gambler plays for gold; but he did not realize that the man who plays with ideas is never gambling; results are too sure. And still another change had fastened itself upon him. He no longer was subservient, humble to those above him. He talked to them as one talks to men across a card table. Likewise, to the vice president and to the Big Man himself of the corporation, he held a sneering man-to-man mien which said as plain as words: "You are nothing to me. And your money is less." He knew that no man's money could buy him more life, and they, recognizing in him a strange devil-may-care attitude, wondered—and respected him for it!

He lived each week on a lone ten-dollar bill which he took from his envelope which contained fifteen. The torn envelope with the remaining five he tossed back into a tin box which locked with a key and which he kept in his desk. He continued to play with ideas. They worked. They brought business. When those above him told him of the success of his ideas, very respectfully, he laughed a laugh which made them talk together in low tones. To himself he merely whispered: "And she deserted me when I was done for!"

The character of the nerve-racking pains which had assailed him for so long changed gradually. One day he ran across his family doctor. "I'm sorry to hear from your letter about Professor R.'s diagnosis," the latter said, "but I **do** want to say this: If you go a year, and"—he named a certain condition —"has not developed, then the diagnosis is wrong, and the condition instead of being—well—malign, is benign."

At the end of the year, however, the expected condition had not developed. It was then that Barton suddenly awoke to a strange fact. He was successful. His opinion upon every matter was consulted by the officials of the corporation. He was addressed by his first name, and he himself addressed the president by the latter's initials. He had assistants, whose salary he named. He was not to die now, for the year had gone, and the diagnosis, like thousands of others rendered by great specialists who are sincere enough, was proven to be again an error. And in his tin box were dozens of five-dollar bills, together with tiny pink envelopes which had been enclosed with the salary, and which he had never even opened, thinking they were printed slips saying, "Salary enclosed herewith, etc." These envelopes containing bonuses, starting with green fives, had risen to the point where they contained four and five yellow tens.

Today Barton has found that thing he defines as success. But he could not have found it until he was driven, not down, but literally OUT. This brought him to the mat, a fighting creature who was shorn of all the desires and fears and petty doubts which defeat men in their race. And he is happy—at least, as happy as a man can be who has had his trust in some one displaced, who has been deserted in his black hour and cannot find some one in his sunny hour upon whom to anchor his faith. This is the one unpleasant ending to the unusual story of Barton, the man who went OUT and UP.

This ended the typewritten script.

And David Rand, seated in his taxicab, re-reading his script again, saw that he was almost at his destination.

With which he folded it up, and put it back in the hip pocket from which he had extracted it.

"Melbourne couldn't have done better," he grumbled to himself. "Especially if he'd had to cover that whole page 5 in **Ultrapolitan**. The real Melbourne, that is. And here—**my** brain child—has to come out—under the name of a fake Melbourne. Oh—well."

The cabby turned about.

"We're home, sir," he announced. "72 West Oak Street."

"Home?" said David Rand. "Home—yes—at least till tomorrow—when I'll be living in an apartment hotel. For I was just made G. M. today, Bud—general manager!—of a flourishing business. Which—but here's a dollar—and keep the 60 cents change!"

CHAPTER VII

"First Alibi Checker"—His Duties!

David Rand, leaning back against the head of his bed—applying a cold wet rag to a bump on his head—curiously surveyed his friend Terrence O'Rourke, "A.C." man of the Chicago Detective Bureau. The other, seated near him, in the old-fashioned furnished room with its flowered wallpaper, in a big stuffed chair, surveyed him placidly back from two steel-grey eyes that surmounted a close-cropped red mustache.

And David Rand asked a question.

"What is this new job of yours? First Alibi Checker?"

Terry O'Rourke grinned.

"Easily described, me boy," he said. "Me job is to sit, in a large private room of me own, at a desk with twenty or so telephones on it, all connecting to th' outside world through a special little one-girl switchboard in a two-by-four room at the other end of the hall; with two telegraph call-boxes on the wall ferninst me elbow—one a Postal Telegraph box, and one a Western Union box—th' same terminating in th' two offices downstairs in the Detective Bureau Building; with three pushbuttons in me desk, bringin' me pages to run hither and about the Detective Bureau or across the city, and three more buttons that bring me hard-boiled operatives capable of inducin' folks to come in for a temporary chat. I am under nobody whatsoever—nor beholden to nobody—but me superior, Sinjohn Mackenzie, a Scot what's been over here in America some 12 years or so now—he come here, in fact, direct from the homicide department of the Edinburgh Police force. And has th' position he has for th' reason that he's a friend and proteegee of Chief of Police Michael J. himself! Not, however, that Sinjohn hasn't the ability to handle a homicide case. Far from it! But anyway, getting back to meself, me job is to do nothing, unless—and until—a murder breaks in Chicago. At which time, as ye know, in the event that th' murderer wasn't caught redhanded in the durty deed, everybody, left and right, gets dragged in to the Bureau—everybody, at least, who might have known the deceased—the while the homicide squad is blindly collectin' an additional hatful of names of everybody what's ever had any dealings—or ever was going to have!—

with the same deceased. Me job is to keep all of these people from bein' use-lessly locked up and glutting the cells downstairs—when there is no sound reason at all for lockin' 'em up. In other words, I have to juggle them phones like a juggler in th' State-Lake Theatre tosses his gold-an'-black Injun clubs up and down, around and about—ask questions—check statements made by arrested people—and check the statements, too, of them as has apparently checked statements themselves!—telegraph to other cities —send out mes-sages—bring people in for a talk—weigh this ag'in that—and sort of elimi-nate them as obvi'sly hasn't had the chance of a snowball in hell of having had anything to do with the same homicide. In other language —I use my own judgment—see? And since Sinjohn Mackenzie was the one who got me in as A.C. man on his trick, he thinks I have fair to middlin' judgment. Now have I made it all clear?"

"I think so," David Rand granted. "You're a sort of a sieve-wielder to sift off the innocent ones?"

"I'd say," O'Rourke ruminated, "that I'm a sort of sieve-wielder—yes—but one that sifts off th' guilty ones—not the innocent ones!"

"A matter of rhetoric," Rand commented, "however it's put." He paused. "Haven't you made any mistakes at all in judgment—thus far? Or haven't you been on the job long enough?"

"I haven't made no mistakes yet," O'Rourke said gravely. "But that's not meaning anything. For we've standing instructions in the A.C. room to this effect: when in any doubt whatever—hold the suspected part for further investigation."

"What's the idea back of this new office—if it's never existed before?" Rand queried. "Surely it's not just a matter of keeping the cells from being glutted up?"

"That's problem enough," said O'Rourke curtly. "For the cell space at the Bureau is limited all right—and they need it all for the regular hoodlums and heisters who're getting pulled in all the time—and not for the thousand and one people whose names get dug up in connection with a homicide. But th' real theory, Rand, on which the office was orig'nated by Chief Shee-han —and he's quite right about it, too—is that the time to check a man's story as to his whereabouts is at the time of his first story—before he's had a chance to change it, and think things over, and fix things up. If you lock a man up in the Bureau, and get to him next day—or the day after—when he's regularly reached in the routine investigation of the case—by that time he's prob'ly fixed up a water-tight yarn, and maybe even his buddies outside have fixed it up—and gotten some message in to him. Oh yes—they get messages in, by a thousand methods."

He was frowningly silent a minute. Then went on.

"No, 'tis the best department—that new A.C. department —that the Bureau has ever worked out. Not because I'm one of the three men who handle it, day after day. No. But because of the fact that one man can do one thing to perfection—and do it fast and furious—providin' that's the only thing he's got to do. Except," he added, with a quizzical raising of his reddish eyebrows, "it's one hell of a bore—that job—when there's nothing doing in the homicide line. And one hell of a collar-wilting, nerve-wracking job—when there is a homicide."

Rand looked at him inquiringly.

O'Rourke laughed reminiscently. "Ye know, Rand, it beats the divil how, when you've given the special girl orders to get a bunch of people for you on the wires—or some of the boys to fetch certain ones straight in— how everything'll fall at the same moment. It's nothing to have four or five people conducted right inside the very room, at just the minute that three or four long-distance connections are throwed in, and a couple of local ones to boot. I'm tellin' you, you miss the time of your life in not seeing yours truly jugglin' telephones."

"I'd like to," Rand proffered.

"And I'd like for you to sometimes," O'Rourke said. "But unfortunately you'll prob'ly never have the chance—for in th' hours of my trick when most of the homicides bust, you're generally asleep. And even if you wasn't, there wouldn't be time to get you down there."

To which David Rand mentally assented, not knowing in the least that within 8 hours—more or less—he was to be treated to a perfect example of how Terry O'Rourke, "night A.C. man on the Chicago Detective Bureau" worked on an actual case!

CHAPTER VIII

Bad News!

Jack Kenwood murdered—

His skull split in half by a hatchet blow—

David Rand, standing in the telephone booth in Mrs. Sprudelganger's dark hallway, the clock up the hall showing the hour to he approximately 1 in the morning—could not yet believe the dumfounding news that O'Rourke had just handed him.

Kenwood—murdered whilst he—Rand—and Aline Creston had been walking along the lake. Murd—

It wasn't possible! Only 8—9—10 hours or so ago that day, he had seen and talked with Kenwood—heard Kenwood make him general manager of **Ultrapolitan**. And now—

And now, for one thing, there would no longer be any **Ultrapolitan**! And for another thing—

And now, in a flood, came the grisly details which, naturally, he had just begged.

"Kenwood's body," [2] O'Rourke began, "was found tonight, at 18 minutes past 9 o'clock—to be abs'lutely exact—lying forward on its chest an' belly on his big flat desk, what sits caticornered in the southwest corner of your office, both hands hanging down over th' front of the desk so's their fingertips barely touched the floor, an' his head hanging down likewise. The head was cleaven—or is clove the right word?—well, it don't matter—right nearly in two, by the blow of a hatchet. In fact, if you **must** have details, his brains was hanging half out of his skull, and th' blood from 'em had poured down onto th' floor under his gapin' cranium, nicely missin' th' corner of the Persian rug what stuck out towards his desk, and then turned sharply rightward—for him, at any rate!—an' run in a stream along the cement floor south-eastward—did you know there's quite some slants here an' there to your floor there in 1122?—well, anyway, the blood had run rightwise, so far as he was concerned, then turned an' run eastward a ways, gathered in a big

2   Publisher's Note: The facts set forth by O'Rourke in Chapters VIII and part of IX only, are set forth, word for word, as they appear in Mr. Keeler's earlier novel "Finger Finger."

pool near about th' middle of the south wall—swelled bigger, and finally touched the south edge of the Persian rug. In fact, it had already seeped into the rug at that point for an area of a couple square yards. All of which facts I'm renderin' you from a Homicide Squad diagram—an' report—lyin' here on my desk, me bein' an A.C. man and not personally having nothing to do with the scene of a crime. And—to get back to Kenwood—your employer, me boy, was drained like—like a stuck pig in the stockyards. He—well, you wanted the facts you know! And he—"

Rand swallowed several times.

"And—and who found him?" he begged. "Was it robbery? Was his body robbed?"

"Not of any big money. Whether he was searched or not, I couldn't say. Most of his pockets was easily reachable. The outside ones held what little change, or gim-cracks, he might have been carryin'. His coat was ev'dently open when he pitched for'ard, and flopped even wider open as he fell; so th' breast pocket thereof was anybody's meat! The change pockets in his vest was about as easily accessible as the rest—just by rockin' his body, on its belly, one way or the other—and feelin' in 'em. For he lay forward, as I'm tellin' you, just as he caught the hatchet in his skull—from across the desk, where the visitor's arm chair in which the killer sat still stood. But about this big money I spoke of. Inside his inner vest breast pocket, what he was lyin' flat on, and protectin', like, with the whole weight of his body, was a flat packet of crisp hundreds and five-hundreds amounting to 2100 bucks. He—say—you wouldn't maybe be in a position to know how much money he had on him, would you?"

"No," Rand hastened to explain. "I did see him, while I was talking to him today, take a sheaf of $1500 in one hundreds and five-hundreds from Miss Creston—a sum she'd gotten for him at his request—and he added it to a sheaf equally thin, equally crisp, that was already in that vest breast pocket—and stowed the whole thing away like—like so much hay. He started to count it—let's see—he got up as far as $1700—and then buttoned it up saying he'd count it later."

"Then you've no idea how much that whole sheaf would be?"

"None. Considering it contained hundreds and five-hundreds mixed, it could have been anything. He always carried a lot of money. He—but who found him?"

"Just a minute till I make a note. Yes. Now who found him? Well, 'twas the night engineer, named Michael Casey, who found him, in comp'ny with the night manager of the Interstate Life Building, Phillip Kinsella, in case you know him. 'Twas just at 16 minutes after 9 that the said Casey got a call on the phone in his engyne room, which engyne room is entered as such in the telephone book under Interstate Life Building. Three other phones was available—but the guy who called up must a been too rattled to pay any attention as to what department he was gettin' hisself connected with. Well, anyways, the noise of Casey's engynes was so bad he had to scream into the phone. An' sprain his own ear-drums to hear, in th' bargain. In fact, he had to slow down one engyne clost to him, to get the drift. All he could make out was 'Mr. Kenwood—murdered—upstairs in Room 1122.' He shut down a second engyne, and tried to get more information, but the party had cut off.

"He rung the night manager at once, they met in the foyer, and up they went. Th' transom of 1122 was lighted up through its glass, but all was quiet. They knocked once hard on the polished, solid oak door that your would-be-ultra buildin' is equipped with. No answer. They opened the oak door up—it wasn't locked at all—and peered in. Kenwood's desk light was on, bright. Ceiling light also. And there Kenwood was too, a dead and bloody sight—as even the homicide squad admits. And they be a hard crew, my boy. A hard crew. Well, Kenwood—"

"How—how long had he been dead?" Rand asked desperately.

"One half hour to three quarters of an hour, by the verdic' of the homicide squad physician who was there inside of 6 minutes after Casey an' Kinsella found th' body. For th' aforesaid Casey and Kinsella didn't even bother to call any of the insurance doctors in the building to see whether Kenwood was dead or not. A guy with his brains hanging out like Kenwood's was, and his blood half drained out of him, was long since beyond physicians. They knew that. They called the Detective Bureau instead, instanter, and Casey posted hisself as guard in front of the door to keep th' scrubwimmen an' busybodies out.

"Three quarters of an hour, to an hour, Kenwood had been dead—that is, at 26 minutes after 9 when the homicide doc took his tests—if it's the verdict of a medical man you want. Or dead from just about 8:20—or 8:30 p.m.—an' only from then—do you want the figures from the known comin's and goin's of him who killed him—and the time Kenwood was last seen, and so on. A perfec' tally, if you'll notice!"

Rand did notice! And was thankful, indeed, that at that hour he and Aline Creston had been with each other on the Lake Front.

CHAPTER IX

The "Injun Chief" Murder

Still on the same wire together.

And on the same subject.

Kenwood's death!

"Was anybody," Rand was now asking, "seen getting off floor 11 to-night, between 8—and 9 o'clock?"

"Yes," O'Rourke replied, "about 40 people! Plus one Filipino necktie peddler! I don't count Flips as people, you see! There was a quarterly life-insurance salesman's conference in the Great Lakes Fidelity Life Insurance Company, which, as I understand it, is down the same corr—"

"Yes, you go down the same corridor as our office is on, around a bend leftward, and to the end of **that** corridor. I know the company."

"Well, there was a quarterly meetin' of life-insurance salesmen of that company. Salesmen from Michigan, Indiana, Illinois and Minnesota attendin'. The main guy was to address 'em—and all to compare notes. The meetin' was for 8:30. And not less than 30 agents got off the 11th floor tonight and went down that corridor between 8 and 8:30, and not less than another 10, all in varyin' stages of lateness, between 8:30 and 9."

"And the Filipino? Is he—by any chance—the kill—"

"The killer? Of Kenwood? Listen, a man's arm, I told you, swung that hatchet—not a mosquito's. This little yellow gnat—I call him a gnat, be-cause you can't go by elevator operators' descriptions of Orientals—he might have been a Filipino, or only a half-breed such, or he might have been some of the other vermin that come out o' the far-East—but anyway, this little yellow gnat, the way he was described, couldn't have cut the whisker off a brother gnat, with a toy axe. And so, as I'm tryin' to get to saying, he wandered in to Kenwood's office at just about 8 o'clock tonight. And left about 3 minutes thereafter."

"Then—how do you know he isn't the kil—that is, just because he was too slight in build? Or—what?"

O'Rourke sighed. "Because Kenwood was seen alive **after** the Flip left the buildin'. And 'twas **after** the Flip left the buildin' that the real murderer come in. Carryin' the hatchet, openly."

"Openly? Good Lord! But how—how could he dare to carry a hatchet without—"

"Here," broke in O'Rourke. "I have always had a penchant in me mind for relatin' things in chromatic order. And here is th' way the whole schedule o' happenings took place."

He sighed, as one who regretted the demands of courtesy, made by friends.

"At a certain time tonight," he pronounced stiffly, "which time will be d'termined by somethin' happenin' a few minutes later, see?—a Filipino with a tray o' six or seven neckties goes up in the elevator, rambles off undecidedly at Floor 11, tosses up a mental coin in his yellow noodle, an' meanders down the north corridor. In which corridor happens to lie th' offices of the **Ultrapolitan Magazine**. All right for that." O'Rourke paused as though to let his hearer assimilate these simple facts. "Very shortly," he continued, "th' said Flip rambles back. And rides down, and goes out. Now please say goodbye to that Flip—because Chicago is as full of 'em anyway, as a dog with lice, and he didn't kill Kenwood!

"For, on th' next trip of the elevator down, Kenwood himself rides down. Shows the elevator man, one Hyman Kovarsky, a silk tie he just bought. For only two bits. From a Flip peddler who'd just blew in his office. And wishes now, he tells the said Hyman Kovarsky, he'd bought more, because after lookin' it over it looked like near a dollar tie—and one fit for a true gentleman!

"With which Kenwood goes to the cigar stand in the foyer, and buys hisself a package of Camels, that being precisely what he rode downstairs for. And he sets his wrist watch by the Western Union clock back of the cigar counter, and asks the clerk, one Cooper Haskins, if th' clock is right, and expresses surprise that his own watch is so far off. And th' said clerk, Cooper Haskins, assurin' him the clock was **always** right, naturally looked at it to see if maybe it'd stopped, and thus noted that it said 10 minutes after 8. And now you know the time that Kenwood rode back upstairs again with his package of Camels.

"'Twas at least a full five minutes after that, that the killer come. And the reason he was able to carry a hatchet openly was because he was dressed up as an Injun Chief. Oh, just a cheap masquerade suit. Consistin' of cotton pants and cotton blouse, representin' buckskin, with brown tatters sewed along the edge representin' feathers. Long red cotton gloves on his hands, to simulate Injun skin. Tommyhawk—yes, the hatchet!—ground beautifully sharp—an iron screwhook screwed in the wooden end of it, and hooked clear through th' cotton cloth of th' blouse, near his wrist an' to'rds th' right hip makin' a striking **toot ensemble**. Is that what it's called? And 'twas that hatchet, of course, that cleaved Kenwood's skull in twain—is that the word, twain?—later. And 'twas them cotton gloves that left not a damned finger-print on anything in the place. Includin' the hatchet itself. Nor th' desk lamp, which I understand was moved about a bit. Nor th' handles of the visitor's chair where the killer sat and talked with Kenwood. For a while at least. 'Twas a fingerprintless crime, me boy. Any comments?"

"So—the killer was an Indian chief?" Rand said bewilderedly. "Well, the elevator man must have—but of course—he undoubtedly thought the fellow was a Hallowe'en masquerader going up to see some friend up-stairs—or to drag him away to a dance—or leave a message. But he must have got a pretty good idea of the fellow's features, even though they were covered with grease paint?"

"They wasn't covered with grease paint. He wore a big loose-fitting Injun Chief mask, same identical thing as the Kresge 25-to-a-$1 stores, the country over, sell for two bits. In fact, the whole suit was bought from a Kresge 25-to-a-$1 store, th' garments proper—outside o' the mask—cos-tin'—only four bits, an' comin' packed complete in a cardboard box in two sizes, known as 'kid' and 'adult'. They been sold for five years now, all over the U, S., so I learned tonight from the Kresge purchasing agent—one Julius Stern—if the name's worth anything to you. On top of which, if 'tis of any further interest, a report I just seen downstairs on Sinjohn's desk from all Loop traffic cops and squad cars indicates no less than 50 such Injun Chiefs was seen tonight, at various times, an' at various points, in th' Loop. And a later report comin' from outlyin' districts shows that—but never mind. About this mask. The **piece de resilience** of the whole get-up! A big shiny enameled affair, with hijeous war paint markings and a big halo—or mebbe you'd call it a festoon—of printed cardboard feathers sticking out all around the edge. Eyes made o' screenwire, pressed outward into a sorta rounded shape—screenwire, that is, with Injun eyes painted on 'em—so's the wearer can look out on this here jolly old world—but nobody on the outside can look past—an' in—an' tell whether he hisself has got blue eyes—or brown eyes—or grey eyes—or any eyes at all. Held to the face, these here masks are, by a rubber band goin' over th' back of the head. Over which head, on Kenwood's killer, was a further appurtenance to the mask, a black cotton half-stocking-like cap, or hood, falling down over th' back o' the neck like Injun hair, with a couple of cotton braids representin' pigtails. With the cot-ton jacket buttoned up around the neck, and this head sack, and that halo o' feathers, he was completely masked. And was—and oh yes, he'd notched a bigger hole in the mouth of the mask—in its left corner—and was smokin' a cigar through it. That was just to give an air of—of **insouicance**. Ain't that the word? Or nonchalance. Is that better? Anyway, the elevator man merely grinned when he got on, and paid no attention to him, other than that he got off on the same floor where most everybody had been getting off."

"From your detailed description of that suit," Rand asked, "you got somebody then—who had the suit?"

"Well—we didn't catch him in it—no. But we got the suit. Doffed in the alley back of the Interstate Life Building it was. When he come out on Clark Street at 8:40 or so, after killin' Kenwood, he ev'dently went around the corner of Adams, down the block west a short ways, and into the alley. Shucked the suit about midway. And come out on the other end—Monroe Street, an entirely diff'rent person."

"Or came out back on Adams Street," Rand suggested.

"Maybe." O'Rourke's answer was mild.

"And the hatchet was doffed—with the suit?" Rand asked.

"Oh—he didn't carry no bloody hatchet back downstairs. No! He left that upstairs on the floor. To make our fingerprint department cuss!"

A few seconds later Rand was asking a further significant question.

"Well now, you say the murderer walked out of the elevator—that is, on his way out after having killed Kenwood—at 8:40. If everybody in the place was clocking him by this time, why didn't somebody—"

"Wait, wait! Nobody was clocking a harmless masquerader. For while Kenwood's killer was upstairs with him, the First Edition of **Midnight Brevities** arrived in the Interstate Building foyer. And a certain old Hershey-bar Jane, who sells apples and chocolate bars and such things around the buildin', for the cigar counter concessioner, was waitin' for them. Waitin' for 'em wit' her board, laid out across two boxes, just to the side o' where the one elevator runnin' at night disgorges its passengers."

"Yes," said Rand. "I know the old girl. She lays out a flock of **News** and **Americans** near the elevator every night at 5—but of course, so late as 8:30, they'd be **Midnight Brevities** only. Well go on."

"Well, it seems that your Interstate Life Building backs the **Brevities** office on Monroe near LaSalle. So it catches just about a real 8:30 deliv'ry every night—as it advertises—by way o' the alley. Right off the presses, in fact. And tonight when the man flung 'em in to Jane in the foyer, he pointed at the W.U. clock and said: 'How's that for service, old gal? An 8:30 paper at 8:30—to the second!'"

"I see," Rand commented. "That is, I don't see what I am to see exactly."

"No, but you will. Well, the **Brevities** come while the killer was up-stairs. Was all laid out on the board, and for nearly ten minutes, by th' time he come down. In fact, he bought one! Not just as he stepped out of the el-evator, though. No, he stopped right square in his tracks, starin' down at th' row laid out t' th' side o' where he'd got off. Like as if somethin' had sort of touched a—a perplex of his."

"A complex, yes," corrected Rand.

"All right—a complex then. Well, he walked a couple o' steps forward, then come back, reached into his real pants pocket through th' usual slit in the costume trousers, fished up a dime in his red-cotton gloved fingers, leaned down, flung down the dime—wavin' off the change—picked up a **Brevities**, and beat it on out, **Brevities** hugged under his arm."

"Well, I—I still don't see yet what I'm to see. I saw that paper tonight. A First Edition, too. Let's see—"

"Did you happen," O'Rourke asked, "to notice the 3 headlines what stood out the strongest, at least from a distance of a human head to th' floor? I got one here on my desk in front of me."

"Well—I remember the main headline. About a 13th Coin of Confucius being recov—"

"Aye!" said O'Rourke triumphantly, like a panther who had just had a drink of blood. "Confucius—China! See! It signifies that—but here—I promised to elucidate ever'thing. There's 3 headlines on that paper what can be seen for a distance. The first, of course, is that big 4-column one in bold condensed letters—Century extra condensed, it's known as—readin' '13th COIN OF CONFUCIUS STOLEN AND RECOVERED!!!' The second is that snappy 2-column stepladdered affair—in bold Gothic—I think that's what it's called—readin' 'BLIND TOM, NEW YORK'S FAMOUS COIN DEALER, BY QUICK THINKING REGAINS ONE OF WORLD'S MOST UNUSUAL NUMISMATICAL ITEMS.' And the third—well this is the broad 3-column 2-line head down at the bottom left of the page, set in a right snappy bold Cheltenham, as it's known: It reads: 'BIG FIRE IN CAPE TOWN SOUTH AFRICA DESTROYS OVER 30 SQUARE BLOCKS OF OLD RESIDENTIAL SECTION. MANY INHABITANTS REPORTED MISSING!'"

Rand was thinking deeply on those headlines.

O'Rourke's words broke in on his thoughts.

"What was that other question you started to ask a while back?"

"I've forgotten, I guess," Rand said.

"Was it," O'Rourke asked, "whether Kenwood's office was ransacked? If so—the answer is no, so far as can be observed. There ain't no center drawer on that table-like desk of his, it says on this diagram here, and the diagram shows, moreover, by certain dotted lines marked in a way we have in the department here, that Kenwood's torso an' legs didn't interfere none with the drawing of either of the two side drawers out—the right—nor the left. The right—the lock-drawer—was unlocked, with its Yale key in it, just as Kenwood hisself would prob'ly have had it while sittin' there; in actuality—the drawer was stickin' out a casual inch or so—and it could have been pulled clear out by anybody who wanted to take th' trouble to step over the narrow blood stream trickling leftward and exposed to view, from front to back, without no trouble. Its pers'nal contents, however, as well as them unpersn'nal ones in the drawer on the opposite end, was all in perfect order, an' every item practically visible without even havin' to rake one over the other."

"Yes," Rand commented. "Kenwood always kept the contents of his two desk drawers laid out like the stock of a Southport Avenue notions store." He paused a second, puzzling. "Then the killer, you take it, wasn't interested—in ransacking?"

"Not at all, I think," was O'Rourke's reply.

"Well, would he—but wait—who, though, do you suppose rang that engine room, at 18 minutes or so after 9, and told this Casey there was a murder up there in 1122?"

"Somebody I think, Rand, whose guts was scared just about entirely out of 'em. Casey had all he could do to get a few of th' words, without tryin' to get the voice tones an' all that. But he thinks, now, that they **did** sound scared. If you ask me, I think one of your **Ultrapolitan** salesmen called— took one look through that door—and blew. Or some life insurance agent then in the building, maybe, turned the handle of the door by mistake— or because he might have known Kenwood—or because he seen the light through the transom over the door, and thought he could write him up—and caught a sight of that body with its brains hangin' out like—like the after-birth of a cow! And fled. In fact, right after 9, they was a gen'ral hejiro—is that the word meanin' ex—exodus?—of agents from a small meetin' being held in the Fraternity Life, on the same floor, at the right end of the same corridor that your corridor intersects with—the corridor that the Great Lakes Life Insurance Comp'ny is at the left end of."

"I see, I see," Rand commented. "And I recall now—remember, O'Rourke, **my** brains are twirling a bit in my own head!—what I was going to ask, was this: How do you suppose this—this—well—fellow, whoever he is—in the Indian Chief suit—got in to see Kenwood—with that alarming layout?"

"Alarming? Not on Hallowe'en. He just walked in, like anybody. Could have said—for instance—had he been a friend: 'Three guesses, Jack—who am I?' And sat down. Or else, had he been an utter stranger, could have pushed the mask back on top of his stockinged head, and said: 'Excuse me, Mr. Kenwood, but I happen to be on my way to a masquerade party, and I'm dropping in like this, if you don't object.'" O'Rourke paused.

"What—what was Kenwood doing, so far as you know," Rand now asked, "when the killer came in?"

"Same's he'd ev'dently been doing when the necktie peddler rambled in a quarter-hour before. Sittin' there at his desk. Which was all cleared of ever'thing. That is, y' understand, I mean clear of all business matters. Some new lease he had on the place lay under a paper-wei—"

"Yes," interrupted Rand. "I know. I saw him put it there after showing it to me late this afternoon. It was a 10-year lease. He was glad because he'd outwitted possible inflation."

"That's what **he** thought, eh? Well, getting back to his desk. It was clear of all business matters. Not clear of paraphernalia altogether—no. For the desk lamp was on it. And th' little red-white-an'-blue appointment calendar that—oh, do you know about his red-white-and-blue cal—"

"Yes," put in Rand. "A dam' fool contrivance—and one, also, which he bought from a peddler. Kenwood was such a good salesman himself that he was fish for all other salesmen. That fool cal—"

"Listen," put in O'Rourke. "I must be a fish myself, then—for I've got one right here on my own desk, and I find it dam' handy, too. It—"

"All right, O'Rourke," said Rand wearily. "Let's never mind stationery appliances. Nor the appurtenances on Kenwood's desk. What was he doing? Working? If so was—"

"No, just setting there, poring over an old marked-up coin catalogue—something supposed to be a catalogue of every coin in the history of the world. Here—let's see: **Bulser's Fits-the-Pocket Listing of Every Coin in World History**—that's its name. 'Twas laying open on his desk, near his body, where he'd set it down, covers upward, to talk with his visitor."

"A coin catalogue, eh? Well, I never knew him to be interested in any way in coins. He—but you don't mean to say there's any connection between—"

"Between it—and that top headline in tonight's **Brevities**? Hell—no! If you read the story, that was New York. And this is Chicago, ain't it?"

"Yes, true. But Kenwood—I never knew him to be interested in coins. Or even to know anything about 'em." [3]

"Well, he was interested tonight. Or else was just lookin' over it to keep hisself from being bored to death while he waited for any of his own salesmen to come in. He'd entered a few digits in pencil on the back of the catalogue, as though to add 'em up—at least our Criminal Investigation Department here reports they're his writing—but they might refer to **Ultrapolitan** profits as much as coins, or to the rent of dames' apartments!" O'Rourke

---

3   Publisher's Note: As was set forth in "Finger Finger," an earlier novel by Mr. Keeler, it was subsequently ascertained that the catalogue had been loaned to Kenwood, shortly around 5 o'clock that day, by Mingleberry Hepp, a drunken author, who had a friend on South Park Avenue who wanted to sell a large coin collection, cataloguing at $2163, for only $400. All the coins in this collection were marked in this catalogue, and it was for Kenwood's use to check the real value of this collection.

paused grumpily. "Well, anyway, that's the way he was keeping hisself interested at the time he met his death."

He was silent now. And Rand too. For the whole thing, in all its cold horror, was sweeping back on the latter again, in a gelid wave. And he was trying to realize, somehow, that never, never would he see Kenwood again. And the Public Administrator of Cook County—in charge of **Ultrapolitan**. And—

"That be a very deep sigh you just gave," said O'Rourke. "Or was it you?"

"Yes," said Rand, "it was me."

"But deep as your sigh was," O'Rourke said, "'twas no deeper than the one th' bloody murderer hisself is givin' this very minute downstairs in Cell Number 39."

"You've—you've got somebody locked up—for the crime?" asked Rand.

"I have," proclaimed O'Rourke calmly. "Though the while he sighs—as you do—he also protests his innocence. And when you come down tomorrow, you can see him. For you'll have to come down, of course, for fillin' in a few details on the mere matter of the business."

"But—but who is the man?" asked Rand. "The man—in your Cell 39? It's about time I was told. I—"

"Yes," admitted O'Rourke, "perhaps it is. Since Kenwood was your employer—and not mine. Well, Rand, the gent who bumped you out of your job—so far as all our professional experience around here is worth a tissue paper dime—is Yin Yi, a Chinaman. And—"

"Yin Yi?" Rand exclaimed. "Yin Yi? Why he had no reas—"

"Your five minutes are up," said Central, in a cold metallic voice. "If you wish more time, deposit another nickel!"

CHAPTER X

"Into 3 Cocked Hats!"

David Rand hastily raced through his pockets, and found a triply-slotted slug that belonged to the Malmgren Drugstores which dotted Chicago. He rammed it into the slot. There was a loud explosion of clicks, and he was back in connection with O'Rourke again. Rather the latter's voice, talking to his switchboard girl.

"Jessica, get this connection reversed as against our number."

Rand heard her say, but not to himself.

"Reverse connection charges, Central, on Police 3333—Line K."

There was a loud clicking supposed to return his Malmgren slug. Except that he noticed no slug was spewed forth, the telephone company coming off, as usual, 100 percent winner.

"O'Rourke?" he said.

"Waiting," came his voice.

"You say you arrested Yin Yi?"

"You know—Yin Yi? I thought you were in New York the last four—five days?"

"Hell no. I don't know Yin Yi. But I do know—" Rand stopped. "Listen, where did you get what information you got about this chap Yin Yi?"

"From Peebles, Kenwood's man," said O'Rourke testily. "And from that red-white-an'-blue calendar that stan' on Kenwood's desk. And from a Chinaman in Indianapolis, named Yin Tsou Li. And from—"

"Wait," David Rand put in. "I suppose you know as much—or even more—than I can ever add. But—well—this calendar. What—"

"Are ye sure ye know what th' red-white-an'-blue calendar is?" asked O'Rourke suspiciously—and a bit peevishly too, so it sounded. "For I don't see how you coulda called it a fool thing if you knew what it—"

"Yes, I know what it is. The sheets are all connected loosely to a pair of brass rings on an iron base. An iron base representing an American flag. And they run in sequence red, white and blue. Red white and blue. Or rather pink, white, and light blue—so you can at least write on 'em. They run for—let's see—3 times 365—that'd be—there'd be 1095 of 'em. At least on

January 1st! Every trio—that is, every red, white, and blue trio—bears the same date. But the red sheets read 'Morning' and are for appointments only up to noon. The whites say 'Afternoon' and are for appointments between noon and 6 p.m. And the blues say 'Evening' and are for appointments from 6 p.m. to midnight, I guess. After which you're supposed to sleep, as there's no further color for midnight till morning again." Rand paused, a bit belligerently—for he found himself thinking suddenly of employment agencies tomorrow. "And you have to tear off a sheet every time the noonday whistles blow—and the 6 o'clock whistles blow. And throw it away. Now do I know what it is?"

"Ye have described a very valuable article," pronounced O'Rourke crabbedly. And lapsed into silence.

So David Rand took up the story himself.

"Well—what did this calendar—this—this God's gift to man—have to do—well—you don't mean that Kenwood had an appointment—that appointment—with Yin Yi—for tonight?"

"Oh, you know he **did** have an appointment, eh?"

"Well—yes. Only that he made some further appointment last Monday afternoon when this Yin Yi was there. He didn't say, at least to me, just when the appointment was. And the girl was out when Yin Yi left. And I doubt if she knows anything about it, for she's not the kind to go riffling over her employer's cal—"

"Let's have no unasked-for eu—eulogies," said O'Rourke stiiy. "For 'tis of no consequence. Yes, Kenwood had an appointment with Yin Yi. For tonight. For 8:30. 'Twas written on the blue sheet, for October 31st. The blue sheet coverin' evening hours. In his handwriting, too. And has been checked, as same, by our C. I. Department, too. It reads just: 'Yin Yi: 8:30'."

"Well—now—let me get things a bit clear. What—what did Peebles tell you about Yin Yi?"

"Did you know that he made a demand on Kenwood for five hundred bucks last Monday afternoon?"

"Yes."

"And that he practically let him know he'd hand him the count if he didn't pay up?"

"Yes. At least he conveyed some sort of unnamed menace. But how about—well—what did Peebles tell you?"

"Peebles? He told me what I just been tellin' you. That Yin Yi put the thumbscrews to Kenwood for half a grand, and let him know it would be just too bad if he didn't come across."

"What else did he tell you?"

"Ain't that enough?"

"Well, that depen—but now, Yin Yi—has he admitted killing Kenwood?"

"Hell no! I told you he was protestin' his innocence, didn't I? But the dam' fool's alibi has blown up sky-high—higher than a kite—higher than a meteorite. He—oh, he'll be putting his name on the dotted line before another hour, and Sinjohn gets done with him. But Sinjohn **must** eat his graham crackers and milk, at 1 in the morning, come what may. He—No, Rand, the damn-fool Chink is so badly involved in his story that he ain't a chance now to fix nothing up."

"What—what was his story? Or is his story? You see—I may be able to throw a little light on things—for I had a conversation with Kenwood today about him—just general—but I must confess I'm—I'm puzzled. You say you've knocked his story into a cocked hat?"

"Into 3 cocked hats! He claims he was in Indianapolis at 8:30 tonight—even as late as 9:30 o'clock—with an uncle, Yin Tsou Li. But hell fire—don't he realize we got telephone directories along the walls o' this very room—directories of every city in the United States—and that we can find with our own eyes the said Yin Tsou Li, and call up Talbot 0303—at Indianapolis?"

"Well he—he—must have gotten scared and—"

"Yeah? Well he didn't think very clear this time—for the Honorable Yin Tsou Li affirms over the phone to no less a person than myself that he is Yin Yi's uncle, and that he hasn't laid eyes on Yin Yi for six months. He's—let's see what time it is—" O'Rourke evidently looked at a wall, to one or the other side of him, for a second. "Yes, he's givin' an affidavit to that effect right now, I guess, to my friend Kelvy O'Connor, the said Kelvy O'Connor being formerly my sidekick here at the Bureau, and bein' now part of the Indianapolis Detective Bureau, the said Indianapolis bein' where his own folks live. Is this all clear?"

"Well then—I pass," David Rand admitted. "I thought I could add a little information—in the Chinese chap's favor. But—but if he claims to have been where he wasn't—well, then—" Rand paused. "Well, it's my employer—and **my** job—that he knocked into a cocked hat—if he did kill Kenwood. And he—Still, O'Rourke, damned if all the Chinamen in the world admit, under your fists and rubber hoses down there, that they killed Kenwood, I'm still betting it wasn't one. It's—it's in my bones."

O'Rourke seemed baffled at his persistence.

"Why—why are you so sure that Yin Yi didn't—"

"It's because Kenwood told me—but then you say Yin Yi's alibi is as phoney as hell? Well—that knocks me for a goal. There's nothing to be said. What—what was his story? Or are you too busy to talk?"

"Busy? Hell no. I've cleaned up all the loose threads on this case an hour ago. My heels are sore from lyin' atop this desk. Now what is it you wanted to know! Yin Yi's story? Here it is—if you want pure Chinee romancin'."

O'Rourke paused. And then went on patiently, like a policeman trying to show a layman how impossible it is to accept any statement a suspected person gives.

"The damn fool was pinched by Detectives Maloney and McGuire, in his bedroom, up above his wax modelin' shop—he's a wax modeler, in case you don't know it—here in Chinatown. Maloney and McGuire had been goin' around there every half hour since Peebles gave us the low-down on the matter. And since we'd found Yin Yi's name in the Chicago telephone book. We'd have crashed the joint by midnight, if he hadn't showed, as well as the other studio he's got. And—"

"Other studio?" Rand interpolated. "I don't think I just underst—"

"Just," explained O'Rourke patiently, "that on their next-to-last trip there, an old Burmese—Maloney, you see, knows all them East Indian an' Oriental vermin, one from another—an old Burmese, as I say, livin' next door, come downstairs in a long cotton nightgown and told Maloney and McGuire that if they was lookin' for Yin Yi, he also had another studio in the Malmgren Company Warehouse on Clinton Street; that he himself— this old Burmese—had brung a package there for Yin Yi once, from the Chinatown studio." O'Rourke paused. "Well, as I was saying, if he hadn't showed by midnight, they'd have crashed the Wentworth Avenue joint. But on the last trip—which was at 11:40 p.m.—the upstairs was lighted up, and the electric latch-release on the shop door was pressed the minute Maloney and McGuire rang, like as if th' guy upstairs thought they was just a friend come to play fan-tan—or—or hooey-hooey-sip-soo. Well, they come up-stairs. Through the shop. The Chink—and it's Yin Yi I'm speaking of now, you understand—was half undressed, sittin' on a single couch-bed in a bare lookin' sort of room with an old piano in it, readin' a copy of—believe it or not!—Shakespeare, printed—so he said—in the new Mandarin Chinese. Amiable as a lark in May. As benign lookin', in the little goldrimmed spec-tacles he was readin' through, as a young Baptist preacher. Which specs, he since says, are just weak plus-lenses from th' 10-cent store, what he uses to insert hairs in the eyebrows of wax heads, and to read with in poor lights. Which latter is the hooey. He had 'em on so's he'd look harmless and in-nocent. Well, anyway, he'd been goin' to bed just as if he hadn't killed a guy nor nothing. Maloney and McGuire they—Listen—**must** you have this story?"

"Listen yourself! You say Peebles told you only that Yin Yi had de-manded $500 from Kenwood? Nothing else?"

"No—nothing else. What more could he have told?"

"Well—I'm not so sure. But go on—you say the wax-modeler's alibi turned out to be worth nothing more than a—apiece of—of old shoestring.

Well—still, I'd like to get the lowdown. Isn't it possible that his uncle might have had a grudge against him—and lied—"

"Nah! I could read him—the uncle, I mean—like a book. He talks like a very fine upstandin' Chinese. He's a guy that ain't framin' nobody—and ain't helping any phony alibis, neither. Anyway, Kelvy O'Connor is probably with him right this minute—or has already been with him and gotten a full affidavit from him. Kelvy'll be calling me shortly, and I'll know all there is to know about this Yin Yi lad. And I'll—but here—here you are—if you want an example of one real fine piece of romancin'."

O'Rourke paused.

"Maloney and McGuire handed it to th' Chink cold—as we do around here. We get better results. Told him Jack Kenwood had been murdered. And with a 100-percent full Chinese technique! And that his—Yin Yi's—name had been given as wanting $500 from Kenwood. And asked him where he'd been the evenin' just gone. And—do you know what the very first words was, that the Chink said?"

"No. What?"

"He said: 'The Fates be praised—that he hypnotized her!'"

"That—that he hypnotized her? What—what did he mean?"

"He dried up entirely on that. Wouldn't explain no further. Told Maloney, in fact, he was referrin' to some dame called Ophelia. Who Hamlet hypnotized, by actin' scrooey.

"In fact—scrooey is what they put him down as, right away. An' they ordered him to dress. And watched him mighty careful, too, so's he couldn't swing any more hatchets. And checked his watch, likewise, what was lyin' atop a rickety old bureau. And—"

"Why—why was that?"

"My request," snapped O'Rourke. "For Yin Yi, accordin' to the ev'dence on the blue October 31st sheet of that calendar had an appointment with Kenwood for 8:30. And this Injun Chief walked in that Interstate Building foyer at just about 8:15, to the dot. Now if by any chance the Chink's watch—"

"I get you. And how was his watch?"

"Fourteen minutes fast," proclaimed O'Rourke exultantly. "Couldn't have fit th' situation better."

"Maybe not," Rand hazarded. "Yet if everybody in Chicago whose watch is fast tonight was dragged into your place—"

"Yeah, I know what you're going to say. No, it don't mean nothing so far as legal evidence goes. It's just one more tiny piece o' straw showing the direction of a sou'easter, that's all. Do you or don't you want this story?"

"Yes, I do," Rand said humbly.

"Well, he told Maloney, while he was dressing, that he'd just come from

Indianapolis. Where he was born an' grew up. That he'd been with this uncle. This Yin Tsou Li. So Maloney went downstairs in the waxworkin' shop, and called me to give me the dope on it, so's I could be checkin' on Yin Yi while he was being brought down. Which I done. And found he hadn't been within a mile of the town.

"They brought him here. About ten minutes of midnight. I fingerprinted him first, in th' room adjoinin' this, and put th' whole set on the wires—yes, photo-telegraphy—for Kelvy O'Connor, who I'd just had on the phone five minutes before, and who'd told me he was goin' off duty and would work on this case—at least an hour or two—on his own time to help an old sidekick make a quick clear-up of matters. You see, I wanted Kelvy to look Yin Yi up and see if maybe he's got a record down there, since he claims Indianapolis as a birthplace. Yin, of course, didn't know nothin' about nothin'. He wasn't even inside this room here, what has all the telephone directories lined up on the wall. And I didn't even tell him the bad news. What his uncle had said. I assured him we'd check all he told us tomorrow morning, and just let him lie hisself into twenty knots within knots. Which he proceeded to—listen—do you really want his story?"

"Hell, yes! And I want to see him hanged if he killed Kenwood. But damn it—I don't believe—"

"All right. Here was his story. Nothing in which explained hypnotizin' business, you understand. He just wouldn't explain that. Said Maloney misunderstood his words. That he'd said—now wait'll I read this. Yes. That he'd said: 'The Fates be praised. I've found th' answer at last. Hamlet hypnotized her!'" O'Rourke paused. "Which happens to be hooey—as I **now** know, Well," he continued, "his story was all beautifully pat by this time—after that ride down in the taxicab—except for the simple an' important matter of fixin' it with his uncle ahead of time, that's all! He said he'd intended to stay in Chicago October 31st, that bein' today of course. Somethin' **very** important! But that he got a bad break—a tough piece of news—late last evening. And besides bein' disappointed half to death, he thought it best to vamoose out o' town. So he decided to go visit his uncle—in the town where he growed up. And he went, he says. Got there at midnight. He says he was at his uncle's—this Yin Tsou Li's—all day today. And that he decided tonight, quite considerably later than the time when the Monon train would have pulled out for Chi, to come home by air—on either th' 9:30 Monon Bullet, in fact—or th' 10:30 Monon Skyrocket—if you know them fast passenger planes which the Monon Railroad runs from Cinci to Chi, by way of Indianapolis, to forestall competition with itself. Big Fokker F-36's, they are—each powered with four Hornet 575 horse-power motors, and capable of carryin', if I remember rightly, as much as 32 passengers. Not that they generally do. No. But since th' Monon Bullet is the one he claims he ult'mately took, let me just say it left Cincinnati tonight right on th' dot at 8 o'clock, come down on the Indianapolis air field 16 minutes ahead o' time—9:14 to be exact—took th' air again at 9:30, its right departure time, and come down on Central Air Field here at Chi at a minute of 11, a minute ahead of its schedule. And started back to Cincinnati at midnight tonight, as an air sleeper, for the same pair of pilots an' porter handles it for the whole 6-hour round trip. It's been chartered, however, for th' return journey, by a bunch o' pill-rollers going to the Cincinnati Druggists' Convention openin' in the morning—and so ain't stoppin' at Indianapolis at all—an emergency plane, th' Monon Arrow, is taking care tonight of the Chicago-Indianapolis last minute traffic—so just wait'll I catch that Monon Bullet by long-distance phone and short-wave. I'll knock that Chink's alibi into its 4th an' last cocked hat. I'll—but never mind. Where am I? About this Yin Yi's tale. Well, this romancin' Chink says that another Chink who he doesn't know at all—a guy just in from Frisco—who fell madly in love with a wax Chinee girl's head in his window and come in several times to gas with him, an' moon over her—a guy with a blind, red, inflamed eye stickin' half out of his head—a guy whom he knows only as Cyclops—listen—who th' hell is Cyclops?"

"No particular person," David Rand told O'Rourke patiently. "A cyclops was any one of a race of one-eyed giant shepherds, living in Sicily, under a chief called Polyphemis. Not in reality, you understand. Just in—in Homeric legend. This Yin Yi must be an educated sort of a bird to stick a name like that on a man?"

"He is. He's up on ever'thing. Well, anyway, he calls this guy just Cyclops. He says Cyclops happened to be in his shop when he got the bad news over th' phone that he'd better blow town, and that Cyclops was grousin' hisself that tomorrow night—that's tonight—he too 'd better dust out of Chicago fast, since some big Chinee tong chief was comin' back to Chi from Frisco, who—if he heard Cyclops was in town—would put the high sign out to ring curtains on him. So he—Yin Yi—makes a bargain with Cyclops. He—listen—ain't this all the scrooiest stuff you ever heard? He bargains with Cyclops that he'll give him fifteen bucks to get out of Chicago with tonight, if he'll do a little callin' up tomorrow—that's today—on some certain numbers—and get a little low-down on something, and phone it to him at Indianapolis—at his uncle's house. Which same Cyclops done, Yin Yi says. Rung his uncle's place at about ten minutes o' 9 tonight—in fact, told Yin Yi he was downstairs in the basement phone-booth room of the Lig-Wall Drugstore on Madison and State Street—and give him the info that it was safe for him to come back to Chi. He—"

"Was Yin Yi mixed up in some tong stuff too?"

"Naw—woman stuff. Irate husband! He come clean about it an hour later—about 12:30—on exactly what he was hidin' out from. I'll give you that later. Now where was I? Yes, Yin Yi there in Indianapolis. Well, he claims he intended to stick right there till his trouble was all cleared up here in Chi—but that he got this long-distance from Cyclops that ever'thing was hunky-dory, after all—an' that the coast was clear—and so he decided to come home by plane so's he could get a good night's sleep and start work tomorrow morning for the Wax Model Exhibit of Histerical Figures—of th' Industrial Exhibits Fair that opens here in four months. That part of his story is true, anyway. He **is** booked to start work tomorrow morning, with four other imported wax modelers. I checked him on that with the employment manager, a guy named Marchisso Fichetti. And he was to make enough coin, during the weeks he'd have been on the job—12 bucks a day!—that he could afford to travel in airplanes. But never mind. You want his story. That sits like a converted pyramid, on a bald lie to begin with. Well, he says after Cyclops called him, he in turn called up his music teacher—or his former music teacher, a Miss—now wait'll I look at this here transcript— yes—a Miss Laura B. Jones, livin' on West 9th Street, in that burg—an' chatted with her for 3 or 4 minutes, an' told her he wished he could have gotten over to say hello—and he asked her a question about somethin' in music—an' that he told his little niece, a—wait'll I look at this transcript again—yes—a kidlet named O Loya Yin—his uncle's grand-daughter, to be exact—goodbye—and went to th' Indianapolis airfield. That is, Lin-Wright Airfield down there, where the Monon planes leave and depart. Took him easily less than 10 minutes, he said, to get there, but seein' th' plane standin' on the field apparently nearly ready for the hop-off, he boarded it without botherin' to buy a ticket at the ticket window. He says he paid cash fare— $14.60—an' that he read a Chinese paper most of the time comin' home on the plane, and that's abs'lutely all he knows about Jack Kenwood. He admits he'd demanded $500, but says that he figured in view of th' warm spot he'd put hisself in in Chi—on another matter—that the Kenwood argument could just as well ride over to another day, anyway. An' so he just let his appointment go, for the time being!"

"And yet his uncle, this Yin Tsou Li, claims he hasn't seen him for 6 months?"

"Yes."

"Well, that's bad. And this Laura Jones. Does she say the same?"

"I'm just lettin' Kelvy O'Connor get an affidavit from her to the effect that she ain't seen her Chink ex-pupil nor heard from him. No use of me tryin' to handle the fool matter no further by telephone when it's gotta be did by affidavits anyway. Kelvy's got the whole layout now of Yin Yi's fool tale—includin', as I told you, a good clear photo-telegraphic set of his fingerprints to see what he may have been messin' up in down there before he come up here to live. Any minute I expect Kelvy to phone me. And then the State's Attorney can come down here to th' Bureau. And have the case presented to him on my silver platter."

Rand was silent. He saw that what he had to add was not much in the face of all that O'Rourke had just told him. And yet—he spoke. "But—now—you say Yin Yi revealed to you a short while ago—what he meant—when he said 'The Fates be praised—that he hypnotized her!'?"

"Yes, that's right. I had him up here again, a while ago. In the room adjoinin', that is. With Sinjohn present, this time. We was both very nice to him. We wanted him to finish the job of hangin' hisself. We says: 'Now listen, Yin—if you wasn't in Chicago tonight, and that's proved up O.K. tomorrow—you ain't got nothing on earth to worry about. We don't want to know nothing beyond that fact. So come clean with us. About this trouble that driv you out. If it's tong stuff—we're off it a mile! If it's woman stuff—we ain't endeavorin' to uncover any useless scandals. Already,' we tells him, 'we got one woman sittin' in this case in a unhealthy light—yet you can ask any of the reporters throngin' around Inspector Mackenzie's once downstairs whether a woman's name has popped up in this case. And they'll all tell you no. So you see we ain't injectin' nothing about no wimmen.'"

"And—and what did he say?"

"He thought a while. Then he says, so near's I can repeat it: 'Well, it is highly logical that you would not be in the least interested in my private affairs if you knew I had nothing to do with this murder. And inasmuch as I obviously had nothing to do with the crime and can easily prove so, I will reveal partly the circumstances of why I left Chicago. But without any actual names, that is.' And with that, he tells the story. It's kind o' vague—not near so clearcut as the story about him bein' in Indianapolis—so, if 'tis based on some kind o' fact like lies often is, I think he's sort of transmogrifyin' some o' the names, suburbs, occupations, an' people what figure in it." O'Rourke paused. "But here 'tis—such as it is!"

CHAPTER XI

How Yin Yi Hastened Indianapolisward

"Yin Yi," declared O'Rourke, "says he had a date for today with a white woman. Wife of a well-to-do business man in Oak Park. She likes 'em yellow, I guess. Lots does! Husband was out of town. So far's I can gather, Yin Yi was goin' out to the house and camp out here most o' the day. However, she had a neuralgy, or headache, or something, and went to her family doctor. Yesterday, that was. The doc gives her a little psychic treatment. Hynotized her out of it, see? But in so doing he got out of her, somehow, that she was gonna meet a lover. Or something like that, anyway. Or at least she got the idea he had, see? For she called Yin Yi up, he says, hurriedly, las' night about 6 o'clock. Told him she'd been hypnotized—was out—blotto!—in that doctor's office for 30 minutes, or so—at least, told him what I been tellin' you—and that hubby was in town—was right in the depot right then. And that their date was off. All off! For the doc, she tells Yin Yi—or, at least, so he says—was an old, old friend of her hubby, and she was cert he'd wired hubby all he found out in the hypnotizosis, and that he should ought to get back pronto—from Waukegan, or Springfield, or Kankakee, or wherever he was at, and hold the fort. She said she didn't have no idea at all, the Chink says, as to how much she'd told. But she advised him to blow the town, for she might've give his name, his whereabouts and Gordamighty knows what!

"So Yin says he was considerably alarmed himself. Didn't pack no duds nor nothing. Up and got out—that's all. But that Cyclops—th' Frisco Chink with the red, protrudin', blind eye was there at th' time—and he give him fifteen bucks plus some extra change for long-distance tolls, as well as his uncle's phone number in Indianapolis, and asked him to ring this dame at different intervals tomorrow—which was today—yes, sure he giv' Cyclops her number—and get the lowdown in case she come to the phone—and the coast was clear for talkin'. Well, he says he put in an uneasy day at his uncle's, laying around and chinning and wonderin'. And at about ten to 9 tonight Cyclops called. Told him he'd got the dame. At half-past 8. And got her alone. An' that she said ever'thing was all right. That she hadn't revealed nothing. That she'd just hinted, at most, at th' state of matters. And that Yin could come back to Chicago safely. And so—havin' that waxworkin' job open—he just decided to fly back. And get on th' job tomorrow. So he give his former music-teacher, who he kinda likes, it seems, a ring, and dug out for the air-field in time to catch that 9:30 Monon Bullet—and come home.

"Well, all that part rings true enough, damned if it don't. For he hedges just enough on the Oak Park part—an' the occ'pation of the woman's husband—and all that, so that it **does** sound like he **is** protectin' somebody. Of course, the village in question ain't no more Oak Park than I am! It could be Ravenswood, right here in town. Or Lake View. Or Englewood. Or what not. One thing's cert, though—if there **is** any basis to **that** tale at all—some woman, sittin' in a parlor somewhere tonight with her hubby, shortly after n o'clock, when the first news flashes come over the home raddios—and th' first stories about Yin Yi's name bein' mixed up in this murder case was on th' street downtown—you see, Rand, th' Interstate Life Building gettin' a tip-off the way it done, give th' homicide squad a perfect 'in'—and full possession f'r over an hour, and kept the reporters out just that long, so that the story wasn't out till shortly after 11—well, what was I saying?—oh yes, that if Yin Yi **is** mixed up in any way with any white woman, she sure put one dainty hand over a beatin' heart tonight, if she had her raddio turned on—and locked her pretty lips good and tight, I'll say!" O'Rourke paused. "But about that story—or any other story—well, Yin Yi's alibi about his uncle is n. g. That's the rub!"

"Then," David Rand commented, "this woman-story is what he meant when he said 'The Fates be praised that he hypnotized her'? He meant—"

"He meant that if she hadn't a got hypnotized, she wouldn't a got scared—and he wouldn't have got out of Chicago—and so might have got jugged—and imprisoned for life to boot!—for killing Kenwood. Just a beautiful stall—if you ask me."

"But nevertheless, as I understand it, you're trying to check the plane on which he claims he came back to Chicago, so as—"

"Listen, Rand, we check every detail of a yarn around here, especially when one detail goes blooey. The bigger a damn liar we can make out of a bird, the more sure we can convict him. I'm demolishin' every point in that Indianapolis tale—through Kelvy, that is—and you can bank your life that I'm doin' the same with the plane. That plane hasn't probably carried no Chinamen for a month of Sundays. They don't ride planes."

"No," Rand said dubiously. "At least not unless they can earn $12 a day!" He paused. "Was no Chinaman at all even seen to get off when the plane landed?"

"She landed at t'other end of the field tonight. Wind wrong! And the passengers clumb out and made their own way toward the entrance gates. Nobody paid much attention to 'em. Them things, on an airfield, are th' same like loaves of bread in a bakery. No, I'm having the main Monon air despatch station—Monon Air Despatch Station No. 1, it's called—at the base of Hoosier Beacon, just outside Indianapolis, call me long-distance just as soon as they get into connection with the plane itself by short-wave—by their auxiliary short-wave, that is!—and hook me direct on to it. It's pretty well in calling distance on that particular wave right now—but not due to come down, of course, before it reaches Cinci. Well, any comments?"

Rand pondered.

"Well, I—I don't want to weaken your case any," I said. "But by all dispassionate reasoning, I ought to now state that—"

The unmistakable voice of O'Rourke's private switchboard girl interrupted him.

"Pardon my coming in on your line, sir. Just a moment. Mr. O'Rourke–"

"Yes, Jessica. What?"

"Mr. O'Rourke, there's several calls all coming in on the board for you at the same time. Detective Kelvy O'Connor of the Indianapolis Detective Bureau is on Line G—about the Yin Yi alibi. That is, he was—a moment ago—but there was an accidental cut-off, and he'll be back on it in a few seconds or so. Monon Air Despatch Station No. 1 at Indianapolis Heights, Indiana, reports that it's just getting into communication with that Cincinnati-bound plane now on their auxiliary short-wave No. 3—you told me, didn't you, Mr. O'Rourke, that I wasn't to ask for the continuous connection that's on all the time with the pilots themselves?—that it was the cabin-phone of the plane you wanted? Yes? Well, they can put you on to the Negro porter and conductor in about another five minutes. The plane's flying about over Malottville, Indiana, now—cutting somewhat northeastward of Indianapolis to save time. Also, the Lig-Wall Drugstore on Madison and State reports that their Miss DuBries who handles the phone-booth room downstairs, is back from her midnight lunch now. And Mr. Malmgren—of the Malmgren Drugstores—was on—but is waiting to be called back at Hyde Park 4462. Also, Mr. O'Rourke, while you were talking, Patrolman Finnehan of that West Harrison Street beat called you to report on that—you know—that Malmgren warehouse matter. On Clinton Street. I told him to call you again in five minutes. And Inspector Mackenzie himself called up—from Mr. Kenwood's ofhce, where he walked over right after his midnight lunch. He wanted you, but hung up right away saying he wanted to check a further matter, and would ring again in five minutes."

"Holy—Mackeral!" Rand heard O'Rourke bite out. "They—they would all come back in at the same time! Well call Malmgren, Jessica, and tell him that we'll call him back again the minute we clean off several long-distance calls—and when we do, you get him then pronto. If Sinjohn calls, don't make him wait a minute, whatever you do: he gets savage as the devil when he gets full o' hot milk. Have that Miss DuBries ring us ag—no, you ring Lig-Wall Drugstore No. 3 as soon as we get the first lull, and get her. You say this Monon air despatch station's got clear short-wave connection with the cabin of that plane now?"

"Nearly so, Mr. O'Rourke. It's just about ready to come through."

"All right. It may be quite a number of minutes at that yet. Take Kelvy O'Connor, the minute his broken connection is restored. And in case the long-distance plus short-wave comes through from Indianapolis Height— we'll just continue to hold the Indianapolis connection with O'Connor—let it tick, that is!—and take the other line—the short-wave affair, while we can get it. Now follow all this carefully, Jessica. I want to clear this thing off complete in the next 10 minutes. I—"

"O'Rourke," Rand said, "before you take any of those calls, I ought to add about Yin Yi, you know—that—"

"Hell—never mind you adding anything! Yours truly is got to juggle them Indian Clubs now that I was telling you about this afternoon. I ain't got time to hear nothing now from people that live only a stone's throw from me. You wanted to hear how we demolish alibis around here—didn't you? All right. Jessica?"

"Yes, Mr. O'Rourke."

"Throw this Mr. Rand right across the whole board by the 'B'-hook-up—so's he can listen to ever'thing. Yes, the steno hook-up that's tapped into all wires. But if he puts in so much as one peep, chop him off."

She giggled.

"Yessir. And—just a minute, Mr. O'Rourke." The briefest of pauses. "Detective O'Connor's connection is restored."

"Good. Put him on. All right, Rand. Stand off—to one side. One word out o' you—and off you go! All right, Jessica. And get me the Lig-Wall Drugstore and Carl Malmgren soon's this connection is over. And don't forget to throw that short-wave connection in the minute it—"

"Yes, I will."

There was a violent clicking. And then a dead silence on David Rand's one wire. Then a buzzing. He guessed it was his connection being taken off, and being thrown back across the switchboard on that 'B'-hookup O'Rourke had mentioned. Then some more clicking. It seemed like all the firecrackers in Chicago were popping. Then all was quiet. And he heard a man's voice speaking.

"Terry?"

"Yeah. Kelvy?"

"Yes, Terry. Well, Terry, if you're holding a Chinese named Yin Yi for murder up there in Chi—at least between 8 and 9 tonight—I guess you haven't got the right man. Or else, if you've got a lot on him, he's been framed, somehow, for the murder. For one thing, Terry, you didn't have the right uncle. The one you called up was Yin Tsou Li. Of 2421 North Meridian Street. The one who's in the telephone book. Yes. Talbot 0303. But he's got a brother—so that gives your Yin Yi another uncle. **His** name is Yin Tzu Lei—" O'Connor spelled it out rapidly. "Sure—it's an old custom among Chinese. Same names for brothers—but spelled a bit different. I'm at Mr. Yin Tzu Lei's house right now. At 1034 South Senate Avenue. His phone's not listed in the directory. So you'd better make a note of it. Drexel 3051-R. And I've got about all the witnesses, right here now, that anybody in the world needs to clear your Yin Yi of anything."

In the dead silence that followed the Indianapolis detective's firm statement, David Rand could picture with no trouble the chaos of thoughts that were tumbling through O'Rourke's sandy-thatched head. And at last he seemed to find his tongue.

"For—for crying out loud!" was all he said. "For crying out—Yin Tzu Lei? Oh for—listen, I—don't believe it yet. This killin' up here is Chinee murder—an' nothin' but! Who—who've you got there that says this Yi fellow was in Indianapolis tonight?"

CHAPTER XII

Miss Jones—of Indianapolis!

David Rand heard the Indianapolis detective's voice coming back over the wire.

"Well, I'll tell you, Terry. For one thing I've got—"

Crackle! Crackle! Crackle! Pop. Sputter. Silence.

Then the switchboard girl's voice.

"Sorry, Mr. O'Rourke, but the Indianapolis connection seems to have got broken again. There may be a green girl on at the Chicago long-distance board—or at Indianapolis. Or maybe it was coming in from an emergency board. I was just about to tell Patrolman Finnehan over on West Harrison Street to call back again. Do you want to take him on in the meantime?"

"Well—try and see if by any chance that Indianapolis connection is back on."

Silence.

"No, Mr. O'Rourke. It's dead. Disconnection somewhere else along the line."

"All right. Let 'em back on by themselves. That guy O'Connor is nertz anyway. I—yes—give me Finnehan then, in the meanwhile. He—"

Another set of clickety-clicks. And an Irishman's voice, with a brogue that could he cut with a knife.

"Who th' hill be I talkin' to now?"

"Hello?" This from O'Rourke. "This you, Fin?"

"Finnehan it is. Who th—"

"Have you forgotten my voice, Fin? O'Rourke. Night A.C. man at the Bureau. Terry O'Rourke. Sinjohn's out just now, feeding up on graham crackers. So you're to report to 3333 instead of 4444. As you ev'dently know. Well—what report have you to make?"

The patrolman spoke slowly and ponderously, but methodically.

"Will, Tirry, Oi had a little throbble in getthin' th' key to the doomp. Oi shtill couldn't raise th' h'id store-kaper an' warehouse tally-man—the wan whose name ye p'aple at th' Booreau got from th' different Malmgren Droogstores—livin' on Wist Harrison Street, just wist of me own bate. He wur at a party. So 'twas Malmgren's sicrytary I had to wait for, afther all. An' he waited f'r me on the wrong coorner—the furst wan east. If I hadn't wondered what a Roll-Royce wur doin' in thot desoorted warehouse region, I'd a-been waithin yit. Annyway, we got in a few minutes ago. 'Tis joost a big stoorage warehouse full av tillyphone booths, ixtry counters, ixtry shilvin', sody fountains, cashiers' wickets, an' all the paraphenaly o' them there Malmgren droogstores. Wid two locked rooms at th' hind ind. Wan big slidin' dure—big enough for a team to back up in—l'adin' direct out onto Clinton Sthrate—an' one regooler soized ordinary dure, to th' side o' the main room, l'adin' out into a cobblestoned coort wid wan narrow gate givin' out itsilf to Clinton Sthrate, but connectin' in back wid th' wide noorth an' sout' crosswise alley joinin' both Harrison Sthrate an' Van Buren. The stoof in th' warehouse is stacked pretty nate, wid a fair loight boornin' all th' toime; and there be an aisle cleared from th' small side dure ladin' out to th' cobblestoned coort. I wint into both av the locked rooms, usin' bot' th' spicial key Malmgren sint down, an' th' key ye people tuk aff th' Chineeman. They be gr-rate big rooms, too. The wan to th' nort' has in it the valyable foornishin's—like cash-registers, typewriters f'r writin' perscriptions, as well as a few addin' machines, an' a case or two of valyble impoorted droogs, although 'tis not this partic'lar warehouse where th' droogs be kipt. That wan is on East Illyni' Sthrate. 'Tis only ixtra foornishin's an' odds an' inds of shtore equipment they kape here. They—"

"Hey, Finnehan—make it snappy! We've a couple of long-distance calls may bust in on us at any time. Get to his nest, snuggery, studio—or whatever it is. We're only interested in that hangout in the Malmgren Warehouse, what we was told down in Chinatown he had. That's the room I want a report on. That other locked room than the one with the typewriters an' cash registers."

"The same, Tirry, if ye'll give me a chance to catch me br'ith. Well, 'twas fitted up very illigent, Tirry, if you ask me. Wid a Chinee roog an inch thick. A big canopied bed, big enough for a rigiment to go to bed in all at th' same toime, and as regal as anny king iver slipt in! A coople—no three!— Chinee hangin' lamps, castin' a soft glow. A heavy rich gowld-embr'idered dhrape, cuttin' aff a gilted three-hole gas boorner big enough to cook things on—or to h'ate vittles up on! An' a dish closet ferninst it. An' on its ither soide, a square porc'lain washbowl—or sink—wid hot an' cowld roonin' water, and big enough to wash dishes in. A foine big room! O'd loike to live in it mesilf for a week."

"You say it's at the rear of the big interior of the warehouse? Do its windows look out on the cobblestoned court—or the north-and-south alley?"

"Both—yet neither, Tirry. They don't look out on nothin'. For they be covered up wid black felt."

"I see. Can't see in, nor see out, eh? A love nest, hey Finnehan?"

"Will—'tis rich, an' sweet smillin' just loike a lovenist should ought to be! True, there be a little pidistal wid some clay on it, an' a loight-fixchure hangin' over, w'at can be shnapped on, an' a couple av queer lookin' tools lyin' nearby, like th' place was for doin' a little work in. Oh yis—it says on the dure 'Studio'. But the clay ain't been wur-rked for a long while."

"Any signs of fresh food—or cooking?"

"None, Tirry. The washbowl—or sink—is quoite dhry."

"Was the dishrag dry?"

"Dry, yis. Oi tuk spicial note o' that, Tirry, knowin' exactly w'at Sinjohn wanted to foind out."

"No food lying around? Or containers?"

"None, Tirry. Oi did pick up a brown Chinee noodle aff the flure."

"Well, that could be a month old. Any smells—like perfume—or recent occupancy of human bodies?"

"Just a smill of d'id incense, Tirry, loike as if incinse had been boorned in th' room an' doi'd, wid th' room never aired out afterwur-rd. Sort of h'ivy an'—an' did-loike, wid a faint shwate-loike tinge. There wur a brass incinse dish in one coorner av th' room, wid a potbellied brass god sittin' over it."

"I see. I see. I know that dead trapped incense smell. It can be a month old—or an hour. It—" I heard O'Rourke pause, helplessly. "Then, in short, Finnehan, you could find no signs of occ'pancy—recent or otherwise?"

"None, Tirry."

"All right. Report back to your own beat then, over there west of the river. I take it you've returned Malmgren's own key to his secretary?" I heard Finnehan's assent. "I'll have Malmgren himself on shortly, and will be findin' out how in hell a Chink happened to have a love-nest—for that's cert'nly what it is—downtown—or at least just west o' downtown—in one of **his** warehouses. I think, in fact, I'll—"

The switchboard girl's voice came in on the wire.

"Excuse me, Mr. O'Rourke, but I got Mr. Malmgren while you had Finnehan on the wire. I didn't think Finnehan would be having such a long report to render. But Mr. Malmgren's available now if you—"

"Oke, Jessica. I'll take him. Goodbye, Finnehan. Give me Malmgren, Jessica. On any instrument but Number 4. Keep that one entirely free, Jessica, for that comb'nation land-an'-air connection when it comes through. For some reason Number 4's the clearest talkin' circuit we got on the desk here."

A series of clickings followed, and a very dignified voice came on the wire.

"This is Carl Malmgren speaking. President of the Malmgren Drug

Stores."

"Oh yes, Mr. Malmgren. We've been trying to get hold of you. This is O'Rourke—Terrence O'Rourke—of the alibi checking department at the Detective Bureau. Thanks a lot for fixing us up with that key to your warehouse on Clinton Street."

"Not at all, sir. Glad to oblige. What else can I do for you?"

"Well, as you've probably gathered from your secretary, this Chinese fellow who had a studio in there is in a jam here—and we're trying to get the lowdown on him. He claims to have been in Indianapolis tonight. Maybe he was. But I still doubt it. But what can **you** tell me about him? How on earth, Mr. Malmgren, does he happen to have possession of that locked room that forms the south-west corner of your warehouse?"

Carl Malmgren was silent for a moment. Then he spoke.

"Well, Mr. O'Rourke, that's easy to explain. And painful too! But of course your job is your job." He paused. "Now about this wax modeler. Some time ago—about two years ago—we were approached by the head of a proprietary medicine firm here who claimed to have a new internal treatment that would absolutely cure psoriasis. Which, as you undoubtedly know, Mr. O'Rourke, is a very disfiguring skin disease. This new internal treatment was based on an ovarian extract. Rather a derivative from the corpus luteum of the ovary. It was, in fact, the accidental discovery of a doctor here in Chicago, in the Diana Court building, who found that a young girl patient of his with psoriasis who responded to absolutely no treatment whatever, suddenly got well after some man got her into trouble. And stayed free from the psoriasis all the time she was pregnant. He reasoned, therefore, that the hyperactivity of the corpus luteum in her body created some sort of a combative influence on the psoriasis. Anyway, this firm wanted us to make an exclusive contact with them to handle their remedy in all of our 1649 stores scattered over the United States. And offered to treat and cure the worst case that could be found in Chicago as an evidence that the treatment was meritorious.

"Well, we found a good case without any trouble. And when I say good case, you understand I mean a very bad case! So bad, in fact, that my general manager suggested that it would be a mighty advantageous thing if we could make a 'before-and-after-treating' pair of wax models. Complete, you understand. Head, torso, forearms and hands. For it **was** a terrible case. At any rate, the name of this chap Yin Yi was given to us by someone connected with our stores—I don't know who, now—as being a wax-modeler who was an artist as well as a craftsman. So we called him in. He made a fine reproduction from the diseased patient, from which, in fact, we later made 30 casts for drugstore exhibition, and on all of which casts the Chinese chap did all the handwork required for the skin lesions. After a month's treatment the patient recovered completely, and Yin Yi made the second mold. From which, of course, we made 30 more casts."

Carl Malmgren paused.

"That, in short, is how I first met him."

He paused again. There was a deep sadness in his very pause.

He resumed speaking.

"This—this is somewhat painful, Mr. O'Rourke. For it's about my little daughter. Six months after I met Yin Yi I learned that she—" The man's voice nearly broke. "—that she—she couldn't live. I won't go into the medical reasons why. She commenced to fade right away. And it came to me then that I could have all the photographs in the world made of her—but that none would be like—like a photo of her in wax. My wife—my wife thought the same. Well, naturally remembering Yin's work on the difficult psoriasis modeling case, I called him in. And, to cut a long story short, he made a very wonderful reproduction of—of—" He was silent. "Of our little Dondrea. Right in our home here, too. One of our rooms, in fact, was converted, for the time being, into an improvised studio." The drugstore chain president was silent again. Then he went on. "Poor little kid. She died 6 months after, Mr. O'Rourke. And we have a room here—in our home—right today—her playroom—where we still keep the model of her, as she was in life."

He was silent again. Rand could see how difficult all this was for him. But that he could see, too, that murder was murder.

"When I went to settle up with Yin Yi, after we'd recovered a little bit from our grief, I asked him what he wanted. Practically told him to name his own price. While working on the job, however, he had ordered some special material for it, shipped over to our Clinton Street warehouse. And going over there to inspect it, he had seen that big empty lock-room in the south-west corner. It was never then used for practically anything, but a few light-fixtures, now and then. And he asked me if I would give him a 5-year lease on it for a nominal rental, as a downtown studio.

"Which I did," Malmgren said, a little defiantly. "We practically didn't use it anyway. For we had a twin room next it, more than big enough for all valuable items of store furnishings, like cash-registers. And so forth. I didn't fear his moving out any showcases or big stuff on me through the side door that gives onto the cobblestoned court. For I could see with half an eye, during the time he lived in our place, that he wasn't that type of person at all. Besides, our store furniture is specially made for the Malmgren Drugstores—all of it—and it wouldn't be salable anywhere in Chicago. My manager fixed up a lease, yes—for 5 years—terminable only if the warehouse ever has to be torn down. $4 a month is what Yin pays. He didn't seem to want to name a price on the job he did for us—and I wanted to repay him as best I could, at least for what he gave my wife—anyway. And besides—besides all of which, Mr. O'Rourke, I had in mind to have him right handy for doing certain waxwork pieces for our show-windows, when they came up. That's—that's all."

"Ever seen his room?" asked O'Rourke brusquely. "It's reported to look more like—like the harem of a Turkish sultan than—than a studio."

"That's nothing to me," said Malmgren testily, "how he furnishes his own studio. He's done all we asked him—and we've done what he asked us. He can make a parlor or a pigstye out of it, as far as I'm concerned. Just so long as he doesn't block up the entrance way from the big main front door of the warehouse,—so we can move our stuff in and out—he can do exactly as he damn pleases!"

Mr. Malmgren, Rand could see plainly, was now getting angry.

"All right—all right, Mr. Malmgren. No offence meant. We're just doing a routine checking job. And as far as I'm concerned, I'd rather see the Chinese come clear than not. Except that if he comes clear—well—then I gotta do more work! See?"

"Quite. Anything further, Mr. O'Rourke?"

"None, Mr. Malmgren."

"Very well, I'll retire then. Ring me if you need any further information. If the chap needs bail—I'll have my attorney look into it."

"All right. Maybe he won't need it. And maybe, too, he won't get admitted to no bail! I'll—"

"Excuse me, Mr. O'Rourke," came the switchboard girl's voice. "The Indianapolis connection—no, the one with Detective O'Connor—is on again. I was just getting that Miss DuBries at the Lig-Wall drugstore for you."

"Well, cut the Lig-Wall connection for the present. Let the Indianapolis one come through. Thanks Mr. Malmgren—and goodbye." There was a loud crackling. Then the unmistakable voice of Kelvy O'Connor again. "That you, Terry?"

"Yes, Kelvy. What the hell happened?"

"We got nipped off in mid-air. That's all I know. Your girl there must have jerked her plug. Well, Terry, getting back to cases, your man, I tell you, wasn't in Chicago tonight. There isn't a doubt in the world about it."

"Oh—yeah? Well if you'd of seen what Homicide Squad Number 2 seen tonight—I didn't see it myself—but I heard about it—you'd have said: Chinee murder—and nothin' but! And now you—well where are you now, anyway? I mean—the address?"

"I'm at 1034 South Senate Avenue, Terry—where Mr. Yin Tzu Lei lives. A very fine old gentleman, about 50—he's stepped out, for the moment, to the alley, to rout up a little nigger girl I want to talk to. So I can speak freely. This is a 2-flat building—9 rooms to the flat—he lives on the first floor, and an old couple—white—live upstairs. This floor's furnished more or less in old Chinese style—handcarved, inlaid teakwood furniture, and all that—Chinese rug in the parlor and a grand piano, to boot—the whole family are musicians, I guess—and the back parlor here, where I'm talking from, is covered—all over its walls, that is—with books, English as well as Chinese. I—oh hello, Mr. Yin—did you rouse her up all right?"

"Put this uncle on the wire," rasped O'Rourke.

There was a pause. Then a very dignified—it might even be said to be, thought David Rand, scholarly—voice came on the wire.

"Hello?" Its tones were mellow; kind.

"Hello," came O'Rourke's voice. "Are you Mr. Yin Tzu Lei? Yin Yi's uncle?"

"I am, sir."

"Yin Yi, the wax modeler, you mean?"

"Yes, sir. The one who lives at 2170 Wentworth Avenue, your city."

"Yes—that's right. Was Yi there tonight?"

"Up to about 9 o'clock, yes. That is, he was here with me all day, as well as last night. He left here, however at 9 o'clock tonight, to try to board the 9:30 Monon plane for Chicago."

"Your wife and family all seen him too, I suppose?" There was a decidedly sarcastic ring to O'Rourke's tones.

"I regret very much to say, sir, that I live here all alone. With my books and musical instruments. Outside of a small colored girl living on the alley back of this house, who comes in to do my work, I—"

"Well what's this about a niece—or was it granddaughter of yours? What lives with you?"

"You mean little O Loya Yin. She does not live with me. She lives a block to the south, on this same street. With her mother. But she was in tonight, and saw her uncle. That is, she calls Yi her uncle; in reality, he would be her second cousin. But whatever she may call him, she knows him very well. And—oh yes—Professor Wunderlich next door saw my nephew too. He is here now—as is the child."

O'Rourke's attitude, Rand could perceive, however, remained very hard-boiled.

"I see. Well, I'll listen to his two-cents' worth in a minute. Were you there tonight when that long-distance call come in from Chicago?"

"I was, sir. I answered it, in fact. A voice asked, in Chinese, for Yin Yi. I called Yi to the phone. He said it was a man called Cy—Cy—yes, Cyclops."

"I see. Well what did he do after he hung up?"

"He said he would go back to Chicago after all. That some trouble that was threatening him was past and over. He then called up his old music teacher, Miss Jones. Miss Laura Jones. She is here now."

"O.K. I'll talk to her too. And what did he do after he talked to her?"

"He tried out a piece of music on my piano—just the end of the piece—the way she told him it was to be played. He was very elated. He said—let me see—yes—that she had given him the logical way of playing it."

"Logical? That's all I ever hear in connection with your nephew. He—but say, Mr. Yin, why didn't your brother—this other Yin—Yin Tsou Li—tell me tonight, when I had him on the phone, that there was another Yin Tsou Li in Indianapolis, only spellin' his name just a bit different?"

"Well—Mr. O'Rourke," said the Chinese gentleman, a bit apologetically, "there—there is a bit of a schism in our family, and he would not have referred to me unless he had been specifically asked—or unless he had known that Yi was in trouble and had given in the name of an uncle. As I understand it, he told Detective O'Connor here that you asked him only if he had seen Yi today, and he replied that he had not seen him for 6 months. And—"

"That's correct," grunted O'Rourke grouchily. "I didn't want him hemming and hawing and saying that he had seen him. Blood is thicker than water, you know."

"So it is, Mr. O'Rourke. Yellow blood, particularly." There was marked irony in the Chinese recluse's tones.

"Well, you can make an affidavit anyway, about all you've told me, for Detective O'Connor there. Tomorrow morning. Now will you put him on the wire again, please?"

"Surely."

A silence. Then—

"Terry?"

"For crying out loud, Kelvy—do you think I'm going to waste my time with a lot of Chinks' lies about Chinks? Why don't you put some white people on the wire?"

"Well, Terry, you asked to speak to Mr. Yin Tzu Lei yourself, you know."

"Well, p'raps I did. Who's this Miss Jones? Know her?"

"Know her? Why everybody in Indianapolis knows Laura Jones, Terry. From the president of the Fletcher Trust down to Sallamagundy on Sallamagundy Alley! She's taught music to everybody in Indianapolis who can play chopsticks—or—or Chopin—on their piano."

"Yeah? But do **you** know her? You say you got some white dame there who claims to be—"

"Here—here—you wild Irish mick! I've got Miss Jones herself here. And I ought to know. She taught my kid sister music for years, and every time I came home to this burg on a vacation I saw Miss Jones at the house."

"Oh—well—that's diff'rent then. Lemme talk to her."

There was a silence again. And in the silence Rand wondered curiously just what O'Rourke would say when he put the finishing touches to this demolishment of his beautiful theory about the man whose name was written on the October 31st blue sheet of that red, white and blue calendar!"

CHAPTER XIII

Miss Jones Comes to the Rescue

The silence continued for the fraction of a minute, and was then broken by a feminine voice, very honest sounding, and very straightforward.

"Laura Jones speaking, Mr. O'Rourke. That is—this is Mr. O'Rourke—of the Chicago Police Department, I believe?"

"Yes, 'tis, Miss Jones. Miss Jones, do you—oh, what's your full name and address, Miss Jones? Now that I'm talkin' to white people, I'll make a note or two." O'Rourke sniffed audibly into the telephone system.

"Laura Bartlett Jones, Mr. O'Rourke. 225 West Pratt Str—well, no, it's called West Ninth Street now. 225 West Ninth Street."

"Um. Yes. Now Miss Jones, you know this fellow Yin Yi?"

"Oh yes—very, very well. I taught him music for years. He's from this city, you know."

"So I understand. Well you know he's in a murder jam here in Chicago? Or was—up to about five minutes ago!" I could almost hear O'Rourke scratching his head.

"So I understand, yes. That is why I got up out of bed, and dressed, and came over here at Mr. O'Connor's request."

"Well, Miss Jones, I'll try to make this brief—so that you can get back to bed. I understand this fellow called you up tonight?"

"Yes, that's correct."

"What time, about?"

"Oh—about 9 o'clock. I naturally didn't bother to go look at the clock because of a mere telephone call, but it was just about at 9."

"What did he say?"

"Well he said he had been in Indianapolis—had expected to stay longer, but had suddenly received news that called him back to Chicago, and regretted that he could not see me. He–"

"Listen, Miss Jones, do you **know** you were talking to him?"

"Well—I'm sure I couldn't mistake his voice. He has a very, very distinctive voice—you can't mistake it." She paused, helplessly. "Please remember, Mr. O'Rourke, I've seen him off and on—or gotten a phone call from him—when he's been visiting in Indianapolis. So I couldn't mistake his voice." She paused again. "But besides this, Mr. O'Rourke, he—he jokingly asked me whether I'd ever yet gotten the circular white stain off my grand piano where he set the glass of water down. Also—he asked me a purely technical question about piano-playing—that was quite typical of him."

"How do you mean—typical of him, Miss Jones?"

"Well now, that's a long story, Mr. O'Rourke. And as I understand—the costs of long-distance connect—"

"No—go ahead, Miss Jones. We've the whole night. This is our business here—to clear people—or to indict 'em. But when you get done, I may tell you some interesting stuff about how ev'ry amateur murderer does just the thing this fellow did—and in the same way he done it. But gettin' back to our topic—what did you mean—typical of him?"

"Well, I mean typical of his queer-acting brain. For he was always a queer character, Mr. O'Rourke. He thought in channels altogether different from other people. At least he did, when a boy. And I say boy because he still seems like that to me. I met him, you see, first in his latter teens. And he proceeded to grow up, while we here in Indianapolis watched him. His teacher at the Shortridge High School, a Miss Quinane—I know her quite well—told me that he would go into a brown study in the middle of a recitation period, and would not know his place or anything; would not even get up when the dismissal bell rang. And he was always maintaining the most bizarre views on all commonly-held subjects. Like the swan, for instance. He claimed that the swan was, in actuality, the most graceless and uncouth creature ever constructed by Nature, and proved it moreover by pointing out its bad proportions and lack of harmony. He—"

"Oh, 'scuse me for interrupting, Miss Jones, but I hafta hop onto things at the moment I think of 'em. Outside of his being Chinee, and naturally havin' a deep interest in ever'thing that is Chinese, did he—now—have any kind of a perplex on the subject of Confucius?"

Miss Jones seemed momentarily nonplussed by O'Rourke's psychological terminology. Then she answered.

"Oh—Confucius? Confucius was one of his heroes. Intellectual heroes, at any rate. He quoted Confucius often. Considered him the wisest of all the old Chinese sages."

"Ahrarah!" I'm sure I heard O'Rourke at that second licking his chops. "Just a minute, Miss Jones. Till I make a couple o' notes in Irish shorthand. Um. Ah. Yes. Now go on, Miss Jones. You was sayin' he was always queer-actin' in school?"

"Not altogether so queer-acting as—as independent in thought. He was always quitting subjects, for one thing, because they did not hold—well—

he called it logic. He disappeared nearly a year from my tutelage at one time—and the only clue I had as to why he disappeared was his tremendous disgruntlement because the chromatic scale was evenly divided—divided, that is, into 12 mathematically even steps. It was the day I gave him his first lesson in the physical aspects of harmony. He had then studied with me—I think—about a year and a half. I had a splendid set of tuning forks to demonstrate my points, as well as a Swiss vibrating wire capable of having artificial nodes incorporated in it at various definite locations. With these devices I was able to show him that the octave was double—in vibration frequency, that is—the fundamental note; that the perfect fifth—to which we referred countless times—and which thus far had been just a phrase to him—was the interval between any fundamental note and its second harmonic—reduced an octave, that is. Perhaps you are familiar with music theory, Mr. O'Rourke; if so, you'll understand, of course, how I showed him how the true musical scale is derived—at least theoretically, anyway!—from the sounds emanating from vibrating strings whose lengths have simple ratios to each other, like 1, 2, 3, 4, 5—and so forth. And possessing, as I did that day, two like tuning forks, I was able to dampen one very slightly with a bit of wax, and show him objectively exactly what discord—or dissonance—was: that it consisted of 'beats', or pulsations, in the air—beats equal to the difference of the vibration frequencies. He was tickled—well—stiff, to learn how every common relationship on the piano had a scientific basis, founded on the relative lengths of vibrating strings. But then, of course, I had to tell him that the very piano on which he was playing—and all other pianos, as well—did not have those exact relationships. That they had been tampered with—tempered, as it is called. So that music could be shifted from one key to any other, without a relative change in the melody. Or the harmony. Likewise, I had to tell him that C and G, although presumably a perfect-fifth—was actually, on all pianos, a slight discord. That G was flattened by about 2/1200th's of an octave. And that the 3rds and 6ths were much sharpened. The 3rd by so much as 14/1200th's of an octave. And just because piano players had deliberately altered the true musical scale into the equal-tempered scale. And—my goodness!—his face grew black as a thundercloud. I thought I had offended him. He went away like a person who had been struck in the face with—with a fist. And I couldn't, for the life of me, figure what I had done or said. But lo—and behold—a year later—he walked into my St. Clair Street studio at the regular time, hung up his cap, and sat down and began his lesson—which was Beethoven's **Fur Elise**—exactly where he had last left off. I asked him where on earth he had been—and why he had come back to his music—and he told me blithely that he had been delving into the mathematics of music at the Indianapolis Public Library. And—well—do you know what that boy had done, Mr. O'Rourke?"

"I'll bite," said O'Rourke, cheerfully.

"Well, he had dug up a table of actual vibration-frequencies for every key on the piano—or else, taking the known frequency of 256 for middle-C, had worked his table out with the use of his highschool trigonometrical logarithms, by using the 12th root of 2. And he had taken a simple piece of music, and re-written it into every possible key. Then he had painstakingly figured out the total error in true vibrations—and oh, he was logical, too, for when an error carried over a full note, he gave it 4 times the number of error-points as when it appeared only in a quarter-note—well he had, as I say, figured out the total number of vibration-errors created by playing the piece in all its keys on the tempered keyboard, and compared it with the total number of vibration-errors obtainable by trying to play it in all its keys on any one true-interval musical scale. And had found, much to his surprise, that the tempered keyboard was nevertheless vastly superior. Providing a less number of errors, that is, on this test. I could have told all this to him, of course, a year before, if he had only waited—but he'd gone off that day like a person absolutely—well—disgusted with the whole art of music, and particularly the piano. And I daresay it was all for the best that it happened this way, for his long-dragged-out computations proved the efficacy of the tempered scale to him in a way that I never could have done; at any rate—having—as Yin Yi himself put it—found that piano music was logical—logical in its illogicality, was the way he put it!—he returned to it."

O'Rourke was quite silent. David Rand could see how all this was rolling off O'Rourke's helpless back. But Irishman-like, he came back for more punishment.

"Well, you're pretty sure, Miss Jones, that 'twas him talked to you tonight, I guess. And as a matter o' fact, Miss Jones, now I want you to be sure—where a minute ago I didn't. Because if I can clinch it that he—an' nobody else talked to you—and add to that fact the fact that—but never mind all that for the moment. This here—now technical question about music. That he put to you tonight. If you don't mind tellin' me—what was it?"

The faintest of half-ripples of amusement emanated from Miss Jones' end of the wire. And she spoke.

"Just, Mr. O'Rourke, that he was dissatisfied with the fingering—at least for the right hand—given on the wind-up of Delibes' **Pizzicato**—from the Sylvia Ballet. Which, as no doubt you know—at least in the Appleton edition—runs 5—1—3—1 and so forth, and winds up, on its climactic note just before the final chords: 1—2—3—4. He argued that the fingering certainly was illogical, and that the more he studied it, the more he was convinced that it upset the gravity of the right hand. And I told him that the fingering, as given in that Appleton Music Book, **was** illogical—that he should begin the wind-up—the last line—with 5—1—4—1 instead of 5—1—3—1, and wind up 1—3—4—5, instead of 1—2—3—4; that it required the weight of the hand on the 5th finger for a real climax—not on the weaker 4th. He was exceedingly happy to learn that the printed music **was** wrong—or at least inefficient—"

"Illogical, that is," grunted O'Rourke. He pressed immediately on with his questioning. "I'm afraid I muffed all o' what you just told me, Miss Jones. The mouth organ is **my** musical instrument! But now tell me where you met this fellow? And excuse my persistence—for I ain't convinced yet, you see, that he hasn't pulled a fast one up here in Chicago. A hatchet murder in short. And—"

"And," said the Indianapolis music-teacher, with marked spirit, "if it's a case of that boy getting any false accusations for murder riveted on him, you can just count, Mr. O'Rourke, that I'll be a witness for the defence."

"Come, come, Miss Jones. Regard me purely as a neuter. All I gotta do is get the right and the wrong. I ain't the judge. Well, I think I asked you where—or how—you met him?"

"Yes, you did. Well, my friend Rosamond Van Camp—of the Indianapolis Van Camps—was delegated quite a number of years back, in some casting work she did for the Civic Theatre here, to fill a number of parts for a production of some play laid in California in the early days of the Gold Rush. Was it a play of Bret Harte's now? Well, I don't know. But anyway, she needed a young Chinese to take the part of a Chinese idiot. She advertised. Yin Yi appeared. He told her he was a great potential actor. So she tried him out."

"Was he any good as an idjit?"

"Just perfect, to be frank. A natural born actor."

The estimable Miss Jones did not see, it was plain, to Rand, that she had said something quite damaging to her ex-pupil.

"A natural born actor, eh?" O'Rourke was commenting. "That's very good. **I'm** glad to know that. Well, Miss Jones, suppose I should tell you that one of the tricks of murderers is to call a party up by long-distance from—say—Chicago to Ind—"

"Listen, Mr. O'Rourke, may I ask **you** a question? Do you know that in Indianapolis it is the custom, on a long-distance call, for the operator to say 'Long Distance—Chicago calling'?"

"Right!" admitted O'Rourke blithely. "And half the time they say 'Hold the wire a minute, please,' instead. And the other half the time, people who are called are rubbing their eyes with sleep, and ain't—"

"Mr.—O'Rourke! I wasn't asleep. At 9 o'clock—at night? I was feeding my two Blue Persian cats. And the operator did not say either of those two phra—"

She stopped, as a man's voice sounded somewhat off the circuit.

"'Scuze me, Miss Jones. Just let me have that receiver for one second. Thanks." Now Kelvy O'Connor's voice came directly into the speaking circuit. "Terry, I'm getting a report on that very thing from Bill Chandervain, night long-distance superintendent of the phone company here. Miss Jones' phone is Lincoln 4063. So the point that's eating you will be settled conclusively."

"Yeah, and the report's gonna show that Yin Yi took a long chance tonight and called Miss Jon—oh well, put her back on."

But Miss Jones was already coming back on the wire. And her indignation, concerning this investigation of her ex-pupil, was thoroughly aroused. "See here, Mr. O'Rourke," she was saying, "I—I know how you police work. I know that anything said here tonight that might be in favor of Yin Yi will be absolutely ignored. And anything that hurts him will be recorded against him, to the last dot, over the last 'i'. But don't think for a minute you're going to hang him. Because you're not. He never committed any murder there in Chicago. I'll—I'll stake my life on that. I intend to testify at his trial—if it goes to that—that he called me here tonight—October 31st— and by local phone only: and if you don't subpoena Mr. Bill Chandervain to back me up—I may so much as say that Bill Chandervain's wife is a friend of mine—and he'll go to Chicago himself, at my request, and testify. Don't you worry! You Chicago police aren't—aren't going to hang an innocent man. And even if you **did** have even a 100-percent case on him—you still couldn't hang him, considering all the abnormality in his family. So you might as well pull in your horns. You—"

"What—what do you mean, Miss Jones. Abnormality? It don't look so certain, so far as I can see, that we're going to hang anybody. What do you mean? Insanity—in his family?"

"Well—not insanity—exactly. But—both his mother and his father not normal. His mother—but that can come out in the trial."

"Listen, Miss Jones. You're sure Yin Yi called you tonight—and that it was Yi himself—and that he was callin' you from across the city. I ain't sure of nothing till I get the report from this Chandervain. But your story and the proper report would just about near unlock the cell door on Yin Yi. So let's be friends, in the meantime. I gotta fill my records complete. That's my job. I haven't nothing to do with anything. So what is this—about his mother—and his father?"

Miss Jones became less unfriendly now, but remained, withal, cool.

"Well, his mother had some rare pituitary gland disease. She died here in Indianapolis. Big Mena, she was known as. She ran a very fine Chinese restaurant on the Circle. Off Soldiers' Monument, that is. She was such a big woman—due to the pituitary disease, of course—that when she died they had to make a special coffin for her. And it took 10 pallbearers—not the usual 6—to carry her out to Crown Hill. And Yi's father—well—his father was Yin Gee, a rapid calculator."

"You mean—he was on the stage?"

"Oh no. He was just a cook in Big Mena's restaurant. But he did give performances around clubs and soirees and teas all over Indianapolis for years. Just himself and a blackboard. He charged $5 for a 30-minute exhibition. He could multiply, add, divide, extract square roots, and do everything—with the most enormous figures—right in his head. It was positively amazing. And he did not know how he did it. But he surely could make his audience sit up and take notice!" Miss Jones paused. And added meaningfully: "Don't think you can ever hang a man with a family history like that, Mr. O'Rourke."

"Well, you may be right on that, Miss Jones. At least not if our best criminal mouthpiece defends him. Now—just a minute. 'Till I fill out the family-history blank on this card. Mother a huge woman, you say—with pituitary gland disease. Father a rapid calculator. Yes. Well, that's that. Well, Miss Jones, here's hoping you won't ever have to come to Chicago to testify on no murder case. And maybe you won't—if Mr. O'Connor there has a few more witnesses like you. Would you put him back on, please?"

"Yes. Mr. O'Connor, Mr. O'Rourke wants you—"

The switchboard girl at the Detective Bureau—that is, O'Rourke's own switchboard girl—came suddenly into the circuit.

"Excuse me, Mr. O'Rourke, but I couldn't hold it off any longer. Indianapolis Heights has good contact now with that plane Monon Bullet, on the auxiliary short-wave, and the connections are all hooked up. You'll either have to have me cut the Indianapolis one, and take the plane, or—"

"No, never mind cutting the Indianapolis one. I told you to hold it. Kelvy?"

"Yes, Terry."

"You got some other witnesses there too—that you claim will clear this hatchet murderer? For I think, b'God, that he's guilt—"

"Yes, Terry. I told you I had. Two."

"I see. Well keep 'em there and have 'em ready. I got to shove you to one side a minute while I catch a plane in midair. I'll be right back on with you in a minute. All right, Jessica. Hold this Indianapolis connection—as is—and check the time on it, too. And put me on the Indianapolis Heights wire."

"Yes, Mr. O'Rourke. Take that Instrument Number 4."

There was silence.

Then some sharp clicks.

And of a sudden David Rand could hear a terrific rattling roar like a battery of paddle-wheels cutting water at high speed. It lasted but a second thus, dying away swiftly to sound like the buzz of a giant bee—and then seeming to be suddenly occluded altogether, although a continual low humming drone kept sounding in the circuit.

And a second later a Negro's rich, sonorous voice came on the wire.

CHAPTER XIV

And a Little Chinese Girl Speaks Her Small Piece

The negro spoke, at least, as one accustomed to speaking from plane to ground.

"Dis am Hennery Jackson, de potah, conductah, an gin'al man abohd de Monon Bullet. Kin you heah me—wheah you is at?"

"Yes, Henry. What was all that roar a minute ago?"

"Oh, dat? Dat wuz de p'opellahs. Ah had open de triple-encase' glass doh ob dis little closet a min', aftah de lil green light flah up inside an Ah had ansah'd it. But Ah is sence close dat do' tight, so de noise ought to be pretty well shet out now. You havin' trouble to heah me, sah?"

"No, not at all, Henry. I hear you fine. Well, Henry, this is the Chicago Police Department. Yes, at Chicago. T. O'Rourke speaking. Detective Bureau. I'm investigatin' the movements of somebody who took your plane tonight."

"Oh—" You could hear Mr. Henry Jackson's voice lower subconsciously. "Somebuddy—somebuddy is aboh'd dis plane now—whut is wanted?"

"No. Nobody in there, Henry. It's a Chinaman—that we got locked up here in Chicago—for murder. We understand he was coming tonight from Indianapolis to Chicago. Now what can you tell me about that? Was there a Chinaman aboard your plane on the northbound trip tonight?"

"Whooie! You spectin' me to git messed up wid some ob dem tongs, is you? Ah—"

"Come, come, Henry. Give me the facts. I can talk to the pilots, you know, on the regular wave length."

"Huh? Dem boys? Dey so—so snooty, 'cause dey is pilots, dat dey don't nevah gib eben half a look back in de cabin. Dey ain't int'rusted in nothin' but weathah, an' dey flyin' signals, an' de groun' beacons down below. Dey couldn' tell you nuffin 'bout nobody!"

"Well, **you** can. Now come clean! Was there a Chinaman aboard that plane tonight? Or—was there none aboard? You'd better talk up, now, or there'll be a police officer at Cincinnati waiting for you, and—"

"Well, yes—dey—dey wuz a Chinaman 'boh'd de plane, Mist' Detictive. An' Ah suah nevah dream he 'uz goin' up t' Chicago to mu'der nobody, neithah. Now Ah—Ah 'spose Ah gonna ketch me a axe in de haid!"

"You're a good crime expert, Henry. Axe in the head—you know Chink murder all right! What—what did this Chink look like?"

"Now see heah, Mist' Detictive, if'n you is 'spectin' me to sen' some po' man to de rope, whut you is got lock' up, Ah jes' ain' gonna make no testifyin'. All Chinamens dey looks just de same lak, to me. Ah don' know de diffunce 'tween one ob 'em an' anothah ob 'em. An' Ah—"

"Come, come, Henry. Nobody's asking you to send anybody to the rope. You're willing to clear a man, ain't you?"

"Suah—if'n he ain't guilty ob nothin'—co'se Ah is willin' to cl'ah him. But Ah tells you, all—all Chinamens dey looks ahdentical to me. Wouldn' be no use to git me in fo' no trial. 'Sides, Ah is gotta sleep days 'count ob dis night run. An' Ah—"

"Now listen, Henry. If this Chinaman you carried is the man we got locked up—then we got to let the man we got locked go. This murder wasn't committed after the plane got to Chicago. It was committed in Chicago— shortly before the time the plane started from Indianapolis."

"Well—dat's a lil diffu'nt. But still, Ah cain't 'dentify nobbodah. All Chinamens looks des de sa—"

"How old was this Chinaman you carried?"

"Well—he—he 'bout thutty yeahs ol—so neah's Ah kin judge. But Ah tells you, Ah ain't no idea whatevah w'ut he looks lak. Ah—"

"Did you note anything peculiar when he gave you his ticket?"

"Gib me his ticket? Well now—he didn't gib in no ticket. He gib me a ten-dollah bill an' a five."

"Ah! Paid cash fare, eh? Well, did you give him a fare receipt?"

"Yassuh. Suah did. But Ah fin' de receipt undah de seat aftah de pas-sengahs is go. Ah—lissen—if'n you is some smaht aleck on de Monon Aih Suhvice tryin' to check mah honesty 'bout cash fahs, you ain' gonna git nowah. Fo' dat fah is already entered up on mah sheet what Ah is tuhn in at Chicago. Ah is wuk fo' de Monon Railroad fo' thutty yeahs, an' is known as Honest Hennery."

"Good. Honest Henry is what we want. No, Henry, this is the Chicago Detective Bureau. Now come on with more details about this fellow. What kind of features did he have?"

"Features? Dat mean face? Hm. Well, he des' hab a soht ob flat face. Soht ob—Chineseh, if you don't min' dat abjectiv'."

"I might put that down at that, Henry. Chinaman—with a Chinesy face! Well, flat. That's somep'n. Now think further. You may be the means of releasin' a man who's abs'lutely innocent. Surely you noticed something?"

"Well—Ah ain't notice much ob nothin', 'cause he spen' mos' ob his time readin' a Chinese newspapah. 'Cose, he is weahin' lil gol' specs lak w'at you gits f'm de ten cen' stoh."

"We're slowly getting somewhere, Henry. Notice anything about his features? Anything striking about his face, when he looked up to pay his cash fare?"

"No, didn' notice nothin' at all. 'Cose, he hab a gold toof in his haid, an'—"

"Where? Where was the gold tooth?"

"'Bout—'bout de exac' middle ob his uppers. It wuz a soht ob a dull gol' toof. Ah membah thinkin' it look pretty nice dataway—an' dat us colohed folkses meks a big mistek to git ouah gol' toofs shiny de way us does. But as Ah say, Ah ain' notice nuffin at all 'bout dis Chinaman, an' cain't tell you nuffin' at all."

"Well, you've told enough, Henry, to get yourself modeled in wax—free someday. Maybe! All right. Now call at the Cincinnati Detective Bureau the minute you come off that run, and swear to an affidavit. I'll phone down there how the paper is to run. Ask for the affidavit clerk."

"Affidavit? Yes, sah. Ah'll go thah soon's we lands at Cinci. Now is that all, sah? If'n Ah hangs up, it'll automatic-lak break dis auxil'ry shoht-wave connec—"

"Yes, that's all. Hang up. I can't hang up here because—Jessica—you there in the wire?"

"Yes, Mr. O'Rourke. Did—"

"Put me back on that Indianapolis connection—the one with O'Connor—so I can wind up things. Throw it over on this phone Number 4, will you?"

A clicking and sputtering.

And David Rand heard Detective O'Connor's well-modulated voice on the wire once more.

"You back on there again, Terry?"

"Yes, Kelvy. Sorry I had to keep you waiting. Well, Kelvy, it keeps looking more and more, all th' time, as though Yin Yi **did** come to Chicago tonight on that plane. At least a guy come in that tallies with him, in a lot o' ways. I won't fall off my chair with surprise, though, if it turns out, by that toll report you're gettin', that this Jones music-teacher was half-asleep when Indianapolis Central told her that Chicago was on the wire. It's an old last-minute trick of panic-stricken killers, who don't never stop to think about them other phases of it. You see, Kelvy, there's a whole string o' factors here in favor of this guy pulling this killing. On top of which he tells a fearfully rickety—vague—story about a woman in Oak Park, and a doctor of hypnotizosis, an—'"

"Well, I don't know anything about all that, Terry. I just want to clear up your docket for you, and go home. The minute Harry Weiss gets over here with the print, I'm blowing for bed. I've been out two hours now on my own time, already."

"Harry Weiss? Who's Harry Weiss? And who else you got there?"

"Who's Harry Weiss? I thought I told you about him. He's second-shift fingerprint photographer, as well as third assistant fingerprint expert, at the Bureau here. Lives right around the corner here from Yin Tzu Lei. So knowing he had a battery of cameras, as well as a photo-laboratory at home, I just—well, you sent me this Yin Yi's fingerprints, didn't you? And I thought surely you'd want 'em checked with—well, you asked who else I had here. I've this Professor Emil Wunderlich who lives next door. Kindly old man, with a shawl across his shoulders, and—no, he doesn't hear what I'm saying. He's pretty deaf except when he uses a phone. Or an electric ear-trumpet. And his trumpet's lying in his lap just now. And I've a sweet little kid here, too, named O Loya Yin—and I don't think I can keep her awake much longer. Her mother's here—brought her over, in fact—but has nothing to do with our matter. Then there's a coon kid—a girl—about 16—named Tarbaby Watkins. She's a little religio-maniac, so I understand—reads her Bible all the time. Mr. Yin Lei says she's thin as a piece of string licorice, and wears a single cotton dress and a pair of sugar-sacking step'ins. And—"

"Hey, hey—is this a radio-broadcast performance?"

"Do you think I can get a job as announcer, Terry? No? Well, anyway, Tarbaby herself is not here—but she's due in a minute—for she lives on the alley right back of Mr. Yin Tzu Lei's place here—and on the alleys is where practically all the Negroes in Indianapolis live!"

"Well, you sure are workin' hard, Kelvy, for this Chink I got locked up. You ought to get free chopsuey somewhere for life. Well, put 'em on in turn, and let's get clear."

"Okay. Professor Wunderlich? Miss Jones, will you please tap Professor Wunderlich on the shoulder? Yes—this way, Professor."

There was considerable of a pause, and then a man's voice came on the wire—to Rand, obviously a man at least 60 years of age. The latter's articulation was decidedly German in accent.

"Hul-lo? I—I am shbeaking to the Chicago Bolice Debartment?"

"You are, sir. The Detective Bureau at Chicago. And you are—"

"Brofessor Emil Wunderlich, sir, bresident of der sdringed insdrumend debardment at der Eendianahbolis Musikal Konservadory."

"Oh yes—let's see—you were at Miss Jones' house tonight when—"

"Nein, sir. I know Miss Chones vell. I haf met her by many musikals. Unt she dit accompany me vunce ven I indroduced, for der furst dime in Eendianahbolis, der Hankel zither-bancho. I lif next door to Misder Yin here."

"Oh—yes—I remember now his saying you were from next door. Well what light, Professor, have you to throw onto this murd—"

"Chust, sir, dot Yin Yi vass here in Eendianahbolis—in dees house to-night. At leasd at a qvarter afder 8."

"He was, eh? You talked with him?"

"Nein, I dittn't talk mid him—no. But I see him. I know him chust so vell like I know Miss Chones. We haf dot music in common, you see. Unt he can blay some uf dem Chinese sdring—"

"You mean you saw him then, from your front window? On the side-walk?"

"Nein, nein, nein. I see him—ride here in dees room here—vere ve are dalking now on der dellyphone. Dru der vindow-glass uf dees room—vot looks out on der passageway between dees house unt mine. Und dru mein vindow, vot looks oud on dot same passageway. Iss dot clear?"

"Yes, I get you now perfectly. Well, what was he doing, Professor, when you saw him?"

"He vass sidding on der vindow zill here, blaying der **erh-hu**—der dwo-strindged **hu**, dot iss!"

"The two-stringed **hu**? Well, explain yourself, Professor. I don't speak no Chinese, and don't play no stringed instruments neither."

"Vell, der issn't nodding to exblain. I know Yin Yi chust so vell nearlike as I know his onkle, Yin Lei. Bod uf dem are musicians of no mean apility, I can dell you dot! Dey haf a natural abptitude, unt blay many insdrumends, including der piano." The Professor paused a second. "Vell, I vass come in my back parlor tonight, to sid in mein rocking chair—dot vass long afder der lights vass on—unt I see Yin Yi ofer here in dis room blaying her **erh-hu**. I see him achually sit down on der vindow-zill unt bow it back unt fort' mit der bow. Unt—but you vass ask me vot her **erh-hu** iss, eh? Vell it chust iss nodding more as a modification of der **hu-ch'in**, or Chinese violin. Yess! Eggscept it hass lower tones, unt blays louder on der pentatonic scale. It is a vooden frame from bamboo, mit snakeskin sdredtched ofer der ends, unt dwo sdrings each apout a foot unt five inches in length. You blay it mid a bow, somevat like as you blay a violin. Yess. Dis **erh-hu** vass Misder Yin Lei's **erh-hu**—only dot he doesn't not make very good by it." Professor Wunderlich paused helplessly. "Vell, dot bow vass go so smoodly unt—unt nimple-like ofer dot **erh-hu**, dot here—I sais—iss a man vot can blay dot instrumend like a masder. Unt so I knock hart on der glass uf my vindow to addract his attention. He dittn't hear me—pecause he vass behind glass himselluf—until I rap mid a conch-shell. Den he looks arount, unt vave hello mit his hant. Unt I vave dot he come around into mein house, mid der **erh-hu**. He look at his vatch—unt nod dot he vill be ofer. Unt get up, unt leaf der vindow-zill."

"But he didn't come?" asked O'Rourke, and though his question was distinctly of a fact-pursuing nature, it was evident by his voice that he was floundering himself now, at least in his thoughts.

"Nein. Afder apout an hour, his onkle come ofer unt make apolochies for Yin Yi. He dell me dot Yin Yi vass going to come ofer lader—about nine o'clock, or so—but got a dellyphone message dot he must come by Chicago at vonce—unt dot he go qvick by der airfield. To catch a 9:30 areoblane. Unt vould come ofer next time he came by Eendianahbolis. Unt dot iss all I know. But id iss impordant, so far as I can see, unt I vant to add vot I can for him."

"You couldn't hear him playing!" Rand never realized before how ruthless and searching a police inquisitor could be.

"Ach nein. How coot I? Two glass vindows—unt me bartly deaf for longer distanzes! But I coot see he vass blaying der vay der blaying **shoot** be. Vot—vot more can you vant?"

"Nothing, I guess, Professor. And you think you know Yin Yi real well?"

"**Ach—du lieber Gott!** Dittn't he deach me some dricks, vot I dittn't know, on der **yueh-ch'in**—dot's der Chinese moon guitar?"

O'rourke sighed deeply. And again Rand wondered how much more deeply O'Rourke would sigh when he, Rand, should give the other further interesting information about this case. But Rand remained silent, for he remembered O'Rourke's injunction that one peep out of him—and he was out!

"All right, Professor Wunderlich," O'Rourke said after a pause. "Tell Mr. O'Connor to put on anybody else he has to put on."

There was silence once more. Then O'Connor again.

"Terry, wish you could see the sweet little kid in my arm here. Little Chiny gal—'bout 3 years old. Big brown eyes—with the corners pointing 'way skyward! Black bangs, too—some doll! Bright as a dollar, and nothing but. And speaks English, too! Mr. Yin Lei's granddaughter, from up the street a block. Here, O Loya, you speak to the man in the wall."

A pause, while a receiver was adjusted to a small ear 190 miles away.

"Hello—Mister Man." The voice was tiny, threadlike, treble, piping.

"Ah—hello, baby," said O'Rourke, with marked diffidence.

"You—you know my uncle Yinny Yi?"

"Sure I do. He vellee nice oncle! You see you' oncle lately!"

"Uncle Yinny Yi here tonight. Gi' me lil doll. I got lil doll here."

"Oh—so Uncle Yinny was there, eh?"

"Yes—but he go 'way—'way off—on choo-choo train."

"Did Uncle Yinny Yi have his beard on?"

O'Rourke—O'Rourke! To try, reflected David Rand, to snare an innocent child!

"Uncle Yinny Yi don' got beard. Uncle Yinny Yi lives in Sycago. I been in Sycago. Wif my grandpaw. 'Way off on choo-choo train. Uncle Yinny got store. With big wax dolls. Like mens and—and ladies. He paints 'em. He give me board to paint."

Take that forever, O'Rourke, thought Rand, in case you think a child doesn't know its own uncle! Or that—

But O'Rourke, manifestly chastened a little bit, was speaking.

"Ah—what was Uncle Yinny Yi doing tonight, baby!"

"He play pinano. Make music. Des' lil bit of moosic. Then go 'way off—on choo-choo train."

"And what did you do then, baby?"

"Tarbaby take me home. You know Tarbaby? She brings me here when grandpaw wan's to see me. Tarbaby take me home. And I go to bed. With my doll. Can you see my doll—what I got here?"

"It's a swell doll, baby."

"Are we gonna hav' ice cream? When they waked me up, they said—"

"I hope you are, baby. But don't eat too much of it, if you do. You—"

"All right, baby," came O'Connor's voice, one-sidedly into the transmitter, "I'll let you down now." Now he spoke directly into the instrument at his end. "Well, Terry, if I could only get a report now from Harry Weiss, I'd—wait." There was a silence. "Wait, Terry. It's Harry himself. Hold the wire."

Another silence. Which grew and grew. And at last Rand heard O'Rourke say: "What the hell—is everybody dead? I say, Jessica, is that line gone—"

Then O'Connor's voice came back on the wire again.

"Terry, it was Harry Weiss. In connection with those fingerprints you wired me to look up at the Bureau here. I let that slide for the time being—but I'm thinking now that you won't want any further search made on your man. You see, when I called Harry over here, from his dugout around the corner, and he heard the general facts Mr. Yin Lei had to give us, he quick made a dusting of those piano keys with white fingerprint powder. That is, the black keys. He used the super-powdered black plumbago for the white ones, of course. And he had his kid brother fetch over his over-hang camera. He—but do you folks up there in Chi know what an over-ha—"

"Yeah. I know. We got one here, in our C. I. department, now. One of them new contraptions, if I ain't wrong, that rolls along a floor, and photographs fingerprints along the whole edge of a table—as far back as you want? Six inches, ain't it!"

"Yeah, that's right, Terry. I didn't know you folks up there in Chicago were even that much up-to-date! Well, Terry, every fingerprint on those keys that isn't blurred by another print on top of it—all those that are distinct—off to one side, that is—or on a key all by themselves—is one of those on that set you sent rue. Fact. Harry's got a white-and-black photo-print here now, covering the whole range where they show up."

"He has? Hm. Well ask Yin Lei how many pieces his nevvie played."

A silence.

"Yi didn't play a whole piece, he says. Just ran over the final bass of it—the way Miss Jones told him to—and got up very elated."

"Elated, eh? Miss Jones' way o' playin' it musta been logical. Hm! What range of keys is them fingerprints on? Not that I understand nothing about music, but Miss Jones there–"

"Here—they're all devoid of prints entirely—except from the second E-flat below Middle-C, to the third E-flat above Middle-C. Harry's photo-print alone runs an octave below and above that, and everyone's negative outside of that range."

"Hm. Put Miss Jones on again, will you?"

A pause, and the voice of Laura Jones appeared on the wire.

"Yes, Mr. O'Rourke."

"Miss Jones, what range on the pyano would the last bars of that there piece—Delivery's **Psitticosis**, wasn't it?—that you demonstrated to Yin Yi, cover? This is Chinese murder up here in Chicago, Miss Jones, and I'm not overlookin' any bets."

"You **certainly** are not, Mr. O'Rourke! Well I happen to know that piece quite well. While I can't visualize the notes, I just played it for Mr. Weiss here from memory—silently—that is—on his photostat of the keys—the last six or seven bars, that is—and the music covers only the range where the fingerprint markings appear."

"Thanks, Miss Jones. Better people than me have lost their jobs up here because they slipped on some fine details! Can I have O'Connor again?"

O'Connor must have been, Rand said, right at the phone, for the other answered immediately.

"Kelvy," O'Rourke asked, "are them fresh fingerprints? Or maybe a week old?"

"Fresh, Terry. Quite. Made within the last few hours. They just snapped up the f. p. powder."

"Hm. Now—let's see—how come, now, there ain't no other fingerprints on them keys? Put Yin Lei on, will you?"

Another silence.

Then the dignified voice of the Chinese recluse.

"Yin Tzu Lei speaking—again."

"Mr. Yin, when was them pyano keys washed last?"

"About—now—let's see—about 6 o'clock tonight. I called Tarbaby in—that's Tarbaby Watkins, the Negro girl on the alley. The one who runs my vacuum cleaner, and keeps my house clean. I asked her to run the vacuum once over the parlor rug, and wash the piano keys. I found them very sticky. Syrup or something. The baby was here yesterday, and had evidently been playing with them."

"Put Mr. O'Connor back on the wire."

A strange voice came on, however, instead of O'Connor's. It was a brisk, youthful, alert, and slightly nasal voice.

"Harry Weiss, second-shift fingerprint man, Mr. O'Rourke, at the Indianapolis Detective Bureau. Kelvy went out to the alley to speed up this nigger girl a bit."

"That's good. So far as I can see, Weiss, your stuff is the one incontrovertible bit o' evidence. That Yi himself, that is, and nobody else, has been up there. The Jones woman of course, is telling the truth—so far as she knows. They're all telling the truth, so far as they know. But that pyanoboard stuff can't lie."

"No, but remember, Mr. O'Rourke, those impressions could have been made this afternoon. Kelvy's wrong when he says I say they've been made the last few hours. They've been made in the last 10—12 hours, all right—that's all I can say. I'd venture, though, that—well—here's Kelvy himself, with a nigger girl in tow. Hold the wire please—and I'll give a look over that **erh-hu** instrument too, for good measure."

There was silence again. And jumbled-up voices off from the phone.

Then O'Connor's voice in the instrument.

"Hello, Terry. I've got Tarbaby. But I'll have her talk to you direct. She thinks she's 16 years old, but doesn't know! But she knows her onions, anyway."

"Put her on."

A silence. Then—

"Dis is Tah-babah Watkins talkin'."

"Hello, Tarbaby. This is the Chicago Police Department. Do you know what you've been drug into the front house for?"

"No, sah. Don't know. Ah ain' done nuffin."

"I know you haven't. Well, Tarbaby, we want one piece o' information from you. What time this morning—or rather yesterday morning, I mean—did you wash the piano keys in this house?"

Stealthy, wily, vulpine O'Rourke! Rand determined then and there, as he listened to this long-distance conversation, that if ever he was arrested for murder, to watch the questions put to him far more than his own answers.

Tarbaby came back, however, quite vociferously.

"Yistiddy? Dis mohnin'? Man—Ah done wash dem keys tonight—just 'fo Ah et mah suppah. Dat 'uz 'bout 6 o'clock. Us ain' got no clock in ouah house, but it wuz des got dahk a lil w'ile befo'. Evvahbody 'roun' heah seem t' be talkin' 'bout dem fool keys! Dey ask muh w'ut Ah wash 'em wid—and how many Ah wash—and all dat foolishment. Cain't say no mo' dan dat Ah wash 'em all—evah one ob 'em—wid wahm watah wut is in a tin pan, an'—an' Ibory soap—all de white **do**'s, and de white **re**'s, and de white **me**'s—and dem sharpses an' flatses. Den Ah run de vacoom once ober de—"

"Did you see Yin Yi, Mister Yin Lei's nephew? Do you even know him?"

"Yes, Ah knows him. Dat is, Ah've seed him. Didn't see him tonight. 'Cause he uz layin' down in de baidroom. But Ah huh'd Mistah Yin Lei talkin' to him in de baidroom. In Chinee talk. Lak as if he gibin' him a lec-tuah fo' all his sins."

"Did you hear him answer Mr. Yin Lei?"

"Well—Ah heahd now an' den one ob dem grunts lak whut de China-mens sez w'en dey means yes—o' no."

O'Rourke's reply came swiftly and rocket-like.

"See here, Tarbaby. How you gonna spend that ten-dollar bill?"

"Whut ten dollah bill?"

"That ten-dollar bill you received for telling this whole story?"

"You mean—Ah's lyin? Say—lissen—w'ite man—Ah wouldn't lie fo' nobody—not fo' all de money whut dey is. What good is money, if'n you buhns in hell fo' etunnity? Huh? Ah don't lie, an' Ah don't steal, an' Ah don't cah'y on wid boys, an' Ah—Heah! Hol' dat phome a minut'." A brief pause. Then—"Ah got Mist' Yin's Bible heah. Whut Ah is tuk from de shelf heah. An' mah han' on it. Ah' clahs t' God, an' may Ah buhn a million yeahs in hell—if'n Ah ain' tellin' de truf—dat Ah is wash dem pyano keys aron' about 6 o'clock tonight, wid wahm watah an' Ib'ry soap. So he'p me God, and all de ang—"

"All right, Tarbaby. You win! Go back to bed. Put the gentleman that fetched you in there, back on."

Kelvy O'Connor came back on.

"I lost most of that, Terry! But hope you got what you wanted. I was signing, at the front door, for a report from Bill Chandervain. He sent it up here by special messenger—a lad I know, too."

"Well, you might as well put the kibosh on the case. There's not so much left, now, to hold Yin Yi on. What did Chand—"

The switchboard girl—the one O'Rourke called Jessica—came into the circuit. "Mr. O'Rourke, Miss DuBries—over at that Lig-Wall Drugstore—calling. No, I didn't call her. She called back, because she heard you wanted to talk to her. Will you be off soon—or shall I tell her **we'll** call back?"

"Hold her, Jessica. That is, as long as you got her. Don't know that I need her so much now, but—Anyway I'm just closing this conversation now. So you can hold her. Kelvy, you there?"

"Waiting, Terry."

"Well—do we hang him?—or don't we?" But I could see plainly by

O'Rourke's facetious tone that he had no hopes of hanging anybody now.

"I'm afraid not. You better hang whoever framed him, Terry. But here's the report. There's been no long-distance calls whatever put through to Miss Jones' number—the Lincoln 4063—tonight. And one only to Drexel 3051-R—that's this South Senate Avenue number. This one was from Chicago, at nine minutes of 9 tonight. Chandervain checked it all the way back to your own town for you, and it came from the Lig-Wall Drugstore, 2 South State Street."

"I see. Well, that's the call from Cyclops telling our Gay Lutheran to come back to a good burg. Well, Kelvy, thanks a lot anyway. You've done a good night's work. And I'm grateful—even if there ain't nothing left to hold my man on. Outside the fact that he **did** have an appointment with the bird who was killed—and he **did** have a dam' good motive to bump him off! Never mind running down any record on him at your Bureau with them fingerprints. Oh—what does your Harry Weiss find on that **erh-hu**?"

"What do you find, Harry?" This was addressed away from the phone.

There was an indistinct sound of talking. Then O'Connor in the phone again.

"There's dozens of old fingerprints on that **erh-hu**, Terry. It never has been washed. But Harry finds a couple of Yin Yi's thumbprints, at that, with his magnifying glass. Fresh, too."

"All right. Well, Kelvy, wonder if you'd mind seeing to it that these folks come down to your Bureau tomorrow, and see that your affidavit clerk gets the proper affidavits. You know now exactly what I want. And forward 'em on to me, so I can pin 'em to this Yin Yi card. And have Weiss send me the fingerprint photostat, and a departmental record form properly filled out. And thank all of 'em, please, for me. And apologize to Miss Jones in case I was a little brusque. And ask her—but only after you hang up!—if I can take her to dinner next time I come down there—providing I don't split no infinitesimals!"

"I'll tell her, Terry. And will send you her answer with the affidavits. Shall I hang up now?"

"Yeah."

"Goodbye, then." A click. Several clicks, in fact. And almost before Rand knew it, a new feminine voice. "Miss DuBries speaking. Lig-Wall Drugstore Number 3."

"Miss Dubries—say—this ain't Lucy Kilgallon, formerly on the Racket Bureau switchboard, by any chance?"

"Yes, Mr. O'Rourke! I just wondered if you'd know me."

"Well—well—well! What on earth, Lucy, are you doing under the name of DuBries?"

"That's my right name. Kilgallon was my stepfather's name."

"Well—well! So you're over at the big Lig-Wall store! And in night-charge of the phone booth room! Well this **is** a small world, I'll say! Well, say, Lucy—I've just a small question to ask you—and I'll let you go. There was a Chinaman in there tonight, wasn't there, calling from one of the long-distance booths?"

"Yes—there was one, Mr. O'Rourke. In long-distance slot-phone booth Number 3. He got $3 in quarters from me."

"What kind of a bird was he, Lucy?"

"Oh—a terrible looking creature, Mr. O'Rourke. That is—his left eye. It was evidently blind—and red as fire. Stuck partway out of his head, and all the little veins in it were like—like incandescent threads. The pupil was glazed like—like a cataract. He wore a striped sweater. And—if you're trying to pick him up—he's minus some of his front teeth. He flirted with me in the phone booth—tried to anyway. Grinned out at me while he was waiting for his Indianapolis connection."

"Oh, we're not trying to pick him up, Lucy. Just making a routine check-back on a story here at the Bureau. I might want an affidavit from you on this later—but in all probability won't want it. Because—" O'Rourke's voice dropped. "Oh say—Lucy, you didn't catch any fair lady's names—or anything about Oak Park—from this booth, did you?"

"Oh, Mr. O'Rourke, those long-distance booths are triple-glassed. Utterly sound proof. You can't hear a thing from outside."

"Oke! Just tryin' to toe up a little scandal that's in our fair burg, that's all. Except that I'd a-had to forget about it even if I did learn a certain dame's identity. Well, come in some day, Lucy, and look us over. But come between 8 in the evenin' and 4 in the morning."

"Not so easy, Mr. O'Rourke. My own hours here are 6 p.m. to 6 a.m.! And an hour off any time in the night I want to take it."

"Well, come in on that hour sometime. I'll let you go now. Thanks."

"Goodbye." The two goodbyes came practically simultaneously. And David Rand heard O'Rourke speaking again. And this time it was in his direction. "Rand! You still in—or have you gone upstairs and to bed?"

"Bed! Well—hardly! I'm here."

"Well, now you've got your wish. You see now what we do around here? We check ever'body against ever'body else. And, like you said today, sieve off the innocent ones, now an' then. Like t'night, f'r instance. Now you take this bird Yin Yi. He had all the reason in the world to kill your boss, and yet–"

"Well O'Rourke," Rand put in, "this may surprise you—but now I'm going to toss you a little further information. That will knock your motive, too, into a thousand pieces. For Jack Ken—"

But the switchboard girl's voice came into the circuit again.

And Rand waited patiently, while the outcome of a certain burglary attempt was all detailed to O'Rourke. And when Rand heard the old familiar sound of receivers being deposited, he resumed his sundered speech.

"I'm still here, O'Rourke," he said. "And I was going to tell you about Yin Yi's supposed motive. Now he—"

But again he was interrupted. Jessica once more!

"Mr. O'Rourke?"

"Yes, Jessica."

"Inspector Mackenzie."

"Sinjohn! Oh yeah—he's over at Kenw—"

"Kenwood's office, Mr. O'Rourke. He walked over there—you remember I told you?—after his bowl of milk. He wants you again. He cut himself off the last time he called. But he's on again. And he's—he's peevish. No, he can't hear me."

"Peevish, eh? That's that damn—darned—hot milk. I wish he'd leave that stuff alone. Well—Rand?"

"Here, O'Rourke."

"Pipe down, till I get done with the Old Man. Then I'll be with you again." A pause. "Put him on, Jessica."

Another clicking. And a Scotch voice with a very decided burr insinuated itself into the circuit. And by its very first tones Rand could see that it was irritated by something.

CHAPTER XV

St. John Mackenzie Adds a Fact or Two

"Terr-ry?" the Scotch voice called.

"Here, Chief."

"I'm oover-r at Kenwood's office. From th' lay'ot o' things here, I think ye'd better call up Dr. Charles F. Read, the alienist, and have him come oover-r and give this Chinese a mental examination."

"Mental examin—well—how's that, Chief?"

"Because th' Chinese must be cr-razy as a bed-boog, th' way he committed this cr-rime."

"Well—now—Chief, about Yin Yi, now—but wait—what do you mean, Chief—the way he pulled the crime?"

"Why—th' deerect trail he left! To himself. Naboody boot a lunatic w'ad poot a rope around their oon neck."

"Ho—how do you mean, Chief? Put a rope—"

"Joost this. Hitterlee, of that Homicide Examination Squad, made mighty careful location mar-rkings, in our washable green stain Number 2, of everything here—the poseetions of the desk-table legs on the floor—the poseetions o' all the chairs in the place—and the movable articles, of course, on the desk-top itself. Including, Terr-ry, line-oop mar-rks on each—an' the place it sat—to show the exact way everything faced. They've been a bit diseur-rbed, naturally, but I've had them all laid oot again, the way they were when Kenw'od's killer left here. They—"

"What articles d' you mean, Chief? You mean that coin catalogue Kenwood was reading when he was sloughed?"

"Yes, and the goose-neck desk lamp here—and one of these red-white-an'-blue appointment calendars like ye hav on yer oo'n desk." St. John Mackenzie paused. "Listen here, Terr-ry. Have ye considered th' fact yet, that the evening sheet on that calendar—for October 31st, that is—the blue one, in fact—was lying exposed to full view when the squad came in? With 'Yin Yi: 8:30' written on it in lead pencil?"

"Well—yes—no—yes. That is, Chief, you mean maybe—you mean that Yin Yi would have ripped it off? But takin' Yin Yi—just for an example now, that is!—f'r things has been movin' along some in my department—and how!—he obvi'sly didn't see the notation! He nor nobody else, I take it. For lead pencil on blue—even if it is a light blue—don't stand out like lead pencil on white."

St. John Mackenzie was a bit slow in answering. Evidently he was pondering on something. He seemed to collect himself suddenly.

"Deedn't see it, did I hear ye saying? Listen—do ye know wha' that crack-brain Chinese did aroond this place?"

"No—what, Chief?"

"Well, he unscrewed th' oreeginal light bulb oot o' th' desk lamp—'twas only a 60-watt frosted bulb—and stood on a small rolling table here—at least he must ha' stood on that—and unscrewed th' big 200-watt **un**frosted bulb in the ceiling, and—well, he changed both bulbs, that's all."

"Changed 'em, eh? How you know that, Chief?"

"Both have the smoodge mar-rks of the red dye in those cheap cotton gloves, where he gripped th' bulbs har-rd to screw them in, if not oot. More-over-r, I had Dotson here count the cross-thread mar-rks under his magnifyin' glass—they show in the smoodges here an' there—and called oop the C. I. Laboratory over there where you are. That was the fir-rst time I was trying to get ye, and coot mysel' off till I could get more infoormation. And do ye know what they repoort?"

"Same number o' cross-threads per inch, Chief?"

"Exactly! And a vera slight scoorchin' of the soorface of the fingertips of the right glove. Hot bulbs, see?"

"Well—I'll be damned, Chief. Kenwood's killer must have wanted plenty of light on that table top. He must have wanted to search for somethin' mighty bad."

"I theenk not, Terry. For fr-rom th' way he laid oot the goose-neck light —an' the calendar—one—or th' ither—or maybe both—he deedn't want th' light on th' table top—but on that calendar! He wanted that appointment sheet to show up like—like a hoose afire, the minute the police came in on the place."

"Well—200 watts, unfrosted, ought to a-made pencil writin' on blue paper stick out like a sore thumb."

"It does! 40 newspaper reporters and 40 flatfeet couldn't have muffed it, Terr-ry. Now, Terr-ry, wi' the lights th' way they ar-re—an' th' absolute positive evidence that 'twas the Indian—th' Chinese, that is—and not Kenw'od, who changed these bulbs and put them in their new poseetions—what conclusion can we come to? Only, that th' fir-rst, last and absolutely sure theeng Yin w'ad a'done—was he right in his head—wa'd ha' been to tear off that little blue paper square showing he had an appointment for 8:30. He couldn't have failed to see it Terry—for 'twas the last poseetion the lamp was left in. It wa'd ha' hit him squar-re in the face. Terr-ry, he's crazy, joost as I suggested an hoor ago. He—"

"Wait, Chief. Now so far as I can see—the lamp was so fixed that the examinin' squad couldn't fail possibly to see that blue top sheet!"

"Yes. And—"

"Well, Chief, I gotta lot to tell **you** about the Chink. He's all in the clear. So far's opportunity goes, that is. He was in Indianapolis tonight, and I've checked him a dozen ways around, an' back and forth across the board as well. True, he had reason to bump Kenwood off—there's positively no get-tin' away on the motive—but he's one damn lucky Chink that he wasn't in this burg tonight."

"So he's in the clear?"

"Posilutely, Chief. That is—all but as to the motive, y' understand. He ain't in th' clear there."

"Well—I'll be damned! Hm! Well, Terr-ry, all I can say then is that who-ever keeled Kenwo'd went to one hell of a lot of trouble to rivet it on Yin. Of course they moost have seen that Chinese name—the appointment, that is— while they were talking to Kenwo'd. And prepar-red to take full advantage of it when they shoold strike him down. And but—hm!—they came here prepar-red to keel Kenwo'd in Chinese fashion. For 'twas Chinese fashion, Terr-ry, regar-rdless of what they called it. 'Twas Chinese fashion, regard-less of th' suit they wore and their motives f'r doin' a quiet job. Chinese stuff, that head-splitting. No getting awa' from that. And—well, Terr-ry, it's begeening to look like a sort of half prepar-red—half-impromptu—plant of some sor-rt, eh?"

"I'm afraid it is, Chief. A little while ago I wouldn't-a talked this way. But now I'm thinkin' on a new plane. And furthermore, th' way I look at it now, th' last thing Yin Yi would ever have did—if he'd been in Chi, and bent on murder—would have been to bump Kenwood off in any fashion even remotely suggestin' Chinese."

"Unless he hasna' his proper weets, I'd say. But you say he's in the clear?"

"Yes. And that makes it all smack, somehow, of a sort of orig'nal inten-tion, on somebody's part, Chief, to hang it on him. Or, rather, on any luck-less Chink that might know Kenwood. And then grabbing off the chance of a lifetime—that name on the calendar. The funniest dam' frame-up I ever encountered yet, in this man's town. But not so funny for the victim—con-siderin' he had a motive to do th' very thing he was framed for. For he did want that five hundred bucks, Chief—and Kenwood, never in this world, would-a been likely to have paid out any five hundred berries on anything like that. For the Chink had no real legal claim against him whatever."

"Well, we'll look into that fur-rther. But in the meantime, ye can bank on it that only an insane man—or somebody trying to frame him—w'ad ha' laid oot these fixtures and light-bulbs th' way they ar-re laid oot right now. Well, I'll see ye in a shor-rt while. I'm cooming back over to the Bureau now."

There were a couple of brief goodbyes, and more clickings.

And Rand heard O'Rourke now fishing again in space for himself.

"Rand—you there yet?"

"Of course I'm here."

With which O'Rourke rattled his receiver-hook deafeningly in David Rand's ear. Jessica came on.

"Yes, Mr. O'Rourke?"

"Take Mr. Rand off the 'B'-hookup now, Jessica, and put him on direct."

In a moment they were talking again as they had first talked, a full hour before.

"And now, Rand," O'Rourke said, "what were you starting to say about motives—when Sinjohn came on the wire?"

"Just, O'Rourke," Rand told him, "that I'm in a position to demolish every vestige of any motive on the part of Yin Yi to kill Kenwood."

"You are? Why didn't you say something about it before?"

"Every time I tried to, somebody came in and tossed me over onto a 'B'-hookup—or told me to pipe down—or moved me here or there."

"All right. Well, what do you know?"

"Just this, O'Rourke. When I came back from New York today, Kenwood spoke to me at some length about the Yin Yi matter. Which had come up while I was gone, of course. He told me he intended to pay Yin Yi off. The whole $500. He was quite earnest and resolved in this too. In short, O'Rourke, even if Yin Yi had gone there tonight—he'd have gotten every cent of the money he thought he was entitled to."

"Well—I'll be damned. Are you sure o' that?"

"Sure? Why of course I'm sure. Furthermore, the girl was sitting near-by, and heard the whole conversation."

"Well—what do you know about that! And Kenwood had the coin, as well, on him tonight, to have paid Yin Yi off with. $2100 in five hundreds and one hundreds. Well, I'll let the girl give her account of the conversation tomorrow—but while I turn over this Yin Yi card here, and use a little Irish shorthand, give me every bit you can remember of that conversation. Where it touches on Yin Yi, that is—and that $500. And where it shows Kenwood did intend to pay the Chink off—or didn't."

"There isn't anything to tell about him not going to pay Yin Yi off. Everything he had to say was to the effect that he was going to. And he was a chap, O'Rourke, who didn't change his mind—once he came to a decision. He—but here—the whole conversation is fresh in my mind now. And I'll go back to the beginning of it, while it is that way. The beginning, that is, where I asked Kenwood what had happened in my absence." Rand slipped back, in recollection, with no trouble to that conversation in the sunny once, late that afternoon. And reason enough, too, perhaps, that he could, so easily, and so clearly, since the conversation was associated in his mind with a most highly pleasing thing—his triumphal return from New York with an agreement that helped his purse—and ego! And with no hesitation whatever, Rand spoke.

"Well, in the first place, Kenwood was tickled stiff—that I had signed his cousin up. I mention this because later on he said that Yin Yi was the 'hunch-back's hump for J. Kenwood, Esquire'; and that something told him he was going to have good luck for the rest of his days for settling in full with the Chinese fellow. And he—but to get back to the beginning. He was tickled stiff, as I say, at my luck. And pleased at the order he got in Topeka. Then we went over to politics. He bawled the very devil out of me—and all Democrats included!—said we all ought to be—but never mind. He razzed us to a fare-you-well. And I speak of that alone, because later on he complimented Yin Yi's intelligence for at least being a Republican, like himself! He—"

"Slow up a second. Till I jot that down. I might as well clear the Chink all th' way around, as half-way. And that Republican stuff ain't so nonsensical as a Republican himself is! I know one good Dimmicrat to shoot a Republican dead. And over nothing but tariff, too. Two years ago. Colonel Vetters, if you recall it. But now go on."

"Well," Rand continued, "Kenwood first introduced the matter by saying that something had come up that was costing him five hundred berries. That was **his** phrase. And he said—let's see—yes—he said: 'I'm paying it out of my own sweet, kind heart—with no grousing or grumbling. In other words—invited guests please omit sackcloth and ashes!'"

Rand paused. "Then he told me all about how the Chinese got roped in. On the gravestone marble ad. A stockselling proposition, see? And I recall he said regretfully—concerning one Golden-Tongued Kelly who once worked for us 'he took the poor Chinaman for his wad'. And added—let's see—yes—the words 'took him lock, stock and barrel!' Then he went on to tell about Yin Yi's visit to him. He did say there was a sort of silent menace about the fellow's visit. But, if you ask me, it seemed to amuse Kenwood more than anything. In fact, he complimented the Chinese fellow again: said, rather admiringly, that the Celestial was too perfect an actor and psychologist to make cheap threats. And—oh yes—it was right there he said that Yin Yi had the most confounded clear logic he'd ever encountered. That it was impossible to get sore at the position the latter took. And—yes—it was right there that I kidded Kenwood back, and found that he was only too willing to attribute Yi's logic to his being a Republican—like Kenwood—

which had come out in their conversation. Now where was I?"

"About Yi's logic."

"Oh yes. Well, Kenwood said then that when Yi got done with his argument, that he—Jack, that is—was absolutely sold himself—not only that he owed the Chinese $500—but 6 percent interest on it for 29 days!—and 7 percent accrued interest as well! I—oh, yes—that's where I kidded him again—as to why he didn't hire Yin Yi for our outfit—but he took me seriously, and solemnly said he would at that—if people weren't so asininely prejudiced against Chinese. In fact, here were his words—catch 'em before they fade from my mind: 'The Chinese—the Chinese in general —yes—are one dam' fine race, I've—I've always gotten along fine with 'em—in fact, I like Chinks; they're such philosophers, patient devils, they—they—yes—intrigue me—they appeal to me in some peculiar way. And as a rule they like me too.'" I paused. "Did you get all that?"

"Yeah, I'm entering the high spots. Yin Yi ought to hand this ticket down to his grandchildren."

"Well," Rand went on ruthlessly, "then Kenwood said that Yin Yi was in a position to do us a lot of injury in case he sued us—the publicity and newspaper sob stories, you know. The which I later confirmed. Then he told how he had learned that he hadn't lost that ad—the gravestone ad, that is—on a supposed hundred-M run. That a defective electro had saved him from a $1600 loss. Tickled stiff, he was. And then—let's see? Yes—he said: 'Then I did some hard thinking. Here, we've run along beautifully all—all these months—without any trouble'—no, that wasn't the phrase he used; he said, instead: 'never hitting a single snag or catching a dose of publicity of any sort; and one poor Chink'—no, he called him 'one poor devil of a Chink'—'and one poor devil of a Chink' he said, 'gets accidentally into our smooth-running machinery—and hurts himself—and thus us.' And—let's see—yes—he said: 'So I said to myself, says I: Having saved a neat chunk of money,' etc., etc. 'Thanks to that electro,' etc.—'and being just about to expand in New York as well' etc. etc.—'if David brings home the bacon, I'm going to pay the Chink off'—yes—'his whole $500 loss'—he stated that specifically, O'Rourke—'and consider it cheap'."

Rand paused.

"And it was after I told him that it really was cheap—that $500 was less than a third of his month's takings—that the said 'Virtue'—yes—'virtue is always rewarded!' And pointed out how he got back the old advertiser for that 2nd cover. And that good order in Topeka. And said that the Chinese fellow was his lucky fetish now. And then—let's see—yes—it was then he called over to Miss Creston for some hundreds and five hundreds she had for him. Of course he knew at the time he had a meeting with Yin Yi for tonight—but neither of us—Miss Creston nor I, that is—knew that. At any rate, he added the money she gave him, to what he already had. That's all—oh—no—here's one more thing."

"Shoot the works," O'Rourke ordered whimsically.

"I said—I said: 'Jack, you've got enough there to pay off a dozen China-men!'

"And he said—let's see—yes—'God forbid. The one doesn't worry me—he's my lucky talisman now!—but a dozen would.' And went on counting to seventeen hundred—and got weary of his own money. And that's all," I finished.

"Well you've said enough," O'Rourke commented, "to file Yin Yi's card with Joan of Arc's and some of them other famous Martians of history that got a right royal framing! Nothing else for me to ask, I guess. Unless—well, let's see—Kenwood was a bit sweet on your Creston girl—at least he musta been if, as you told me, he wanted to marry her. Now Yin Yi didn't make goo-goo eyes at—"

"No, he didn't," Rand said wearily. "I kidded her about that very thing myself. Asked her outright, in fact, if Yin Yi made love to her. And she said that Kenwood stepped out once while Yin was there—and she tried to be nice to him—but that he only scowled at her."

Rand paused, and finished:

"No, O'Rourke, I'll stake my life—from what I know of Jack Kenwood—that had Yin Yi stayed in town and really gone there tonight, he'd have been paid off—and off in good humor too. For Kenwood was in the best of humor—every way around the board. Lady Luck was just beaming on him this week."

"Well, between you an' me tonight, Rand, Yin owes us plenty. And you say the girl heard the whole conversation, too?"

"Every word of it."

"Couldn't be better. I'll read off these notes to her tomorrow, and she can check affirmatives for everything she recalls."

They were both silent now. And O'Rourke spoke.

"And what," he said, "before I hang up—shall we make Yin do for us—his saviors? Model us in wax?"

"God forbid!" was Rand's answer. "As far as I'm concerned, I'll be content to have the best Chinese dinner that can be bought in Chinatown."

"I likewise," said O'Rourke. "I'll go down to his cell now—and tell him that he's going to be our host! What day will suit ye?"

CHAPTER XVI

"Your Announcer Speaking."

Sebastien Zing, squatting deeply in the huge sheepskin-lined bag with which each member of the Elliott Muncibar Tibet-bound party was provided, huddled even tighter in it, there in the midday encampment at Pass 171, in the Himalayas. The noonday tea would soon be passed about by the cook Fung Soo, and he, Sebastien Zing, would, he knew, then be feeling more cheerful.

In view of the fact that it would be another month before the party could possibly make Tibet—and that its single short-wave sending radio, by which it could telegraph back to civilization, was completely and entirely out of commission, Sebastien Zing should have felt exceedingly lonely as well as a bit cheerless. But no—the compact 14-tube radio in the ground in front of him was at least bringing in the jolly strains of a most jazzy orchestra, clear from Shanghai.

But now the music came to a stop, and a man's voice—a bit British in enunciation, but quite American in its choice of words—spoke from the tiny box.

"And now, ladies and gentlemen," it said, "you have been listening to the Royal Scots Band, in the Chung Sung Luncheon Club of the International Settlement, Shanghai. Which club—thanks to the generosity of Mr. Chung Sung—is also radio station EW-18. And before putting on the air that marvelous little London tap dancer, Patricia O'Hearn, I want to give you all a most interesting announcement that is right now being carried—according to the classification under which it had just come to the Shanghai office of the Amalgamated News Service—in thousands of extra newspapers in far-off America where, of course, at this moment it is approximately midnight. That is, it is now 1 a.m. in New York, 9 p.m. in San Francisco—and exactly midnight in Chicago, the locale of the news in this particular news item."

Sebastien Zing pricked up the ears which were affixed to the head protruding from the warm bag.

Chicago news!

"It is, my international friends," the announcer went on, "that the strange hatchet murder, six weeks ago, of that American—J. Kenwood—who published that equally strange quack magazine, has at last been solved. Through the capture of his murderer due to a slip made by the latter—and the murderer's confession, rendered in full but 30 minutes ago. He was captured, it seems, in Chicago—that undoubted home of drama and melodrama!—through having been held up in the Negro section—and because of having notified the police immediately by phone that he had been held up! And because of the fact that his despoiler was thereby instantly picked up by what is known, over there, as a 'squad car'—some sort of roving car, don't you know, which travels bad districts with police in it, and is in continual touch with its headquarters by short-wave radio. Anyway, upon this black holdup man's person was found about 3 pounds in American currency and a beautiful dappled fountain pen, which was ascertained by the Chicago police to have obliterated lettering engraved on its gold band, reading 'Jack Kenwood'. It—"

The speaker paused.

While Sebastien Zing caught his breath.

"My God!" he said. "Dappled fountain pen—what—Chicag—what—"

But the announcer with the British intonations and the American phraseology was again speaking.

"He claimed, did this black holdup man, that he had found both pen and money upon a sidewalk, bound together by a rubber band, where the packet had been dropped by the man who subsequently claimed to have been held up and who, he said, had been walking ahead of him. The police were not, however, interested in this childish and naive Senegambian-like argument, nearly so much as they were as to **how** the man who was held up got the pen. The latter's explanation, when he called at the Detective Bureau headquarters for his possessions, failed utterly both as to **where** he had bought the pen second-hand—for that place, it seems, had gone out of business before the murder of this J. Kenwood—and with whom he had been that night of the J. Kenwood murder—for that man, a bridge instructor, and famous expert, was dead on the day before the J. Kenwood murder. And so Kenwood's murderer confessed all.

"His confession was that he went up there that night to the Interstate Life Building, garbed as a North American Indian chief, intending to go to the room across the hall from J. Kenwood, and—"

"Thank—God!" said Sebastien Zing. "One—one of Hippolytus' nut clients."

"—but went into J. Kenwood's office, which was lighted up, instead. He himself was in the Indian suit, he claims, so that he could go over to the Negro district to complete some business transaction. And thus openly, and legally, carry an axe for protection. It being, you will all remember, that quaint American holiday known as Hall-of-the-Eeen. He entered J. Kenwood's lighted once, wanting to find out from J. Kenwood if he could rent the latter's office, then or later. For he had discovered that his own name, and J. Kenwood's room number, and the street where the building stood, and the building number itself, all numeralized into a magic number that spelled huge success could he knit them all together by occupancy thereof. But he found, of course—as all you who read the fine journalistic pages of the **International News** here, and who remember that bizarre case, and the 10-year lease that lay on J. Kenwood's desk—that J. Kenwood had leased the place for 10 years the day before. And, in desperation—not knowing any other way to obtain the office which filled out for him only, the exceedingly lucky combination—he killed J. Kenwood. Only to see, the next day, the building manager change all the numbers in that corridor, and exclude the fatal—though for him, the murderer, lucky—number.

"His profession," the announcer went on, "before I put you back onto some music—for Miss O'Hearn is only just now putting on the first of her tap shoes—was, as will be surmised, that of Numerologist. A Numerologist, in fact, whose office was directly across the hall from that of J. Kenwood. And his name was Hippolytus Zing. And—oh all right, Scotty —give us the music, then, for Miss O'Hearn's entrance."

And the music from the Royal Scots Band soared forth.

"My—God!" said the man in the sheepskin bag, reaching forth one arm and turning off the radio. "He—he—he did it! He—did it! Whew! Well I only hope he didn't make a mistake on his dates—and that the killing didn't take place on a night when he had no class or anything. For he could be hung—yes!—under those new speedy Illinois execution laws—before I'd even get in touch with civilization again. My God, yes—here's hoping."

And he reached forth an arm to his radio and turned it back onto the music from the Chung Sung Luncheon Club, Shanghai. For it was cold, and very cheerless, there on Pass 171.

CHAPTER XVII

In Which D. Rand Visits T. O'Rourke On a Wintry Day

Sealskin cap deep down over ears, gloved hands sunk far within the warm pockets of his great winter coat, David Rand surveyed curiously the old-fashioned 4-story apartment building on South Ashland Boulevard where Terry O'Rourke now lived. Its grey Bedford-stone arched doorway, and white marble vestibule, including white marble steps leading up to and into its front hall, were decidedly not the architecture of those ultra-modern structures that were rapidly filling Chicago; but it was well kept up, and had a certain dignity about it. Its transom glistened; every square inch of its white marble was spotless. The mailboxes, though old-fashioned, and accessible to every thief who might wish to insert his fingers, were polished to a high brassy radiance.

Snow, in great heavy flakes, had been falling all day, this day of February 7th, and the leafless trees on either side of Ashland Boulevard seemed cotton-encrusted. An occasional automobile plowed its way along the wide boulevard, and far down the street an actual sleigh came sliding along, its bells tinkling gaily, steam coming from the nostrils of the prancing black horse which drew it.

What, David Rand wondered, did Terry O'Rourke want of him—that he should ask him to call there at 3 o'clock sharp, on the afternoon of February 7th—and without fail?

He turned into the vestibule, and pressed the button of that second right-hand mailbox which bore the name of T. O'Rourke. And then, peeling off his fur-lined gloves as he walked, proceeded up the carpeted inside stairs that wound their way past walls covered with old-fashioned lincrustawalton.

Terry O'Rourke greeted him in the doorway at the 2nd floor.

"Glad you got here first," he said. "Thought at first you might be one of the two other chaps I invited also. We're all going to hold confab. But that won't prevent you an' me from chewing the fat a bit first." He stood aside. "Enter my bachelor diggin's."

David Rand entered the apartment. It was pleasantly warm; and he heard a radiator sizzing somewhere. He hung his coat and sealskin cap on a mission hatrack that confronted him in a tiny hall.

"In this way," directed O'Rourke proudly, indicating a narrow back-parlor with ancient bead portieres cutting it partially off. "My livin' room. I keep my parlor room for a gymnasium!"

Still considerably puzzled, Rand entered the living room. A fine large room, but hopelessly without the touch of woman. A flamboyant rug, expensive obviously, bedizened with huge red and yellow roses, covered the floor. Two tall windows gave forth onto a vacant lot at the south of the house, and a huge rubber plant sat between them, but in such position as not to obstruct the generous light they gave. The doors to the parlor—or gymnasium, as O'Rourke had made it—were locked, and studded with photographs of everything from Hollywood screen actresses to baseball players and pugilists. Not a chair in the room matched any other chair, or anything else, in fact, much less the rug. A huge deer head hung upon one wall, with antlers spreading forth into the room, and a pair of pajamas hung on the tip of one antler. A fireplace in the wall separating the room from the dining room had been converted into a sideboard, by a set of terraced cigar-boxes covered with red 10-cent store tissue paper, and banked with wine glasses, liquer glasses, cock-tail glasses, and more glasses of every shape and tint. A row of quart and 5th-size bottles stood along the entire front of the fireplace.

Across the room from the side-windows was apparently an alcove, or den, or smoking niche—although exactly what it was was not revealed, for two heavy black drapes occluded its doorway, operated by cord pulls running down rings on the side. The only room adjoining that was visible was a dining room, containing a built-in sideboard and a large round table, in its center a half dozen ash trays, a poker-chip box, and at least seven decks of cards.

"Quite a place you've got here," Rand offered.

"Ain't it!" said O'Rourke enthusiastically. "I'll show you about later on. Including my smokin' den over yonder there, abaft the drapes. Which are designed to sequester him what looks too long on the wine when it's red. I call it the 'pass-out' room. Never a party, but some dam' fool guzzles too much over in me fireplace bar. So I stick 'em in there—in the 'pass-out' room, that is—on the couch. Turn off the lights. Draw them there black drapes—and let 'em sleep it off while th' party goes on, joy unrefined."

"You're absolutely human, O'Rourke," commented Rand wonderingly. "I thought you were a policeman. And here you like parties—good drinks—poker."

"An' why not?" countered the other, a bit nettled. "Is there annything immoral about them things? Sit down."

Rand dropped into an occasional chair.

"I didn't understand your note, O'Rourke. It said positively 3 o'clock—

and must be the 7th. I plowed all the way over in this snowstorm by street car and foot, to fulfill the terms. Didn't even try to bring out my car. For the streets with street car tracks on 'em are the only ones that are being kept clear. Was it something about the manuscript I wrote up for you? Your note intimated that—"

"Hold!" said the other. "When it comes to not understandin' things, I don't understand why your wife—when I just now rung you—said I might catch you at 'your desk' in the Amalgamated News Service. How the billy-hell—"

"Just," said David Rand sadly, "that Kenwood's murder brought me—indirectly—success. In more ways than that particular one set forth in the 'story' you asked me to write up for your 'grandchildren' [4] For, as you'll remember, you police found an **Ultrapolitan** cover in Kenwood's drawer on which he'd lettered, in ink, 'An Exclusive Editorial by Gilbert Melbourne'."

"Sure," admitted O'Rourke. "And when th' reporters connected with Gillie—he blew smoke out of his eyes and swore he'd never agreed to write nothing for that quack magazine, and then they—th' reporters—contacted you, the Gin'ral Manag—"

"Ex-G-M then," Rand corrected the other. "For with the passing of Kenwood passed **Ultrapolitan**!"

"Right! Well they contacted you—and found that 'twas to be another Gil Melbourne that was to father th' article, and that you was to write it—had already writ it—an'—"

"Yes, and that fellow Dog-Face, of the **Chicago Tribune**, swiped my article from my room—and ran it complete in a huge 2-page Sunday supplement feature story he wrote entitled 'Quack Publishing'."

"And from that has come—somethin'?" queried O'Rourke helplessly.

"More than something," declared David Rand. "For when 'Mal Gamate' of the Amalgamated News Syndicate died last week—he was, you know, Frederick vanHosley, and did stuff very much like Melbourne to ape Hearst—they found nobody who could quite exactly imitate his style. And then the Old Man—I work for him now, and can call him 'The Old Man'—reading over Dog-Face's feature article again, read my article that had been intended to sort of—of copy Melbourne—he realized that it at least aped the dead 'Mal Gamate'! So he called me in—had me write a half dozen sample short talks—anyway, I was hired day before yesterday—at $5000 the first year, and $10,000 the next and thereafter if I stick. And now I'm 'Mal Gamate'—of the Amalgamated News Syndicate."

"Well, 'tis a swill wind," said O'Rourke, "that blows the smell of gar-

---

4   Publisher's Note: The strange and immediate effects of Kenwood's murder upon David Rand's life and fortunes are set forth in the earlier novel by Mr. Keeler entitled "Finger Finger."

bage in any direction! Or, as maybe you might say it, it's an ill wind that don't blow nobody any bad. And it—but you were just now asking about the manuscrip you writ for me. For me grandchildher. Detailin' the odd events that come out of Kenwood's bumpoff. No, twasn't about **that** I wanted to see you today. For your manuscrip is a crackerjack—ending included—and how!—but only so far as it goes. The longer you writ on it—the more you writ like an author. But I find now that it don't cover the whole case. An' me grandchildher will want to know it all, from A to Izzard. How it all **really** started. How it all really **ended**. How—"

"Well—it seems to me that I started it correctly, anyway. First, an accidental exchange of raincoats aboard the Chicago Fly—"

"Accidental, eh? Well, not so's you can notice it, me boy. Nothin' accidental about it at all!"

"Why—what—what do you mean, O'Rourke?"

"Well, it's a long story. Which I got to make short. A one-time guardguide in the Cyrus Weatherford Mooseum in New York—fellow named John Walsh—got a bit daft over some young chicken up there, commenced squiring her around—and his wiff sued him for divorce. About 10 days ago, that is. She—but say—do you know about this here 13th Coin of Confoocius!"

"Why—sure. What I've read in the papers, that is. I read how China got up on her ear a couple of months ago, and kicked a number of Jap dictators out with such force that they never came down till they were volplaning over Nippon. And you told me yourself, you'll remember on the phone, that this chap Yin Yi said in his postal to you from China that China was all agog. Then too—there was that newsstory the night Jack Kenwood was killed. In the first **Midnight Brevities**, you know. About the blind numismatist in New York who—"

"Yeah. Never mind recountin' it. That's what I'm touchin' on now. About John Walsh's wife. Well, as I say, she's suin' him for divorce. It'll prob'ly be patched up. Them things gen'ally are. But the things that escapes in the heat o' emotion—stays escaped! See? An' she went to th' District Attorney down there—some 10 days ago, as I said—an' spouted a lot o' dope to him. It was her hubby, Rand, who snitched that coin. And not no mysterious German with square silver-rimmed specs an' a high-pitched voice. Her hubby, she says, snitched it in exchange for a cancelled mortgage, of 400 bucks, on their bungalow at 142 West 123rd Street. And a wad of 50,000 bucks cash—which, however, he never got! Trouble is, Rand, after he got let out o' th' Museum for carelessness, he got to drinkin'. Then goin' to night clubs. An' met this chicken. And stuck another mortgage on his place. So's he'd have coin to squire her around. But he'd told the wiff all the facts of the museum affair, after he'd been let out. Pretty good pals the two of 'em was, you see—at that time. And so, when the blow-up between 'em came, she spouted—with a vengeance!" O'Rourke paused. "Since which time," he continued, "four of us—Police Assistant Cadwallader, of the District Attorney's office in New York—Fed'ral Inspector Curtlan of New York—Assistant Fed'ral Inspector Monz at Chicago—and your humble yours truly—has been workin' together quiet-like, all in cahoots, on this case—an' at both ends at the same time—fillin' in every detail that the wiff has given a lead to. An' together we've just about dug up the whole darned picture."

"But I—I don't see, O'Rourke, how that New York case should touch anything in your line of work—here in Chicago?"

"No? Well when Cadwallader's and Curtlan's investigations in New York brung out, five days ago, the startlin' fact that on October 31st last, certain individuals here in Chi was ordered to pull off a murder—**a la** Chinese—same to be a delicate plant against any luckless Chink who might have the bad fortune to be entangled in any way with the victim, 'twas me who was delegated to work with 'em. For the Kenwood murder was just such a murder. And I'm still in charge of the remains of that case—such as they be! An' I ain't never really stopped workin' on it, Rand, because I knew, of course, that Hess [5] never done it. Even as I knew, at the very time the son-of-a-bitch confessed, that 'twasn't old Doctor Hippopotamus Zing that—"

"Why—" put in Rand, in surprise, "—did you know Zing didn't do it—at the time he confessed?"

"God—yes!" said O'Rourke. "But th' newspaper boys had done me a big favor th' week before, an' I'd promised to give 'em a red hot story soon—an' I wasn't deliverin' at all—had nothin' to deliver. And whin that down-at-heel noomerologist sung like a canary—I just paid 'em back, each an' ivery one of 'em, so damned well that I understand half of 'em succeeded in drawing a week's pay in advance from his cashier's office. The old codger—that Doc Zing! With 7 wimmen comin' for'ard next day an' sayin' he was teachin' em noomerology, at 10 cents apiece, the night o' Kenwood's murder. The old codger! Claimin' we beat the confession out of him! That's what gets me damned mad. I dropped in, last week, whin I was over in the Fine Arts Building, at his office, an'—"

"Fine Arts Building?" ejaculated David Rand.

"Right! And by God—he had a dozen wimmen—these 'uns in furs and silks—waitin' in a grand reception room—to be noomeralized—at, I understand it, $3 apa'ce. An' he had a gal in a smock, keepin' office—and whin he come out of his insulting room, the Doc was wearin' big Oxfordian silver specs, and a long swallow-tailed English coat. My God—but that killin' just made him—after he woke up to what he could do with it."

"Well," commented David Rand, "again, as you say, tis a 'swill wind'

---

5   Publisher's Note: A character in the novel "Finger Finger."

that blows nobody any bad. But you say you've never stopped working on the case?"

"No. Never. Th' time I went out of the city, and left you to write your story in p'ace, I went to New Orleans; but **on** the case. For I was putterin' away an the jigsaw puzzle even then. But not until five days ago did I have the whole boxful of missin' pieces like these fellows in New York was able to supply. That is to say, them persons as is tangled in the Confoosian coin theft, is also concerned in the Kenwood murder. See?"

But David Rand did not see. Other than that O'Rourke was floundering, evidently, as to where to begin his words. Then the Irishman went on. "This Walsh, Rand," he said, "was contacted by a Jap secret agent up at Lac du St. Pierre, Canada. See? For th' Japs didn't want Chiny to get that 13th Coin, and come buzzin' to th' front—exactly th' way she's doin' right now."

"But—but—what's this got to do—with the raincoats?"

"Plenty! Hess' raincoat had the coin in it. At one time, that is. Fact. 'Twas searched—on the train—by a Jap agent who switched another coat into its place. And who was thorough enough to search yours, too. Usin' Hess' to switch with. And so on, yours back to Hess—for certain reasons— ring-around-th'-rosy. S'truth! I've got enough notes and data over there in that desk to tell the whole story, with abs'lutely nothin' left out. In fact, am going to have a certain Chicago author write 'em up into a set of chapters to run in ahead o' your story and—"

"I'll revise my story at once," put in Rand hastily. "And get out of it all my dam'-fool observations on Chance and Life and—"

"You'll revise nothin'," growled O'Rourke. "It's th' very way I want it—th' way it is right now. An' will serve to show my grandchildher never to take nothin' for granted. That everything in the world, happenstance or not, results solely from somethin' what took place ahead of it. And—"

"And in turn creates—what eventuates from it?" put in David Rand, a little disconcerted yet.

"Correct! And that's exactly why you're up here this afternoon. For con- fab. With me an' two others. Relative to what is to come out of it! An which is to constitute another story to edify my grandchildher."

The younger man, however, could but look at the older one inunder- standingly.

While O'Rourke, in turn, looked at his watch. "That confounded author should ought to be here to hear all this." He put his watch away. "Rand, when I seen yesterday I was confrontin' a bigger and curiouser web by far than the one you've so kindly spun for me grandchildher, I had just read in the paper about a Mr. John Macrae bein' in town at the Blackstone Hotel. He's the owner of Duttons, what publishes friction books in New York. So I run over to th' Blackstone and see him. He was in confab at the very time

I got there, with a long tall guy with a fetlock hanging down over his fore-head, that has actually writ a friction book for Mr. Macrae dealin' with them there 12 Coins of Confoocius that's been in Chiny for such a long while. **Sing Song Nights**— or some fool thing like that. Anyway, I let Mr. Macrae read your manuscript. An' give him a rough idea of the events lyin' back of it, and that more has to come from it all. The author he just stayed glum and said nothin'. They're all three-quarter wits anyway, these professional authors, you know. But the upshot of it all was that Mr. Macrae is going to publish the whole thing under two titles 'Finger Finger' and 'Behin' that Mask'—for this here author is to incorporate all the facts now avail'ble into some chapters that's to run ahead of your story. After which yours will come—just like you writ it. An' will constitute this here now 'Finger Fin-ger'. Then the author is to fix up another true story—incorporating th' facts of Kenwood's bump-off—and the further things that's to come out of it. He may even, he says, borry me own description—exact as **you** writ it—of Kenwood's demise. Word for word. So's he—but if you'll excuse me a sec-ond, I'd like to see if he's gone into a dream or somethin'."

With which O'Rourke stepped out in the hall. David Rand heard him calling on an old-fashioned phone for some Bittersweet number. And then:

"May I speak with H. Keeler?"

"Now lissen, smart-gal-on-a-wrong-number, you prob'ly think you're pulling a fast one to get a free earful about something that don't concern you, but it just happens—see?—that H. Keeler is a guy—that is, with the fetlock he wears, he's just short o' being a horse!—anyway, he's a bird with pants, which is prob'ly more than you're wear—

"Oh—I see. Hrmph. Of course. Hazel Keeler—wife; Harry Keeler—husband. H. Keeler. Yes, of course. And don't pay no attention, will you Mrs. K., to my ribbing you that way on the phone?—y'see I knew all the time—ha-ha-ha!—you were the sweet wiff he spent all his time talking about when I met him, and so thought I'd do a little expert kidding—a fact!—you try it sometime, Mrs. K., that same way, and you'll find it's a cinch to make people think they're on a crossed wire, after which the stuff you can pull on 'em is a screa—well do you think you could call to the Old Man—above the roar and rattle of his trusty typewriter—that Mr. O'Rourke of the Chicago Det—

"He—what?

"Oh!

"Oh, yeah? Oh, yeah. Yeah, I know, Mrs. K. I know—O.K.!"

The sound of O'Rourke's disgusted sigh came into the back parlor room from the very hall, as he banged his receiver back. And he came back dis-gruntedly into the room he had just left.

"Con you beat it? His wiff reports he's very busy sittin' in a tub of cold water, with a half dozen bottles of coca-cola and a straw, plottin'. That he can't never be disturbed when a friction plot starts to come. That he has to foment 'em this way—or no—ferment 'em, I guess it was. But that he's left word for me that he don't need to sit in any confabs to write no thrue stories. That we should get all the data, and th' high-lights—now what th' hell are high-lights!—and that's all he'll need to work on." O'Rourke snorted angrily. "Well, you're official collector of high-lights now. An' just one more peep out of that author—and damned if I won't get Mingleberry Hepp to write the whole thing up—that is, if Mr. Macrae agrees."

He sat down angrily. And looked at his watch again.

"Well, I'll try to give you th' facts before our third confabee arrives!

"In the first place, Rand," he began, with no delay, "our man Hess who shuffled off in th' Police Administration Hospital is the man who sold that Confoocian coin back to Blind Tom—of New York. Up to five days ago, there was a whole raft of things that pointed to that fact—if we'd used our heads here in Chicago a little more—and if we'd had what Walsh's wiff spilled to the District Attorney there in New York. But I needed their parts, I guess, just like they needed mine. Anyway, now we've got abs'lute proof two ways goin'—which I'll give you in a minute. Walsh's wiff, in spilling her story there in New York, said that a Jap agent supplied her hubby with that gold-plated lead coin, and that he—hubby, that is—made the exchange himself in the Confoocian case. And was just about to slip th' Confoocian coin into a Jap woman's umbrella—then a bunch of thief-alarm lights went on all over the Museum—some nut elsewhere, you see, tried to steal somethin'—and Walsh got panicky. And stuck the coin quick into a tiny pocket on the inside of the bottom hem of a Dryo raincoat, that some greybeard, with a zipper bag, that'd drifted into the Museum just before 4 o'clock closin' time, had laid acrost a bench. It seems, also, that Walsh, to help this here greybeard out, had read the old boy's Pullman coupon and train ticket for him—when he seen the old boy holdin' it 'way out at arms' length and ogling it—and that's how Japan knew the very train an' coach that greybeard was to go on.

"Remember how Hess told us that after he come from that Jacqueline Kenwood's roominghouse up at 522 West 113th Street around 3:30 p.m.—on his second trip up there—he strolled around a bit? In that neighborhood? Well, this museum is on Morningside Drive—an' smack around the corner from 522 West 113th Street. Do you grasp it all now? And do you remember how Hess told us he finally rode down to West 20th Street, near 8th Avenue, to look up a friend of years ago? And rented hisself a cheap little room right about there to lay down in a while?"

"Yes. Sure I do. And later on ironed that raincoat out! And the rest wouldn't be hard to guess—if you really **can** substantiate that this visitor to the museum was Hess. For the minute his iron hit the place where the little pocket lay underneath, with the gold coin in it—which his iron evidently did at that, for I saw the faint mark of it there myself, later, right where it must have rested a few seconds too long while he was figuring the thing out—he examined the pocket, and found the coin."

"Correct. And he supposed it was some sort of a current Chinese $20 goldpiece, hid there by some Chink who'd forgot all about it, and had sold the coat down around Chinatown—where Hess had bought it in the morning. Off Chatham Square, if you'll remember his dyin' statement. Maybe he thought the Chink who'd hid it there had croaked, and his family had sold the raincoat for four bits—or so."

"Yes. I see. And then he took a streetcar over to Blind Tom's—"

"No, he didn't. Consult your map of New York. The place where he found it is right around the corner from Blind Tom's place at 217 7th Avenue. He just sashayed forth shortly after 6 o'clock on that third and last trip he made up to Jacqueline Kenwood's place, and naturally went to take the 7th Avenue subway, at the 23rd Street station, up to Times Square, where he could transfer to reach the Morningside Park neighborhood. And near that 23rd Street Station of 7th Avenue, he seen the sign 'Blind Tom's Honest Coin Emporium.' That 'honesty' part maybe got him. I don't know. But he went in. And you know the rest. He got, in exchange for that coin, 7 bucks and a Philly Sesquicentennial $20 gold-piece—worth actually $36—except that he thought it was just worth $20.

"But how do you prove all this, O'Rourke, as completely as you say you do? Solely by Walsh's wife's story? Surely she doesn't remember now the train, car, and berth that her husband's museum visitor traveled on?"

"No. Of course not. I'll come, in a minute or so, to how we've clinched it 100-percent. I'm tryin' to show you just now what this author is up against—and, if you ask me, he'd do well to hop out of that tub pronto, shove his coca-cola bottles out of the way, and mosey over here." O'Rourke made a helpless gesture. "But these authors are all the same. They think they're some kind of artist, an' can portray a waterfront better when they're on a desert; an' a desert better when they're on a waterfront. Why, confound 'em, they—"

"Yes," put in David Rand hastily. "But leave him where he is, O'Rourke. I'll collate **for** him. Everything."

So O'Rourke continued.

"Well, this wiff's tale gave the full description of th' middle-aged Jap who contacted Walsh in Canada. And with the limp he had, he was picked up without much trouble. In Brooklyn. Name was Kaisetsu. He was married to a Korean woman named Emiko. The Koreans don't naturally love the Japs too much—considerin' how Japan snitched Korea bag and baggage and called it Chosen. Fed'ral Inspector Curtlan's assistants knew they couldn't crack the Jap in a million years—so they hid him in the cooler a couple of days, and worked on her. She had enough antagonism toward Kaisetsu, 'way down inside her, to start a good bonfire. They told her he was keepin' a Siamese belle named Ruhka, in a flat on Central Park South. And figuring to take her back to th' Orient, and ditch the Korean gal flat. Inspector Curtlan provided the Ruhka girl hisself. She happens to be a United States intelligence service agent. Uncle Sam ain't so dull, you know, as not to have a half of an intelligence service of his own. And when Ruhka finished her spiel with Emiko, the Korean woman was red-headed with rage. And spouted all she could—just like Mrs. Walsh. Hell hasn't no fury like a woman—but you know th' rest of th' sayin'." O'Rourke paused a second. "But Emiko didn't have near so much on her hub as what Mrs. Walsh had on hers! Nothin' but that he sometimes identified hisself, on the telephone, when he rung up certain people, with th' words NY-3, and talked in dam'd guarded tones. Which proves he was a secret agent, see! And she knew a number he called at times. Which was Equitable 44132.

"'Twas checked. And was—at least up to a month and a half ago—that of a big Jap importer named Yamagushi in the Equitable Building. Who has since blown from the United States for Japan. The gov'ment even about then was suspectin' him of having something to do with th' Jap intelligence service here in America, an' no less 'n a few weeks later was puttin' him down on their records as being actually one, Kusumoto. But a long code wire that he sent from his office the same day you was aboard that Chicago Flyer—and of record at the Western Union offices in New York—to another importer here in the Merchandise Mart, Chicago, calling himself Tokonami, indicates he was the bigadabug of the whole system! For it was decoded for Curtlan by an ex-lieutenant in the American army, a cipher expert, named Lieutenant James, who'd been stationed over there in the Orient for years and was so familiar with the Japanese language he could nag his own wife in it."

"But how the devil could he ever decode a spy wire?"

"Well, when Yamagushi cleared out suddenly in New York—Japan, you know, changes her agents often and swift—he left behind him—all tore up, you know—a little cardboard disk with letters on it. What was attached to a cardboard square—also with letters on it—so's it could revolve. An' a thumbed Japanese-American dictionary. Them things was retained by the U. S. Secret Service. And James, who just hit New York a week ago, has spent his life on Oriental cipher messages. So with as much of a lead as he had, the decipherin' of the message was pie."

O'Rourke paused belligerently. But receiving no disaffirmations from his visitor, went on.

"Well, this here Yamagushi had been a life-long friend to a Jap named Shigi Jitsukawa. In New York, that is. Jitsukawa had died. And left a son. Named Shinzo. And this guy Yamagushi was sort of a god-father to Shinzo. See? And Shinzo had just come from Brazil—Inspector Curtlan has the whole story—some skullduggery about a magnetic range finder plan he beat German agents to, on a river down there, only the plan was all destroyed— I'll give the whole blamed thing ult'mately to this author in writing—and was the guy sent out to recover that coin from Hess' raincoat. And—What's that, you say? Oh—where is Shinzo now? Oh, he's beat it for Japan too. But a check-up of the Pullman agents in th' Grand Central Depot brings to light that Agent No. 7 remembers a Jap trying to wangle a berth aboard your coach. He remembers him by his color. Bronzed, he says, like nothin' he's ever seen before. He—"

"Why—I remember the chap," said David Rand. "The bronzed young Jap, that is. A charming fellow. He sat in my seat a while and talked with me. And with Hess, too. Although Hess sort of cold-shouldered him out. Evidently didn't like him."

"No? Well, that bronzed baby is the bird who done the skullduggery about the raincoats. We know dam' well that it was done—quite aside from this here decoded wire—because a further checkup reveals that Yamagushi bought a Dryo raincoat by phone from Saks Fifth Avenue, and had it delivered to his office the afternoon of the night you left New York. Now do you, by any chance, recall your train being stalled next day near a place called Amesburg Crossing, Ohio?"

"Yes. An over-turned boxcar on a line crossing us."

"Well, there's a long-distance message on record to Yamagushi of a conversation from there. The tower man at Amesburg Crossing also remembers giving a young Jap off that train enough half dollars to feed the coin box of that long-distance phone from now till when. 'Twas that message, Rand, what give us what we've now got to work on to get at the bottom of Jack Kenwood's murder. Say—suppose I try to get that Keeler bird out of that cold bath, and fetch him down here? This thing is intricate, I tell you. It—"

"No," advised David Rand. "He'll write up a more convincing picture of the whole thing if he never stirs out of his studio. Really, O'Rourke, he will!"

"All right. All—"

"Just what came out of Shinzo's conversation," asked Rand, "that brought about Jack Kenwood's murder?"

"Well, Shinzo tipped his superior off that Hess had found the coin in the night, ev'dently, and had it in his possession—on his person—instead of in the coat. See? And—but say—you didn't see Hess examining a gold coin aboard that train, did you?"

"No. But I was in and out of the coach a lot."

"Well, this Shinzo obvi'sly did. Only 'twas the Philly Centennial gold-piece Hess got in New York that he was examining. And Shinzo phoned this to Yamagushi. Who maybe I ought to call Kusumoto now, and be done with it. We was puzzled for a while why Kusumoto wired such a long expensive wire that day. Until I found out the other day that there was a small fire in the North Wacker Drive telephone exchange on October 31st. That cut off Tokonami, see, in the Merchandise Mart. An' for your edification, I might also add that not only does Assistant Fed'ral Inspector Monz, here in Chi, maintain positively that Tokonami's description tallies complete with a certain Nisaku Sato, an agent of the Japanese government in Kansas City six years ago, but that the Tokonami-Sato bird folded his wings and blew this town entirely the day after Kenwood's murder!"

"You don't mean to say he is the murd—"

"Naw! Of course not. But he's the head-man for the Jap intelligence service here in Chi. And is eligible to walk the gallows steps behind any of his men who he instructs an' guides in the pullin' off of any little killin's. See?"

"Hm! I'm beginning to see a lot. And yet—but what was the text of this long wire to Tokonami, O'Rourke. Or Sato—whatever you want me to call him?"

"Boy—it was a humdinger! I hope the Emperor of Japan gets the piles, an' has to stand up at his meals for at least a year. It was a humdinger, I tell you. It ordered Sato to put the whole Jap intelligence system, here in Chicago, to tailing Hess to get that Confoocian coin. Even to kidnapping Hess. To bumping him off. To burying him. To following every contact he made—and bumping off any person who that coin might have passed to—except you."

"Except me?"

"Yes, you. Which, quite aside from the wire, shows that Shinzo had your raincoat in his fingers—and your set of sales curves—with your address on its back. And that he used your raincoat to get back the Saks Fifth Avenue Dryo raincoat he'd stuck in Hess' rack. He knew Hess would be bumped off, see? And the Saks coat would be traced to Kusumoto back in New York."

"Well you've certainly handed me a few knockouts, O'Rourke. No wonder Sato faded out of Chicago if, as you say, Jack Kenwood's death resulted from all this. If Sato had all his Japs out to kill a man—any man—"

"Wait! I didn't say the system was all Japs. The wire specifies that not only is the Japs to be put on the job, but three whites also, known as C-11—he bein' a supposedly former NY-15; a C-3; and a C-13; and a nigger called C-7. It specifies out-an'-out that a certain white C-8, an' a certain Persian C-12, is to be left out altogether—because of their unwillin'ness to commit homicide for Nippon. Ain't that a honey?"

"Well—well—with all this compliment of men out for him, how comes that Hess didn't get bumped off!"

"Hell, they didn't have a chance. Broad daylight all the time. The only one good chance they mighta had to run him into their car was right after he fled outa your dump on Oak Street. It bein' pretty free o' people right up in that block. But he pops into the Newberry Library—see?—to get his breath—yes, I know now that Hess' whole story was true—an' pops out later right into a passing taxi. Straight downtown. By way of busy Clark Street. To the Morrison. And from that time on they couldn't do nothin' but follow him about and chew their nails. And—oh yeah—here's a rich one. Harry Morrison, owner of the Morrison, instructed his desk clerk a few months ago to sequester all gold pieces took in, and put 'em in envelopes for him. Before turning 'em over to the G. Since gold pieces is now legally allowed to be kept—providing they are noomismatical items. And Morrison is a coin c'llector.

"Well, Harry Morrison's been in Europe all this while, but we been through some o' the envelopes that was marked an' sealed up about that time. And in one there's a $5 U.S.A. goldpiece, a 2-guinea British goldpiece, and a $20 Sesqui goldpiece, all handed in th' same afternoon that this Ralph Stone of Kansas City—which was Hess, thanks to that phony introduction he was lucky enough to get—registered. That completes the chain, I'd say."

"It surely does. And you've certainly worked things out beautifully."

"Thanks. Now we go back just a little bit to what happened when Hess struck Chicago. Remember that bird Hideo who popped up that afternoon, on the streets downtown in th' Loop, in that old Ford car, an' got pinched, and—"

"Yes. And kept you from getting over to 72 West Oak in time to interview Hess. Then Hideo was—"

"Hideo and nearly everybody else in the Jap system here was out that day on this Confoocian coin job. Tailing, trailing, reporting, an' what not else." O'Rourke paused. "For Kusumoto ordered a killing to get a-holt o' that coin. He ordered every man-jack of 'em—except th' thin-skinned ones—out on the streets. An' get this: He ordered 'em to use masquerade suits—when night come—see? An'—"

"Then, after all's been said and done, a Jap killed Jack Kenwood? And–"

"Whoa, Tillie! Didn't you hear me at all say that white agents was ordered out, too? No, Rand, th' man in that Injun Chief suit never was a Jap. They're one an' all too little. An' the people in the Interstate Life that seen that Injun Chief says he had a good all-round build on him. That tell th' story, don't it? Plus the fact that th' white people Japan has workin' for her in Chicago is desperate enough individuals a-plenty, ready to do anything for th' gold she hands out. And—"

"Then," put in David Rand helplessly, "that Filipino necktie ped—"

"Wait! Speakin' O' Flips, th' Filipino Reilly found buzzing around Hess' floor in th' Paris Hotel wasn't no Flip after all. He—he was a Jap agent. He'd searched Hess' room—even that package Hess brung in—as soon as it was reported Hess was 'way over on the near North Side, contactin' you—who had a perfect whitewash with those babies in this affair. Moreover, th' one-armed Jap gentleman who got out of the elevator with Hess the night of Kenwood's death—on Hess' first trip to Kenwood's office—and went up the hall alongside Hess, was followin' him. Seen him go into Room 1122. All waited up th' hall long enough to see him go out of 1122. And—"

"Oh-oh! I get you! And heard Kenwood say to Hess, as the latter stood in the open door, 'It's mine now—and I'll hold onto it—till I get what I think I ought to have for it—so run along'!"

"Ex-actly! They all of 'em thought, when that was reported to 'em that the coin had just been passed to Kenwood. For remember, Rand, right after Hess left and went back to the Morrison to think things over, a Filipino necktie peddler went up to Floor 11—and into Kenwood's office. A Jap again, see? Or maybe actually a Filipino who's lived in Japan, and calls himself such. He seen Kenwood readin' that coin catalogue whose cover stated that it listed all the coins and tokens in the world. That was plenty—enough! He sold him a tie cheap—just for a stall—and blew out—down-stairs —to a parked car somewhere up the street. Reported enough to prove that Kenwood **had** bought the coin—as a speculation—or as a favor—or Lord knows what—and was going to work out a deal either for himself—or for himself and Hess together."

"I certainly get it all now," commented David Rand, shaking his head at the very devilish perfection with which every detail fitted every other one. "And then a big masked Indian Chief climbed down out of that car—or was picked up further down the street—went upstairs into that office, and killed Kenwood quick. And used a hatchet to—but didn't I understand you to say a while back that that telegram ordered the killing to be invested with a Chinese angle?"

O'Rourke nodded grimly. "Yes. But cautioned 'em to be subtle as hell about the way they dragged th' Chinese angle in."

"I see. I see. And the Jap agent—the white Jap agent, that is—frisked Kenwood's pockets as he lay on his face. Looked in the drawers of his desk. Saw that something was wrong somewhere. Maybe looked up in the tele-phone book the Yin Yi whose name was on that blue calendar appointment sheet for 8:30, and found he was just a wax modeler instead of a banker."

"Or," put in O'Rourke, "has it occurred to David Rand, Esquire, that maybe the killer got a ring on Kenwood's phone at that moment tellin' him to drop ever'thing—and blow?'"

"Why?"

"On th' theory that th' gang outside may have bought a copy of the first issue of **Midnight Brevities**—and seen that the coin was recovered in New York City."

"By golly—you're right. Except that they didn't have time to tell him anything more than that the coin was definitely **not** in Room 1122. And that's why his attention was so arrested when he stepped out of the elevator, and saw by those headlines that not only was the coin not in Room 1122— but that it was recovered, as well, by the authorities in New York."

O'Rourke shrugged his shoulders with an air that said plainly: "Your theory is as good as mine."

"It's all mighty plain now," Rand continued. "Having received the order to clear out of Room 1122—or seeing plainly that a bad boner of some kind was pulled—he nevertheless saw to it that the unknown Yin Yi whose name was on that uppermost blue sheet of the appointment calendar caught the full brunt of the thing—as suspect. Changed bulbs between the ceiling fixture and the desk lamp, focussed the bigger brighter bulb square on the dark blue paper, where the first detectives in there would be sure to see the pencil notation—and got out."

He paused helplessly.

"And what," he finished, "would have become of that luckless Yin Yi if he hadn't lost his date with that inamorata of his in Oak Park—or wherever it was—gone to Indianapolis, and best of all—thanks to me, and at least two others—could prove he wouldn't even have had a motive to kill Kenwood? O'Rourke, those agents must be devils in human form."

"Devils? You don't know the half of it! But, me boy, I am able to tell you now that we know the identity an' th' whereabouts of each man in the entire crew—that is, each of the three white agents here in Chicago, and the Nigger—one of which four must have been delegated to be killer that night. For this Tokonami, head of th' system here in Chicago, didn't conduct his end o' things like this Kusumoto in New York—keepin' his agents, that is, all hid from one another. And a meetin' between the whole bunch, held at Tokonami's office in the Merchandise Mart, sometime back in September, before all this took place, happened to be checked by Monz' men on the half supp'sition at that time that they were maybe part of the Ojira opium smuggling syndicate—if you remember that case; an' while it turned out that they wasn't, th' location of every man jack of 'em who left that meetin' is on record. Fact! An' now that Tokonami turns out to be the recipient of that telegram—why them names becomes worth their weight in gold—in the Kenwood case. See? In fact, every one of the whole four is under surveillance right this here minute. An' don't know it, neither! Any one—or all four—can be brung to this very room within 30 minutes—if I raise the receiver of that phone out there and call Monz. Only I don't want to raise it until—" O'Rourke stopped.

"Until what?" David Rand leaned forward curiously.

"Rand, I'll give you a guess." O'Rourke paused. Then shook his head deprecatingly. "You don't get it, eh! Well, have you stopped to consider that there's more money back of those guys—to save their skins, that is—than your paltry $50,000 could throw even a shadow on? That Nippon's prestige—her very honor itself—is in danger? That if the true solution of this Kenwood killin'—an' the arrest of the killer—is to brand her as a dirty stinking sneakthief, ready to bash a guy's brains out with a hatchet and hang it onto a humble member of the very race she's exploited, she'll stop at no lengths to avert—no, divert—that? Why aside from Nippon's unlimited supply o' coin—one of these white guys alone owns a $40,000 flat-buildin' all clear of debt, that he can fling a $20,000 mortgage on. For his legal defense. Another owns a tract o' land out around Lake Calumet, that'll sell for at least enough to cover the palm o' the first criminal lawyer in Chi. The Nigger—oh he's like all Niggers—broke. But Rand, now that the whole Jap'nese angle to Kenwood's murder lies complete in our mitts—and Hess' whole story therefore can be proven to be true—there ain't no Hess to lay the murder on no more. See? And they'll direct all their energies and coin, therefore, to tryin' to rivet it onto th' next nearest suspect. The very guy who was framed in the first place: Yin Yi. Rand, not only is there all the coin in the world available to hire the most brilliant lawyers there are—fellows that are ex-prosecutors themselves, and can at least try to rivet this case back on Yin Yi, but—"

"But how can they rivet it back on him? His wealth of witnesses can—"

"Listen, poor infant! Ever hear of killin' off alibi witnesses? Th' strong ones, that is? An' buyin' off the weak ones? Remember his life, after all, hangs on the testimony of people. A big bunch of 'em, to be sure. But neverthe—"

"But, O'Rourke, the Japs don't know the names of Yin Yi's witnesses. He wasn't officially arrested. Just held a while for questioning, till released, so far as I understand it. And I well remember how you weren't handing anything out to the reporters that night. And by the time you finally did release the full details of the Kenwood case—the finding of that safe had become the big story—and the reporters didn't have time to waste on the different false leads of a killing then 3 days old. In fact, as I recall it the stories just mentioned that Yin was quizzed and released as not having been in Chicago that night. Am I not right?"

O'Rourke looked sheepish. "Unfortunately, Rand, the matter ain't quite so simple as that. Sinjohn's Chinee friend, Tom Shee, editor of the **Kong**

Shing Yu Po— that's the Chinee Daily News here—called at the Bureau th' day after Commissioner Mike Sheehan ordered a release on the whole Kenwood case, and asked for all the dope pertainin' to Yin so's they could write up a story on how the Gods of Destiny had guarded one of their race that night. Sinjohn sent him up to me, and I give him all there was in the Yin Yi folder of the **dossier**, providin' only that he let me check a translation of his story. Which he done, later, and which I handed back. Well, th' **Kong Shing Yat Po** run a whole half front page—best hunk of journalism I ever see—givin' names, addresses, details of ever'body in Indianapolis an' here too. Which story doubtless was reprinted in Chinee papers the country over. And there ain't nothin' printed in a Chinee paper, Rand, that ain't read by Japs and analyzed. Long ago them babies doubtless figured that if Hess hadn't turned out to be the fall-guy for the killin', and things had got too hot ag'in 'em, Yin Yi would have had to be made fall-guy. Which would involve makin' a number o' midnight calls on certain people in Indianapolis—detailed fully in the **Kong Shung Yat Po** story, and—"

"Good Lord, O'Rourke. You mean that, for instance, if you ordered an arrest of a Jap agent here, Miss Jones of Indianapolis, Yin's old music teacher, might be killed? And–"

"An' don't forget Mr. David Rand, neither, star witness as to Yin's havin' no motive. And Mrs. Aline Rand, same. And—"

"You mean they'd try to wash Yin up completely so far as defen—"

"I mean nothin' else. Rand, if the Jap intelligence system this minute even suspected that movements was under way to hang one of its men for murder in a coin snitching job—and not less than 3 more as accessories both before an' after th' fact, d' you know what would happen—right tonight—in Indianapolis, where, by the way, there's at least a dozen and a half Japanese agents of all colors and nationalities, tailing the Asiatic Conference that's going on in th' Hotel James Whitcomb Riley?"

"What would happen?"

"Miss Laura Jones, who lives entirely alone in a more or less insecure cottage, would be strangled in her bed. Victim of an apparent nigger burglar—probably a white man blackened up—who maybe would be seen comin' from her place. Her little house at 225 West 9th Street is just close enough to the old canal—which is out-an'-out nigger district—and such explanation of her murder would sit O.K. with the police down there. This Yin Tzu Lei, Yin's uncle at 1034 South Senate Avenue, would be shot dead before midnight. Victim of an apparent tong war. At least, all th' evidences of tong stuff would be left scattered around. Like all th' Chinese, he's a member of a tong. A little one—the Dee Lung Tong—but not so small that there ain't plenty hard feelings with their closest enemies, the Bing Kong Tong. The toll records showin' that Yin Yi called Miss Jones from Indianapolis, around th' time of the Kenwood murder, and not from Chicago—one of the strongest points of his defence—would be snitched out o' the filing cases of the Indianapolis Telephone Company before midnight tonight—if they had to cross some clerk's palm with ten thousand bucks. And—"

"And that old musical professor? The one who saw Yin across the passageway between the two houses, sitting on the windowsill playing the **erh-hu**? Would he be kil—"

"No, he wouldn't be killed off at all, if you ask me. Old Emil Wunderlich, we have found, is as honest as the day is long—but he's heavily mortgaged in his place there at 1036 South Senate. And he's out, as head of the stringed instrument department at the Indianapolis Musical Conservatory. I'm saying he'd be given a job at $100 a week—as head of a department like that at the Nakamura Musical Conservatory here in the Lyon and Healy Building. The wires 'd easy be pulled for that. That is, if he just had a mind lapse as to whether he was sure it was Yin Yi he seen sittin' on the windowsill that night playin' the **erh-hu**. With proper work done on him— he wouldn't be sure of nothin' no more."

"But Yin's fingerprints on his uncle's piano, O'Rourke! Those are incontrovertible."

"Sure—except that their value for keepin' Yin from bein' indicted depends wholly on the testimony of Tarbaby Watkins, that she washed them keys at 6 o'clock. There'd be enough coin fed her black parents and a couple o' crooked alienists in Indianapolis to have her declared cuckoo—prob'ly on the subject of religion—and her testimony would be worth nix. As for the little kid grand-niece from up th' street—O Loya Yin—who seen Yin Yi playin' the piano just before he left—she's just a baby girl, and ain't a legal witness for nothin'. No, with Yin Tzu Lei dead—and Tarbaby declared nuts—there ain't no chance, you see, to legally fix the time when the black girl brung the child over to the South Senate Avenue home—hence of Yin Yi's playin' that piano—much less of Tarbaby washin' the keys. See? I'm only tryin' to show you what witnesses would be bumped off—and what ones impeached—and what ones fixed."

"Well now—now take this one-eyed fellow—the fellow Yin Yi called Cyclops? The one who rung him in Indianapolis by long-distance from the Lig-Wall drugstore here that night? To tell him the coast was clear here in Chicago about this white woman? Your Miss DuBries—wasn't that her name?—over there, said absolutely that—"

"Oh, Cyclops? The Jap intelligence system can pick him up somewhere—wherever he is in the U.S.A. Chinks with one red protruding eye an' minus some front teeth can be located easy enough. But hell, Rand, he'll turn out to be the star witness for the state against Yin. From Yin's description of him to me, he's just a sort of no-good, a loafer. A guy like that can be fixed easy—to swear Yin's life away—maybe to say Yin was in Chicago—or at best to disclaim knowledge that Yin was on the other end of that wire—in Indianapolis. A thousand dollars would do it. Lucy DuBries—sure—can testify th' Cyclops was in the Lig-Wall phone room. But that don't mean nothin' at all if the toll-records at Indianapolis are swiped tonight. Cyclops could then maintain, without no chance of controvertion, that he'd been callin' a brother in Davenport, or a woman on Archer Avenue here in Chi, or even Tom Brown of Harvard!"

There was silence. To David Rand, O'Rourke's delineation of the situation seemed weirdly fantastic. But he had no doubt of the other's knowledge of whereof he spoke—associating as O'Rourke had been the last few days with a Federal inspector who knew the Japanese intelligence system.

"Well," the younger man said at last, musingly, "you've shown me pretty well what can happen to nearly each of us. And thanks—for giving Aline and myself first chance to mosey out of the picture. For a while. Where do we go from here? Florida? The Congo? Where?" He smiled, but mirthlessly. "Have you written Yin Li himself yet that he's in grave danger?"

"Danger?" said O'Rourke, and it was evident that he mistook the other's meaning. "Oh, he's in no danger whatever. The Japs would want him to stay alive above all—so's they could get him hung for th' Kenwood killin'—an' whitewash th' Son of Heaven over there in Tokyo. They'd want a live man to stand that crime on. And would—oh, now I get you. Grave danger as to his defence, you mean? No, I've written him nothin'—if for no other reason than that's he's home here in Chicago. And has been for at least a couple of weeks. But if you mean have I told him anything—I'll say I have not. Remember—it's his witnesses—not him—that would got to be looked out for. His legal status—not his life. My phone might be tapped, you know, Rand. Being in touch as I have been, with Inspector Monz. Moreover, Yin's phone in Chinatown may be tapped too. You just can't tell about them things. An' if I told him—at least by way of the phone—and he got panicky—and rung up Miss Jones—and Uncle Yin Tzu Lei—and all them other folks to warn 'em to guard theirselves, they'd laugh at him and think he was scrooey. But can you imagine how fast that Japanese system would work? By morning there'd be one dead music teacher on West 9th Street—in Indianapolis—and one dead Chinese re-cluse on South Senate Avenue. No, Rand, what I'm doin' now is such that it protects him—you—Mrs. Rand—all of you. I—"

The bell of the apartment buzzed raucously.

"There's Yin Yi now," O'Rourke said. "I called him here to show him in full detail exactly what he's up against. An' keep him from making a bonehead play—right off the bat. And now—if he'll work with me completely from A to Izzard—do exactly what I want him to do—then go where I want him to go for the time being, so's I'll be sure of myself—I'll spring the whole thing—even have every Jap agent, white and black, fetched over here right into this flat by Fed'ral operatives, and by evenin' the papers should be carryin' the solution of the Jack Kenwood killin'!"

CHAPTER XVIII

In Which 3 Men Hold Council of War

David Rand sat back in his chair, troubledly, frowningly, while O'Rourke went to the door.

"Come in, Yin," he heard the latter say. "I see the snow didn't hold you back?"

"No," came a cheerful voice. "As Confucius—was it not?—said: 'Curiosity is stronger than the hottest summer wind, or the coldest winter breeze'."

"Confoocius, eh? Well that, in a way, is what I'll be taking up with you. Yes, hang your coat on the rack. In this way."

David Rand had never met Yin Yi face to face. For that Chinese dinner had failed to materialize—owing to O'Rourke going out of town; and then, later, Yin's making a trip to China. And Rand looked up at the newcomer with interest, despite his own disquiet of mind. And concluded a second later that Yin was the most Mongolian looking Chinese that he had ever encountered. A perfect Celestial, in every way. Flat nose, high cheek-bones, extremely oblique eyes, hair a glistening black, and skin a pure saffron. His tallness, and breadth of back and shoulders, indicated that he was of the Northern breed of Chinese. O'Rourke, at the other's shoulder, made an introduction.

"This is David Rand, Yin. He was general manager for Kenwood."

Yin hesitated politely as one desiring first to see whether the white man wished to acknowledge the introduction with only a nod of the head, or a hand, and then, seeing the hand coming forth, thrust his own out.

"Very glad to meet you, Mr. Rand. Although sorry—yes—that we meet this way, ninety days after Mr. Kenwood's death."

"Ninety-nine days—to the day, Yin," said O'Rourke, glancing up at a torn calendar on the wall. "Sit down. Yes, that tap'stry chair there. No, don't bother to turn it around. You'll only get the glare from th' side o' that whitewashed buildin' across th' empty lot—and the snow to boot, if you do. Swing yours around, Rand, and split the difference. I'll stick my chair here. An' we'll have a triangle. I see, Yin, you wonder why all the black curtains!

My smoking niche. Or pass-out room!"

Yin sat down politely. His oblique eyes did stare with dignified polite-
ness on the alcove. But he asked no questions, folding his hands across his
stomach instead, and waited.

O'Rourke too sat down. He was the unlucky one to catch the light from
the snowbound empty lot outside. And blinked grimacingly for a few seconds as he got used to it. But at least the three men were now where each
could see the other, and talk.

"How did you like Chiny, Yin?" O'Rourke asked.

"I found it very interesting. But to one born in Indianapolis and spend-
ing his youth there, then residing in Chicago, I found China not at all a place
to live. No steam heat, as I wrote you. No running water. No phone system.
An American Chinese assuredly cannot endure the still primitive conditions
there."

"But Chiny's considerably pepped up, ain't she, by her possession of
them 13 Coins o' Confoocius!"

"She is indeed," said Yin. "If I gather correctly the meaning of 'pep'!
There is assuredly a new spirit. Everyone I met in Peiping, Shanghai, Nan-
king, Canton, believe now that China has drawn a mysterious source of
power. Like—like a hungry man who has been given a cup of warm inspir-
iting coffee. Japan has lost her grip entirely. And, if you deign to accept my
humble opinion, I believe that any threat which Japan may ever have held
for America is broken, without China as a source of military man-power—
and her coast as a base."

"Good. How did you get along with your relations?"

"Oh—they understand me not. I understand them not. I was glad indeed, after about 30 days there, to book my passage and come back to my
wax-working shop; and glad that I retained my lease. When I put my key in
the door, I said 'Home, very sweet home!'"

O'Rourke chuckled. Then he grew gravely silent.

"Well, Yin, I been tellin' Rand here a lot of interesting dope that I won't
go fully into—because I'm not at liberty to reveal it wholly. Gov'ment stuff,
see?" Yin nodded, but obviously quite inunderstandingly. "But I think I'm
free at least to release to you the fact that all the evidence now available is
that Jack Kenwood was killed by one of four agents of the Japanese intelligence system here in Chicago."

Yin leaned forward unbelievingly, his mouth agape, "The Japanese—
intelligence system? The Japanese intellig—But—I do not understand. You
mean then, Mr. O'Rourke, that it was a Japanese, who kil—"

"No, it wasn't a Jap, Yin. A Jap agent, yes, but not a Jap. The four agents,
of whom one done it, are non-Japs. That is, three are white—and one is a

Negro. And all are still livin' right here in Chicago today."

"But agents—of Japan? I do not understand."

"Well, in brief, Yin, Kenwood was contacted that night by a man whom they knew—or thought—had the 13th Coin o' Confoocius."

"The coin which was sold to the man called Blind Tom—of New York?" O'Rourke nodded.

"And when they seen a coin catalogue on his desk, to boot, they killed him." O'Rourke paused. "Furthermore, Yin—by gosh, I am revealing nearly everything, ain't I?—a long telegram has been decoded from one Jap intelligence chief in New York to a Chicago intelligence chief, ordering him to have his agents kill—if necessary—to get that there coin—an' put a def'nite Chinese touch on the crime."

"The mongrel whelps!" grunted Yin. He was plainly angry.

"The blundering fools, you mean," said O'Rourke. "For 'twas so damn subtle that it overstepped itself. They'd ought to have known you wouldn't bring to light your own engagement with Kenwood that night—and use a hatchetman's axe to do it with!"

"Hardly," agreed Yin. "But I nevertheless give thanks to the spirits of my ancestors that I did not have occasion to go there that night. For it would have been a bad thing for me, I fear."

"Only too true. Your only defense, in that case, would have been that you weren't such a half-wit—or moron—as to draw down attention that you and Kenwood had an appointment; that you'd have ripped off that blue appointment sheet, and took it with you." O'Rourke paused. "However, this killer worked in a hell of a hurry—and didn't see where he was makin' a mistake." He paused again, troubledly.

"Well, with all apologies to your estimable race, Mr. O'Rourke—and my kind feelings to you and Mr. Rand here, understand—the detail you cite proves that a white man—and not a Jap, nor a Negro either—was in that Indian Chief suit. For a Jap would be too cunning to make a misplay like that. A Negro would not think even so far as to create such an apparently perfect frame-up, as you once termed it. Only a white man—begging your pardon again—would make that error." He paused. "But you say you know the names of these agents? So that—"

"Yes, every one, Yin. But two are well-heeled. One can raise $20,000 bucks cash money for a defense. One can raise several thousand. While both can swing a half million defense fund by threatening to squawk that th' Chicago chief of Jap'nese intelligence system put 'em up to the murder. Do you know what all that means?"

"Well—no—I fear I do not grasp its meaning."

"Well it means, Yin, that if we call for an arrest without first takin' care of all your many, many witnesses, your former music teacher and your uncle down there in Indianapolis will be bumped off tonight. Honestly, Yin. I mean it. But we're not making such a bonehead play as that. And I'm giving you the full low-down so's you don't get panicky and trip things up. We're ready to fling a guard of not less than 4 men about each of them two key witnesses of yours down there—and in the twinkling of an eye, too. But, Yin, that don't solve things for you. The arrest will mean that the forces of the best criminal lawyers in town here will be brought to smash your witnesses in court—try to rip your alibi to pieces. Indict you. Then convict you. For only if they can convict you, can they save their own skins. Yin, they'll go to any lengths to send you to the gallows."

"But—but my witnesses will protect me. That is—if you protect them."

"They'll do their best, sure. But the lawyers paid by the Jap system will try to discredit 'em. Look up every incident in their past lives. Try to make their testimony worth nothing."

"But you forget, Mr. O'Rourke, that I have more than human witnesses—fallible though they may be. The telephone toll records. And remember my fingerprints on those freshly washed-off piano keys. And I talked with Miss Jones myself within a few minutes after they must have killed Mr. Kenwood. Everybody in Indianapolis knows Miss Jones. Never can they discredit her. Why they—"

"Yeah, but Miss Jones 'd be testifyin' up here in Chicago—where jurymen don't know her! No, Yin, I guess you just don't grasp the power of Big Money. Big lawyers. They'll go the limit to try to nail you on the cross."

"Nail me on a—oh—you are speaking figuratively, of course? Yes, I see. But—but how about this Mr. Peter Hess, deceased? Who badly wanted Mr. Kenwood's finger? Why—why will they not try to rivet the guilt still further on him?"

"Because, Yin, the complete proof in our hands that the Jap intelligence service was after Hess—an' everyone Hess contacted—proves Hess' dyin' story is th' truth from A to Izzard. There won't be no Hess left for to lay the crime on. They'll go for you. I tell you."

"Hm." Yin looked troubled.

"Well," put in O'Rourke kindly, "cheer up. Now that we know what's coming off—we've got a chance to see if our witnesses for you have any weakness that the lawyers for Japan's side can bust through. After all, Yin, Rand here is one mighty tremendous ace in the hole for you. Considering he heard Kenwood say that he intended to pay you that $500."

Yin turned to David Rand. "Please to guard your health very carefully, Mr. Rand," he said. "And also that of your estimable wife—who likewise—so I understand—heard Mr. Kenwood's statement."

"We will, Yin. Don't fear."

"Well now, Yin," went on O'Rourke, "let's take a survey of things. Like as if we was all holdin' a council of war." He paused. "Now the first thing the lawyers for the accused would do—say—both of you, of course, have heard of Abe Lepinard?"

"Isn't he Red-Necktie Lepinard?" asked David Rand, though puzzledly.

"Yes. That's the fellow I mean. The old hangin' prosecutor, as he was known here for years in Chicago, who always wore a red necktie everytime he had a hangin'—then, later, an electrocutin'—case." He turned to Yin. "Yin, the bird in this quartette of Japan's agents who has the 20,000 bucks to command is a pers'nal friend of Red-Necktie's—Red Necktie bein' now in private criminal practise, you understand. Red necktie has actually took care of him on one or two small cases. And if I don't miss my guess—th' minute he's arrested—Abe Lepinard will be sent for. An' will wind up as chief-of-legal-staff for the defense of the whole crowd, mark my words!" He paused. "Yin, that Red-Necktie Lepinard is the most unscrup'lous and tough fighter they is in America. He wouldn't stop a second from buyin' off any witnesses of yours—if he could! He's one bad actor, Yin, 'specially if puttin' th' blocks to you means saving his own client—in fact, four clients all at one crack! Two men—" He turned to David Rand. "Two men—" He turned back to Yin. "—he sent to the old electric chair, that was innocent. Found to be afterward, anyway. George Scymsczk was one; and T. Bruce Venable was the other. The case wasn't so strong against either one, neither—but Abe Lepinard succeeded in gettin' 'em strapped in th' chair just the same. An' they say he just laughs about it today. An' remarks that they should ought to have kept their feet dry!"

"He must be a man minus all human sensibilities," said Yin indignantly, though with reason enough for his indignation considering that it was his own witnesses who, according to O'Rourke's delineation of things, were being menaced, unknown even to themselves, this very second.

"He is," frankly admitted O'Rourke. "An' he's my pers'nal enemy, too—by the way. That is, he once upon a time alluded to me, in some-one else's hearin', as a dirty, ig'nant Mick—with unwashed ears!—from th' peat-bogs of Ireland." He chewed savagely on his under lip. "An' if Abe Lepinard hangs anything on you at all, Yin, it means the end of my job at the Bureau—because I give you complete clearance, you know. And then I am—for sure—'that ignorant Mick from th' peat-bogs'!"

"You shouldn't pay any attention to him, O'Rourke," advised David Rand.

"No, I shouldn't—but I've been burning up for years about it," burst out O'Rourke. He unclenched his right fist, which had unconsciously closed itself, and made a gesture with that now open hand as of one trying, anyway, to dispel his own emotions in the matter. And turned toward his Chinese visitor again. "So you an' me, Yin, is both concerned—two ways goin'—in anything this Red-Necktie Lepinard might do."

He paused a minute. Then pressed on with his exposition of matters.

"The first thing Red-Necktie would do, Yin," he said slowly, "and before even a legal staff for these here arrested Jap agents was organized—would be to mandamus us at the Bureau for a certified photostatic copy of ev'ry document an' notation in the dossier on Jack Kenwood. Mandamus, Yin, means to get a court order and compel us to do this—or do that. And a dossier is a packet of folders, each folder containin' all that touches on each person or object in the Kenwood murder case. One folder for you. One for Rand here. One for Hess. And so on. Well, we'd have to furnish all them copies in all the folders—photostats of 'em, that is—so long as the accused's lawyers paid the bill, or be under sentence for contempt o' court if we didn't. Then they'd examine everything for holes. Even try to make holes where holes wasn't. Now, for instance, Yin, if them criminal lawyers—headed by Red-Necktie—could locate anybody all who would claim—perjurously, o' course—to have been with you—in Chicago—not Indi'napolis—that whole day of Hallowe'en up to say—8 o'clock in th' evenin'—some 30 minutes or so before the murder, they would have something darned near to convict you on. Am I not right?"

"Arresting me, perhaps. But neither indicting me nor convicting me—of anything. For my uncle—"

"But Yin, an investigation down there in Indi'napolis held durin' the last couple o' days, on th' very theory of anticipatin' any of Red-Necktie's own moves, reveals a certain poss'ble weakness for your case—that is, only if they do dig up a perjurer at this end. You may think, of course, that I'm too fantastic in tryin' to anticipate for you what they'll try to do. But I've sit through a lot of criminal trials myself, Yin. And I know. So now, for Lord's sake, let's see what we can do to consolidate our mutual position here—in case they spring anything on us." O'Rourke paused helplessly. "This here investigation reveals that this here 2-flat buildin' at 1034 South Senate Avenue where your uncle lives was formerly an office for the Wall-Tex Wallboard Comp'ny—before they give it up, an' he bought it and converted it into a 2-flat of 9 rooms each floor. An' they had a small switchboard mounted in what's now th' closet under the front stairs. To connect all the people in them 19 rooms, one with the other. And,the switchboard is there yet—disconnected, o' course. Again, the phone wires to that old couple livin' in the flat above your uncle runs up through his inside front hall. Now—yes, I know this sounds ridiculous—but in a court of law, it sounds different. Someone down there reports that you got a cousin named Yin Oo—what's a mute. Not deaf—so they say—but just mute; th' way it was put to us, he can't do no more talkin' out o' his mouth than a few gruntin' sounds, but since he hears O.K. he gets by with writing his answers to people—or his questions, as th' case may be. Well, this mute part don't have no bearin' on things at all, but this part does—maybe -or maybe not. For they report that he worked for a while as a switchboard-wirer in the Indi'napolis Electric Works, thanks to bein' unus'ally handy and swift on electr'cal benchwork. Is that hooey? Whether 'tis or 'tisn't, suppose our 4 guilty men are arrested here in Chi in the Kenwood murder case tonight—an' by day after tomorrow no less a person than Red-Necktie Abe is demandin' your arrest, too, maintaining that the night you spoke to your old music teacher, you wasn't in Indianapolis at all; that you was in Chicago? Suppose he claims—the hangin' fool!—before th' very grand jury about to indict his clients, that that upstairs phone was stolen—you get my meaning. No, I mean that just the wires was cut off—and the live ends run over to this here switchboard? By Yin Oo—sure—I know it sounds like a nickle thriller. But if such a thing was done, you know yourself that the old people upstairs wouldn't know a single thing about it—if they didn't have occasion to be using their phone. And suppose Red-Necktie—lettin' his imagination go—claims that the live wires leadin' to your Uncle's phone in that back parlor study was also carried over to the switchboard too. Thus givin' him two telephone circuits to th' outside world for the short time either one capable o' bein' hooked into the other across the little switchboard. And that when you called up by long-distance—say, in some depot booth here in Chicago—he held you on the board, and immediately called Miss Jones at Lincoln 4063. And the minute she answered—or even before—plugged you into his circuit with her. So that—as Red-Necktie would claim—you talked to her from Chicago—instead of from Indi'napolis?"

"Well—that could not be wholly gainsaid," admitted Yin thoughtfully, "for the deplorable reason that that none-too-good Chinese I call Cyclops **did** ring Uncle Yin Lei's house that night, to talk to me, and that the long-distance call on Drexel 3051-R—Uncle's own phone—is of record. The Yin Oo you describe **is** my cousin. As to the extremely far-fetched fact whether Oo has ever worked as switchboard wirer—I must say I do not know. For at least a couple of years he and I have been decidedly on the outs. Not even speaking—or rather, to be quite exact, not communicating by word from me, or written message from him." He paused. "Do you really think this coterie of lawyers here would dare to take such a stand as you outline?"

"I do. I tell you they'll dare anything."

"Well—all I can say is that my Uncle would never permit such weird manipulations as all this to be carried out in his home, much less lie to help me, and—"

"I believe that—from what I've heard of him. A sort of a scholard, ain't he? But I'm not a grand jury. So let's follow up Red-Necktie's possible line of attack. For a paper affixed to your section in that Kenwood case **dossier** down at the Bureau affirms, Yin, that you swore to some sort of alibi for your uncle some years ago, and that he wasn't held to the grand jury down there. What was the facts?"

"I am glad to give them. And why not? They are of record. They were as follows: Four years ago my uncle had no wealth. He owned a laundry, employing 4 Chinese; nothing more. And his own half-brother Lee Wai was shot to death in Lee Wai's own home on Pennsylvania Avenue. My Uncle Yin Lei inherited Lee Wai's wealth, gained from a whole chain of laundries. When Lee's body was found, however—at least 12 hours after his murder— two Chinese called Soon and Kuan, of bad repute too, I assure you, came to the prosecutor down there with a story to the effect that around about the very time Lee Wai was killed, they had called at the Pennsylvania Avenue home, and could not get in; but saw Uncle Yin Lei, a revolver in his hip pocket, going out by the back entrance. With my cousin Yin Oo. My uncle Yin Lei, however, had the best defense in the world to such false charges. For one thing, he was a member of the Dee Lung Tong—an opposite tong to the Bing Kong Tong of which his half-brother Lee Wai was a member—as well as were both of these lying persons Soon and Kuan. The Bing Kong Tong, uncle was able to show, wanted to get him out of the way—because he was sole heir to Lee Wai's wealth; and Lee Wai's will provided that in case his heirs died before the customary year of probate of his estate, it was to go to the Bing Kong Tong. Uncle Yin Lei and Oo both were found at my place in Chinatown here—we were eating dinner—and I was happy to swear to an affidavit that both had been with me for 24 hours, visiting me. I dislike to have to add this also—but it is between friends, I trust. Oo desired me to perjure myself—to clear him on something else—a minor matter—to say that in actuality he had been with me for a week. I had to refuse. And stick exactly to the truth. He never communicated with me any more after that. And now I have truly stated the entire case, have I not?"

"Yes, you have," admitted O'Rourke. "Our report says that the prosecutor there, in view of the alibi, plus the obvi'us motive on the part o' them Bing Kong tongsmen to destroy th' one heir to Lee Wai's estate—to swear Yin Lei's life away—refused to bring the case further to the grand jury. But Good Lord, Yin, Red-Necktie Lepinard would wave aside the whole fact that you and Oo are on the outs; he'd say that that was just a friction story agreed upon between you and Oo. In fact, he'd go so far as to charge that since you swore to an alibi for your uncle and Oo—they owed you a like service—in a like case—at any time you wished to call upon 'em. The law of **shong-sung**, someone told me it's called."

Yin Yi made a contemptuous gesture with his hands. "But the Honorable Red-Necktie Lepinard is—or will not be—the prosecutor," he said. "If he wants to infer that everybody lies, he can do so. Assuredly there is among

Chinese a law of **shong-sung**, and I would be glad to give the Honorable Red-Necktie a book detailing its whole history—with my compliments. If he must impugn the testimony of my own people, he certainly cannot impugn that of that innocent little child, O Loya, who—as you yourself told me she said in her very own words saw 'Uncle Yinny Yi' that night—said he went ''way off—on choo-choo train'—and saw him playing the very 'pinano' on which the prints of my fingertips were found."

"That's true," agreed O'Rourke. "Except that your profession goes against you there, Yin. Red-Necktie will claim that you make wonderful reproductions of human faces in wax, from life—or from a photograph—or that you can even do such from your own reflection in a mirror. Not only solid wax castings, he'll say, but wax shells on a stiff cloth base, lifted off of a clay model, modeled—say—after your own features. That is, a sort of a thing that would constitute an exact mask of your own very face, with—say—pin-point holes in the waxen pupils of the waxen eyes. To see out of. In short I'll tell you what Red-Necktie will claim, Yin. He'll claim that it wasn't you who sat in the window that night and was seen, acrost th' side passageway, by Professor Wunderlich, playin' that **erh-hu;** nor yet you who sat on the piano bench just after little O Loya was brung to the house by the colored girl from off the alley. He'll claim it was your Uncle—who plays the piano also—with a mask of your face on, which mask might-a been sent him by air-mail the day before—or might-a been there a couple o' years, waitin' just such an emergency."

"All of this, my dear friend, irritates me greatly," said Yin Yi. "Not with respect to you who so kindly point, it out, but with respect to this Red-Necktie who might try to make such extravagant claims. He might as well try to build a case against ex-President Roosevelt—or the President of China himself! If you are correct in all this, he will no doubt therefore claim that Uncle Yin Lei, acting on my orders, despatched Oo on that Monon plane, wearing goldrimmed glasses, to register as a passenger thereon, instructing Oo to conceal his mutism by the simple expedient of shrugging his shoulders with any strangers endeavoring to speak to him, pretending to be a very grouchy Chinese—or else a Chinese who spoke no English—all of which, my dear friend, is an old, old trick of Chinese the world over when they do not wish to converse. Indeed, your Red-Necktie should have no diffidence in claiming that the said Oo would not even have had to talk to the porter-conductor of that plane, since there was but one stop for the plane—Chicago—and the $15 tendered to the Negro indicated plainly passage to Chicago—and nothing else. All this then, no doubt, Red-Necktie will claim. Since after all, Oo looks a li'l bit like me, that is true. Except—"

"Except he ain't got your upper middle gold tooth. Which the porter on that plane said his Chinee passenger had!"

"No, that is true. But you may send to Red-Necktie, with my compliments, the welcome suggestion that a bit of gold wax can be pressed over a tooth and resemble the dull-gold one such as I have." Yin Yi was scornfully silent a second. "Only don't forget, Mr. O'Rourke," he went on, "that that little religious colored girl, Tarbaby Watkins—deeply religious, at least, with respect to your Christianity—washed those piano keys that night at around 6 o'clock. That little colored girl could not, and would not, lie. I may not be rich, but I at least have money enough to bring her here from Indianapolis, if needs be. And she—"

"Well," offered O'Rourke helplessly, "if she ain't declared nuts, by a piece of dough put in some alienist's hands, and made 'nix' as a witness, then Red-Necktie will maintain that it was curious that she should have been called in at 6 o'clock that night to wash them keys clean. Of course, I know the keys could he sticky. Lord yes!—with a child in the house at least once a day, from up the street. But they'll investigate you, Yin, I tell you, and find that you are not only a wax-worker but that you graduated from th' Rubber Technologycal Institoot of Indi'napolis. They'll get a-holt of a school catalogue—" O'Rourke reached into a magazine pocket attached to the willow chair in which he sat. "Listen to this, Yin. Suppose they get you on the witness stand, and read this out." With which O'Rourke read forth slowly:

"'Also is taught the Michaelson-Faddock Oil-and-Acid Wash Technique for transposing any kind of delicate line drawings, including even fine etchings, to rubber—in either relief or intaglio. 16 class hours and 64 laboratory hours are given to this speciality.'"

O'Rourke looked up, catalogue in hand.

"Hell fire, Yin," he grumbled, "they'll claim that you made a simple pair of flesh-colored rubber gloves, with your own fingertip markings transferred to their tips by this here process; and that the pair either went to your uncle by air mail the day before you hypothet'cally went to Kenwood's office—or maybe was waitin' down there for a whole year, in case of any jam you might ever get into here in Chi. And that while it was him playing on the piano, it was your fingertips—thanks to his rubbin' them gloves in his hair first—that was strewn all over them freshly washed keys."

"All this," commented Yin Yi, with dignity, "is fanciful hypothesis, and will remain fanciful, for the world will know that Red-Necktie is but trying desperately to save his own clients. For after all—I know enough about law to know that hypothesis is not fact. Much less evidence. He cannot prove that I was in Chicago that day when I was in Indianapolis, and that he would positively have to do. Motive, we all know there was none. Nor opportunity, can he prove. Simply because nobody living or dead, sane or insane, man, woman or child, saw me in Chicago. Because, in short, I wasn't here!"

"Yeah, I know that. But if they fix this Cyclops with a thousand bucks to swear—"

"Don't worry! I saw Cyclops in Sichwan, China. I could not believe my eyes. Nor he his one good eye, I guess. But there he was! He'd won enough money on the money I gave him to go to Memphis, to go to some grandfather's at Nanyang—about 10 miles from Sichwan. And so they won't buy him off—unless, perchance, you or Mr. Rand accidentally reveal that he is in Nanyang."

"We will not!" said O'Rourke indignantly. "But do we keep him hid this way—non-existent—they'll use that ag'in us."

"They will? How?"

"They'll declare there ain't no such person. Red-Necktie will say that Cyclops, with his striped sweater that night, was you—wearin' a dickey around your neck. With a hollow wax shell, like a inflamed eyeball, stuck under your left eyelid like—like a sort of monocle. And black wax pressed over a few of your front teeth—so's they looked like missin' teeth when whoever 'twas grinned at Miss DuBries from out th' gloomy inside of that telephone booth. Callin' up to tell your Uncle to shoot the works—establish the alibi—and throw you over pronto onto Miss Jones' wire." Yin Yi, however, looked so utterly skeptical of O'Rourke's bizarre conjectures, that the latter emphasized his next words with a forefinger in the palm of his other hand. "Red-Necktie may, or may not, claim that it was you yourself who called the noisy Interstate, Life Buildin' engyne room and tipped off the murder. So's that alibi would be worth somethin'. But I do know, Yin, he'll claim you was hidin' all day up to 8 o'clock or so in that little cozy studio you got in the Malmgren Company warehouse; maybe slept there the night before; and that you ventured out on the street only about 8 o'clock—and that when you did venture out, you was completely ensconced in that Injun Chief costume."

"Well—let him claim so. Since it is—alas for his rantings!—not the case. For I was not in the Malmgren Company warehouse that day, and nobody can say I was without perjuring themselves."

"And nobody's more glad than me to know that. But as to that, Yin, havin' mandamused your docket—in fact the whole Kenwood **dossier**— that is, just photostats of every document in it—they'll try to undermine you by the little blue ticket."

"What ticket, may I ask?"

"Well, Yin," explained O'Rourke, again a bit apologetically, "we have a rule in the Chicago Police Department that when a man has been hauled up as a suspect in a major case, special investigators empty his wastepaper and garbage for ten days, gettin' there early in the morning ahead of the regular man, with a car. For the police ain't psychics, see? They can't find things hid in the backs of clocks, nor stuck in cracks, nor God knows where else. They're just hooman. But anyway, what junk is picked up for 10 days is took to a special department at the Bureau, and sorted, and anything an' everything that might touch in any way on th' suspect's alibi is attached to his case-history. Unfortunately, you being drug in temporarily as a suspect, as you was, automatically got registered downstairs in the pick-up department, and so—against my wishes, of course, had I happened to think—for the 9 days up until you left for Chiny, all the stuff you throwed out down at your Wentworth Avenue place got sorted."

"I am glad to hear that. For I threw everything out of my place, I am certain, the day before I left. And so the very thing that might have hurt me, under circumstances of guilt, becomes, I take it, my best defense."

"Well, I suppose yes. For nothin' incriminatin' was throwed out. At least nothing that amounts to anything. Except one thing—what might cause you trouble! It's the weighin' ticket."

"What ticket is that, may I ask?"

"Here it is," said O'Rourke, feeling about in the side pockets of his coat. "It's the original item itself—initialled by both of the sorting clerks what found it in your junk. I suppose we could destroy the fool thing—unless maybe those two clerks might spill their mouths to Red-Necktie." He transferred his search to his other pocket. "One o' them automatic weight tickets like the machines in the Malmgren Drugstores spew out for a penny. Destiny tickets they call 'em, too. Oh—here it is."

He fished it forth and handed it to Yin Yi, just a small oblong of tough blue cardboard, one of those typical type-printed destiny tickets which David Rand himself had so often seen on sidewalks. And curious as to what bearing this could possibly have on matters, he moved his chair over toward Yin's. "Mind, Yin," he asked, "if I look over your shoulder? After all, 'twas my employer was killed, you know?"

"Not at all—considering you are my best witness," said Yin, and moved his chair a trifle to make room.

The little ticket, as David Rand saw, was initialled in ink on its two upper corners, and read simply:

WHO holds me for 3 days from the time I am delivered, and then indulges in a game of Chance, do I bring great winnings; and whether I am then held or tossed away, do I bring to him who held me such 3 days, on the 99th day after he first received me, a great change in his life!

Madame Destiny.

Yin gazed down at the ticket, "Ah yes," he commented. "Strange how these little tickets actually seem to control human Fate. Predict the very course of events for their holders. I have never been able to account for it. I found it, as I recall it now, in front of the drugstore just outside the main gate of the air field. Moreover, but 3 days later, did I challenge the very prediction on its face. By playing **fan-tan**. And won $500! With which I went to China."

"Whoa—Tillie!" said O'Rourke amusedly. "Don't let Red-Necktie know you won five hundred bucks, Yin. He'd say it was your $500 you got from Kenwood! If you must let that fact out—do make it any sum but five-hundred even! Well, I'm glad the ticket brought you good luck. But if we let it stay in the **dossier**—it'll bring you trouble."

"Outside of its still further fanciful prediction—how?"

"Well, because," O'Rourke explained solemnly, "a micro-examination of the automatic date print on the other side—like we check typewriter findings—and a comparison with sample tickets took from all the machines in Chi—reveals a contradictory feature. F'r instance: the micro-examination shows a doubly broken 'O'—th' break horizontally acrost it, that is—in th' abbreviation for October; and a missin' upper barb on th' '3' in '31'. An' these two defects—together with four more seen only with a microscope— is to be found only on the steel date cylinders in Machine No. 706. And that machine, Yin, is a machine what was in a Malmgren drugstore on Division an' Wells Street. That is, up to 10:30 o'clock in the evenin' of October 30, when they was a fire an' the drugstore was partly burned out an' had to be closed up. Such valuable stuff as wasn't hurt by water nor fire—like these here weighin' machines which is only leased, under bond, to Malmgren, same as to other places—was put on a wagon an' run straight over to the Clinton Street warehouse, by telephonic orders from Carl Malmgren hisself. Now take this here machine—or any of 'em, in fact. As you know, they run by clockwork. The clerks wind 'em up about once a week. Their date cylinders advance one notch, automatically, at midnight every night. In fact, Yin, when this here missin' machine No. 706 was fin'lly unearthed as bein' in the Clinton Street warehouse—long after you went to Chiny—it had changed every 24 hours up until November 5th, at which time it had run down. So you see, Yin, there must be some mistake. You couldn't have found this here ticket on no Chicago sidewalk. For the machine it come out of was under lock an' key in that Clinton Street warehouse from 11:15 at night, October 30th, till at least November 5th—if not much longer yet."

"That is quite true," conceded Yin, gazing once more at the prediction printed on the ticket. "The ticket I picked up, outside the air field—it all comes back to me now—said something about receiving a letter from a far distance, if kept for such and such a number of days. I promptly threw it away—for, among us Chinese, a letter from far distances can but only mean bad news, at best. Now this ticket—yes—must be the other one. For, after coming in from the air field, I stopped off first at the warehouse—this was around 11 o'clock that night of October 31st—to pick up my searing knob and my wax-smoothing knife. For use on that job I intended to embark on next day. That job which you'll recall Mr. Marchisso Fichetti of the employment department of the Industrial Exhibits Fair, assured you I was booked up to begin. And I obtained this ticket from the very machine which you call No. 706. At least it stood not far from the private door by which I go in and out of the warehouse."

"Well, that clears up that then," said O'Rourke relievedly. "But—but how, Yin, did you get a ticket ever to register like this one done? Now you're a man of about—I take it—165 pounds—no more. Yet look at the other side. Look what's printed there!"

CHAPTER XIX

In Which T. O'Rourke Relates How He Hunted In a Haystack—But Not for Needles!

Yin promptly turned the ticket over. David Rand, peering over his shoulder, could see that it read, partly in type-print and partly in print made by a cylindrical die pressing through an inked ribbon:

Arrow points to your CORRECT weight ONLY IF you stand quiet on platform until red hand stops, before dropping coin. PATENT 2,134,553. American Auto-Weigh Destiny Machine Co., Inc.

===

$$485$$
$$\text{Oct } 31 \text{———> } 486$$
$$487$$

===

Trade at the MALMGREN DRUG STORES. Purest drugs. Cheapest prices. Most courteous service.

"You note, Yin," O'Rourke said troubledly, "that the fool thing registers 486 pounds. How—"

"Yes, I do," admitted Yin Yi, looking up. "All of which is very easily explainable. Just about a week prior to this particular night I had opportunity to pick up a barrel of modeler's wax very cheap. It was reputed to contain 450 pounds. And was so branded. I paid for it, and had it delivered to the Clinton Street warehouse for the time being. But seeing the scales there that night I stopped off for my searing knob, it occurred to me, as I was about to go, to weigh up my barrel and see whether it was correctly branded or not. So I laid a plank from the cement floor to the scales platform, and rolled my barrel up on it, with very little trouble as you know if you have performed such an operation. And on putting a penny in the machine, and taking the ticket it flung out, I found that—as a matter of fact—my barrel was 36 pounds to the good. For which I was very glad. And I kept the little weight ticket. For I half believe in sooth-saying predictions."

O'Rourke's face was the picture of discomfiture. And at last he managed to speak.

"So—so it's only the record of a barrel of wax!" he groaned. "Wurra—wurra! Damn it, Yin, but why couldn't I have learned that before? For I wasted some 60 days—oh, more'n that—while you was in Chiny, doing the very thing that—well Red-Necktie hisself will be doing now. Well, we'll let that baby run himself ragged now. It'll be rich! Why Yin, I searched the country over, runnin' down ever'body who had a weight as huge as that ticket showed, in the belief that only they could-a stood on that weighin' machine platform that day of October 31st—or that night. I interviewed Fatso, known as the Human Mountain, who plays sideshows and books himself out independent. And I got into touch with Big Giant Harry McGill, of Wenner and Humphries' Circus, that covers the South in winter. An' Tweedledee and Tweedledum, the Twin Kings of Fatdom. It took me plenty trouble to locate these people too—the ones who booked independent—because they get work only here and there—and Lord knows where—nor when. But, of course, I was barkin' up a wrong tree on 'em, for Fatso was sick in Vanderbilt Clinic Hospital at New York, the night of Kenwood's murder. No doubt of it. The hospital records was unmistakable. Tweedledum and Tweedledee was in Dallas that night. Big Giant Harry McGill—and the whole Wenner and Humphries' Circus—was playin' Savannah, Georgia, that night.

"Nut that I am," went on O'Rourke, "I even tried fat women. For I thought that maybe—But it don't matter, for as I see now I was all scrooey. But on and on I searched. Market Street Mary, World's Fattest Negress, of Barling's Collection of International Freaks. Well, she was in London that night of October 31st. And Baby Rose, Queen of Fatdom. She was a hard one to reach. I had to actually go down to New Orleans to locate her. Only to find that she'd been in San Francisco, the whole week in which October 31st lay, playin' 7 days engagement with the Middleton Museum there. Skyzmziaka —the Polish Dumpling! Whooey—what a labor! She talked no English—and couldn't write even Polish. And I had to get interpreters on both ends, to get anywhere with all the correspondence that passed. But Skyzmziaka, that night of October 31st, was just where she was when I located her in early January. In Northern Canada. With a pack of relations. Took me plenty messing with Canadian authorities and what not to get the proper depositions on that. Oh, I run 'em all down, Yin, one by one, an' to no avail. There wasn't but one more in the whole United States. She—I don't suppose you ever heard of this party, by any chance?"

O'Rourke stepped over to his small desk, and from its drawer took out an evidently folded lithograph. When he had unfolded it completely, however, and held it up, it showed, in large white letters, outlined in red, and on a black background, the flamboyant announcement:

Little Dolly

Prettiest Sideshow Fat-Woman In The Entire World!!!
See her inside.

"Now this here party, Yin," O'Rourke said, "**was** in Chicago on October 31st last. Positively. In fact, had been here for many weeks up to that time. Livin' at the Hotel State. On South State Street. She come here orig'nally, it seems for to play the State Street Dime Museum for a week, an' at that time, I understand, come to your place out on Wentworth Avenue—in comp'ny with her husband, a bird known as Herman the Demon Sword Swallower and Human Salamander—to sit for a wax head for some Cleveland medical museum who was willin' to pay for it. An' stayed on there at the Hotel State whilst her husband was fillin' an engagement of several months at Milwaukee. Now, of course, Yin, you mayn't have known her by her professional name. An' that's why I asked you if you'd ever heard of Little Dolly. She—but then maybe I can act better than I can talk."

O'Rourke rose wearily, and turning to the curtained smoking niche snapped an electric light button affixed to the rightmost jamb of its entrance way. And this done, pulled on the hanging cord. And as he did so, the two black drapes rolled swiftly apart, revealing in truth a small windowless alcove—but an alcove in which, under the bright ceiling lights, sat two persons. One was St. John Mackenzie, with his long face and his sideburns, looking very grim, with a long revolver laid across his knee. And the other, on a chair made slightly wider with a short piece of broad board, was a huge mountain of girl—or woman—in an exceedingly low necked, short, sleeveless sideshow dress of green gauze, a fan in her pudgy hands. The tremendous area of soft white flesh thus exposed—all curves, and dimples, and mounds—was daintily powdered, and had a texture that was that of a baby's skin. She might have been 24 years of age. Her hair was blonde, made more so by peroxide, and her face was not at all unpretty in many respects: for the blue eyes at least held a childish appeal in their dresden-china depths, and the half-petulant pair of red lips were rosebud like.

"This is Little Dolly, Yin," O'Rourke said quietly. "And St. John Mackenzie—whom of course you know—of th' Homicide Division."

The huge dimpled mountain of soft flesh arose from her chair, by helping herself slightly aloft with the palms of her two hands; which accomplished, she stepped forward with no further trouble from the alcove. Her face was troubled, unhappy. Yin's ever-impassive face, however, did not alter in its expression in the least. She moved forward towards him, slowly, majestically, like a battleship bearing down on a wharf.

"It ain't no use, Yinnie," she said sadly. "There ain't nobody but me in the whole Yoonited States could-a registered that weight ticket that night.

All the other's like me, as in the profesh, was all in different cities as Chi."
She paused, a single regretful second. "No, Yinnie, this man what's been a-
talkin' to you all this time got to me. Ten days ago. In Mobile. Where me an'
Herman went after we left New York. Herman was sore at th' Billboard—
an' quit readin' it—an' he never seen the ads this man was runnin' for people
like—like me." She paused, giving herself a single apologetic waft of air
with her circus fan. "He—he told me, Yinnie, that he had abs'lute proof that
I wuz in a Malmgren warehouse in Chicago on October 31st with—with a
Chink, as he called you, what had a key and—and a little love-nest there.
He says somethin' about you havin' some kinda mother-fixation—whatever
that is. Me, I—I don't jest understand that, of course. But I knowed he was
tryin' to do you some injure, Yin, an' I—I swore I wasn't there. I told him
and th' Mobile chief-o'-police what come to my place with him, that I wuz
in Gary, Injiana, all that day, with my sister Susie. But they helt on to me,
Yinnie, so's I couldn't git to a phone and long-distance Susie. And they got
to her in Gary, see, with another detective. An' she swore I hadn't been there
at all that day, but the day before—an' proved it. 'Count of her havin' give
that special party that time I come—it bein' her birthday. An' her birthday's
October 30th. See? Poor darlin'—she didn't know what 'twas all about. Nor
did I neither, Yinnie. For Herman an' me was already speedin' t'ords N'York
the night the news of—well, you know—come out on the streets here."
She fanned herself again violently. This was plainly a terrible strain on her.
"They tol' Herman all—an' he sez he'd take me back into his buzzum—per-
vidin' I told all. Oh Yin—I hadda tell all. An' did. But—but I didn't know,
Yinnie, that I was hurtin' you any when I tol' 'em, too, about that there Injun
costume and the—the hatchet that wuz both layin' in the bottom drawer
of that chest o' drawers what I peeked into when you stepped outside th'
stoodyo into th' main warehouse to get some clean fresh water from the
other tap—for to make our tea with. Yes, Yin," she added, and the cupid's-
bow lips were sad, "I hadda confess you an' me wuz in the love-nest all that
day from early mornin' up to—to 8 o'clock—when you sent me home!"

There was a tense silence in the room.

During which Yin Yi reflected studiedly. Then he spoke—but apologetically. "Very deplorable, this is indeed. Not with its respect to my fortunes—no. I refer to the fact, Dolly, that you should have had a slight rift in
the marital equanimity between yourself and your husband. Myself? I am
of no consequence. Alas, the wages of super-calculation seems always to
be—trouble! Or, paraphrased, a bell cannot be successfully stolen—because
somewhere it will clank." He looked up at O'Rourke. "In addition to my
many talents, which include that of being a musician, a poet, an artist, a philosopher, and a charmer of the fair sex, I confess to being considerably of a
logician. And therefore realize quite plainly that my entire defense has gone

down—thanks to your hypothetical refutation of every element in it—and your finding Little Dolly. I have not now what is proverbially know as even the—er—Chinaman's Chance. So I quite freely admit I killed him. Which I was almost certain I would have to do when I went there. Indeed, you may write in your case-history that the complete alibi was worked out solely by me—and its paraphernalia sent to Indianapolis the day before. I killed him, yes, in a quite Chinese manner, so to speak, focussing all the attention possible upon my own name and 8:30 appointment, so that your astute detectives would realize I was not so imbecilic as to—er—frame myself. Is that not the word? Yes. And was that not beautiful logic, too? I call it perfect, myself. Too bad, of course, that Dolly must prove to be the eternal feminine and weigh herself as I guided her out that night—and that the weight ticket, thereafter quite useless to her, should contain such prognosticative provisions on its reverse side, leading inevitably to my own retention of it. And—but, ah!—this is a little joke of yours, Honorable O'Rourke, is it not? You have purposely made the day of reckoning between us to be the 99th day after the ticket's date—so that my life would indeed changed. You have a sense of humor."

To which O'Rourke said nothing.

But David Rand did.

"But why, in Heaven's name, Yin," he put forth, "did you kill Jack? He said he intended to pay you off on your $500 claim. And—"

"Oh—that?" said Yin Yi depreciatingly. "True, he did pay me off. As soon as I had made known my identity, and apologized for my festive appearance. In fact, he had it waiting for me in a corner of his desk drawer. A single $500 bill. That was what I subsequently went to China on." He paused the slightest fraction of a second. "Upon his paying me off, indeed, he became quite chatty. No hard feelings—either side. We discussed a number of things, including our mutual detestation, the Democrats. And then the conversation ran over, somehow, upon feminine beauty. He did not seem to possess, however, either tact or diplomacy—much less an appreciation of the salient fact that beauty is a quite independent and personal matter—for each individual. That the sort of scrawny, scraggy creature that calls itself modern woman today—and which he might consider beautiful—I might not even spit upon. And would not, in truth. But I was too refined to dilate in any way upon what might touch **his** emotions. He, however, was not as I. And he commenced to wax suddenly quite virulent upon the subject of fat women—without any respect to my sensibilities—nor even first inquiring as to whether my feelings were being transcended. He said that all such were nothing but great behemoths, at best—and should be locked in dungeons and made to eat nothing but bread and water. He said that they should be flogged daily. And forced, screaming, into steam rooms to steam their avoirdupois off. That he would drown them all in the lake, did he have his way, unless they removed every day, from their bones, not less than 2 pounds of—ah, **kai-dai**!—he—he called it suet! I could stand it no longer. I saw red. I just slew him then and there. For such remarks about fat women. He simply did not have the heart of a poet. Nor of an artist. Nor was he one hundredth the connoisseur of feminine beauty he considered himself to be. For fat women are the loveliest flowers that God has placed in this drab garden of Earth. Their curves are the essence of true estheticism. They have the so-called 'It', a thousand times over. They are great luscious blooms, which unworthy man has the rare privilege of nurturing in his midst. They are delightful, and they are sweet, to their last dimple—one and all of them!"

He made a gesture, of complete finality, with his saffron hands. And Little Dolly broke the silence with a deep sigh.

"Oh Yin," she declared, "but you sure do talk beautiful. You allus did. Never has there been any white men I've ever seed what could say them beautiful things what you can say. And I—I sure do hate to see you get hung."

"I also, of course, shall find it disagreeable," remarked Yin Yi philosophically.

www.ingramcontent.com/pod-product-compliance
Lightning Source LLC
Chambersburg PA
CBHW020648180626
46816CB00003B/1186